VEIL OF STARS

A Wild Hunt Novel, Book 17

YASMINE GALENORN

D1519940

A Nightqueen Enterprises LLC Publication

Published by Yasmine Galenorn

PO Box 2037, Kirkland WA 98083-2037

VEIL OF STARS

A Wild Hunt Novel

Copyright © 2021 by Yasmine Galenorn

First Electronic Printing: 2021 Nightqueen Enterprises LLC

First Print Edition: 2021 Nightqueen Enterprises

Cover Art & Design: Ravven

Art Copyright: Yasmine Galenorn

Editor: Elizabeth Flynn

A Nightqueen Enterprises LLC Publication

Published in the United States of America

ACKNOWLEDGMENTS

Welcome back to the world of the Wild Hunt!

Thanks to my usual crew: Samwise, my husband, Andria and Jennifer—without their help, I'd be swamped. To the women who have helped me find my way in indie, you're all great, and thank you to everyone. To Kate Danley in particular, for running our author sprints that have helped me regain my focus in this current pandemic. To my wonderful cover artist, Ravven, for the beautiful work she's done.

Also, my love to my furbles, who keep me happy. My most reverent devotion to Mielikki, Tapio, Ukko, Rauni, and Brighid, my spiritual guardians and guides. My love and reverence to Herne, and Cernunnos, and to the Fae, who still rule the wild places of this world. And a nod to the Wild Hunt, which runs deep in my magick, as well as in my fiction.

You can find me through my website at Galenorn.com and be sure to sign up for my newsletter to keep updated on all my latest releases! You can find my advice on writing, discussions about the books, and general ramblings on my YouTube channel. If you liked this book, I'd be grateful if you'd leave a review—it helps more than you can think.

Brightest Blessings,
~The Painted Panther~
~Yasmine Galenorn~

WELCOME TO VEIL OF STARS

The Dragonni have established their theme park, but they may not have time to spin out their web because Echidna calls out Typhon, and the Father and Mother of All Dragons prepare to go to war. Ember and the Wild Hunt are there to witness the battle, but when Echidna and Typhon rise against each other, the resulting shockwave sends Ember, Angel, and Raven into the realm of Caer Arianrhod—the Castle of the Silver Wheel. Now, they must find their way out before the Star Hounds of Arianrhod hunt them down and destroy them, and Ember must prepare to face the Gadawnoin.

Reading Order for the Wild Hunt Series:

- Book 1: The Silver Stag
- Book 2: Oak & Thorns
- Book 3: Iron Bones
- Book 4: A Shadow of Crows
- Book 5: The Hallowed Hunt
- Book 6: The Silver Mist

- Book 7: Witching Hour
- Book 8: Witching Bones
- Book 9: A Sacred Magic
- Book 10: The Eternal Return
- Book 11: Sun Broken
- Book 12: Witching Moon
- Book 13: Autumn's Bane
- Book 14: Witching Time
- Book 15: Hunter's Moon
- Book 16: Witching Fire
- Book 17: Veil of Stars

CHAPTER ONE

"IF YOU DON'T STAND STILL, I'M GOING TO STAB YOU WITH A pin." Miss Evelyn wasn't joking. Currently with a mouthful of pins, the elderly woman was as spry as anyone I'd ever met, and more ferocious than most. She stood about five-two, though she looked shorter because of the dowager's hump on her back, and her gray hair was smoothed into a beehive. She should have been in an old-fashioned retro housedress, but instead she wore blue jeans and a gingham shirt—which looked entirely out of place on the otherwise prim and proper seamstress.

I stopped fidgeting. I had been standing on the chair for fifteen minutes, but I fought back a snarky reply because A) Sheila was watching, and since we were being fitted for bridesmaids' dresses and she was paying for them, I didn't want to come off as whiny, and B) I had agreed to this and so I was going to carry through with a stiff upper lip while hoping for as few pinpricks as possible. So far, Miss Evelyn had managed to stick me three times, but then again, I hadn't done my best to stand still and let her work.

I glanced down at Angel, who smirked at me. She was sitting on the sofa of the Lace & Satin Dress Salon, which was the name of Miss Evelyn's shop. I stuck my tongue out at her.

"It will be your turn next, so laugh all you want," I said, holding still as a statue.

"Haven't you ever had a dress made?" Miss Evelyn asked. It was always "Miss" Evelyn. Sheila had emphasized that when she had given us the address. She had also warned against being too flippant. Apparently, Miss Evelyn was a seamstress of some renown and in her younger days had worked in Hollywood as a costumer. She had the awards to prove it.

I started to shake my head, then stopped. "No, actually, I haven't. Though that's going to change soon." Morgana had notified me that her dressmakers were preparing to make my wedding dress and I'd be needed over in Annwn for custom fittings soon.

"Well, then you'll be ready for the next designer," Miss Evelyn said, sounding all too satisfied. "Here, another few pins and we'll be done."

The dress was unlike most bridesmaids' dresses, thank gods. No poufy sleeves, no lime-green neon colors. Instead, Sheila had opted to wear red to her wedding, and the bridesmaids were being fitted for knee-length pale pink chiffon dresses. We would have pink hats and gloves. Viktor's tux was going to be black, and his groomsmen were wearing rose boutonnieres to match our dress colors. This was perhaps the most girly thing I had ever worn. The color didn't suit me, but the dress itself was lovely, and made up for making me feel a little washed out.

Miss Evelyn finished with me and motioned me down from the chair. I cautiously slid out of the dress with her help, only once scratching myself on the pins, and with a sigh of relief, slipped back into my jeans and sweater.

Angel took my place on the chair, and with a flurry of measuring tape and pins, the seamstress began working her way around the hem.

As I watched, the tinkle of a bell from the front of the shop announced another customer. A moment later, the clerk opened the door to the sewing room and I jumped up, squealing as I saw Raven standing there. I held out my arms and she rushed over for a flurry of hugs.

"Raven!" Angel said, standing perfectly still.

"Oh good, I was wondering if you were going to join us today," Miss Evelyn said.

Raven slid out of her jacket. "Sorry, it took awhile to make it to the…" She paused, glancing at me. She had been about to say "portal," but a lot of people didn't know about them. It wasn't in anybody's best interests to alert the general population to the portals, even though their existence wasn't exactly a secret.

"It took me awhile to get here. Traffic sucks." She dropped her coat next to mine on the other end of the sofa and gave me a long hug.

"How are you doing?" I asked, holding her back by the shoulders so I could get a look at her. There was something different, though maybe I was seeing it because I was expecting it. Raven had recently left the Eastside to live in the realm of Kalevala, where all the Finnish heroes and gods hearkened from. Much like Annwn, it was a step

3

away from our technology and modern life. It was hard to imagine her liking it much, but she had an air of contentedness about her that I had never before noticed.

"I'm good," she said. "So's Raj. Kipa's over at the Wild Hunt right now—he tagged along to visit. We'll stay for a few days, then return for the wedding."

I glanced at Miss Evelyn, who was absorbed in her hemming. "You look good. Do you really like it there?" I asked, lowering my voice.

Raven thought for a moment, then nodded. "It's different. I'm still getting acclimated to the new surroundings, but I've begun my training and that's fun. Mostly, right now, I'm learning to identify the different trees and plants in the forest. I'm not sure where this will lead, but I trust that Väinämöinen knows what he's doing."

"How's Raj taking the no-TV thing?"

Raven's gargoyle, who was both companion and pet, had been sorely distressed when he found out they were facing at least a year without TV.

"He's at the house, binge-watching all his DVR'd shows. I promised we'd come back once a month for a weekend, if training permits, so he can keep abreast of them. I doubt we'll pry him off the sofa till it's time to go back," she said with a laugh.

I snickered. "I want to hear all about the training." I paused as my phone jangled. Herne was texting me.

AS SOON AS YOU CAN, GET BACK TO THE WILD HUNT. MORGANA AND CERNUNNOS WILL BE HERE AT NOON TO TALK TO US. BRING ANGEL AND RAVEN.

I glanced up. "As soon as we can, we need to get back to work. I just got a text from Herne."

Miss Evelyn glanced at Raven. "I'll need another

twenty minutes or so. I'm almost done with Angel's dress. Raven, if you would like to change into your dress, we can get right to it when I'm done hemming Angel's."

Raven plucked her dress off the dress rack and began to take off her gear. She was, as usual, decked out in a chiffon skirt over a tulle petticoat, a jacquard corset, striped leggings, and platform boots. You could take Raven out of the goth scene, but you could never remove the goth scene from Raven.

As she changed places with Angel, I kept looking at Herne's text. I texted him that we'd be there within the hour and then settled back to wait, but in the back of my mind, a little voice whispered we were about to dive headfirst into something big.

WE HEADED BACK to the office, stopping to pick up four pizzas. The Make-It-Take-It franchise that had moved in near the office had pizzas steaming hot and ready to go, and they were always fresh. We bought four pepperoni with extra cheese pies, and made it back at the Wild Hunt by eleven forty-five. As we entered the waiting room, Talia jumped up from Angel's desk, where she had been fielding calls.

She pointed to the break room. "Herne's in there with his parents and Kipa. He's asked the rest of us to join them at noon, and by the looks on Morgana's and Cernunnos's faces, whatever's going down is big." Talia looked like a woman in her mid-sixties, with gorgeous silver hair down to her back, but in reality she was a harpy who had lost her powers. Morgana had given her the power of glamour so she could exist in human society, and Talia had chosen the form of a woman she felt wouldn't be under constant scrutiny but who also wasn't old enough to be ignored.

She glanced at me. "I think I know what it is."

Angel took her seat and put her purse away. "Echidna?"

Talia nodded. "I believe so."

I headed to my office to stow my purse and motioned for Raven to follow me. "Come on, you can drop your things off in my office."

I gathered my tablet and a notepad and everything else that I thought I'd need. "If Talia's right, then we're near the end point."

Echidna was the Mother of All Dragons, and we had managed to locate her after much searching. She was the only one who could stop Typhon—her former mate and the Father of All Dragons—from trying to take over the world.

Typhon was trying to conquer on a two-fold front.

The dragons had returned to Earth from their realm after being locked away for thousands of years. Typhon was an avaricious monster, born of two Titans, who was out to enslave the Earth. But he was cunning and had been doing his best to infiltrate society through his children, to win the humans' good will and confidence. But we knew what hid below that spectacular guise—a sly viciousness looking to use humanity for his own private food supply. But the only way we could stop him was for Echidna to go up against him and drive him back into stasis.

"End point. And to what end?" Raven shook her head. "I have a strong feeling of foreboding. I'm grateful I'm living in Kalevala right now. Sure, we're on the doorstep of Pohjola, which is pretty much Evil-Land, but an arrow can bring down some of the strongest opponents. Bringing down a dragon? Not so easy."

I bit my lip. I had been thinking about all of this lately, too. "I wonder if we'll all end up away from our home-land. If needed, we'll pull back to Annwn. I was going to ask you to come with us if we do so, but I guess you and Kipa are fine where you are."

She nodded. "Yeah. It's so different, Ember. Some mornings I wake up to the soft fall of snow on the ground, and I listen but there's no sound of traffic, no sound of planes, and everything feels incredibly peaceful. At other times, I'll be standing outside, looking at the forests that seem to stretch along forever, and I feel a haunting loneli-ness. The land there is changing me. I feel stronger, almost a little harsher but not in a brusque way. I under-stand why the people who live in the northern areas of the world seem so stoic and almost a little brutal. You have to harden up to withstand the cold and the isolation."

She sounded almost teary-eyed, but her eyes were dry and it was then that I realized she was accepting her fate—not fighting it. Some people fought their destiny. But Raven had changed, and she seemed reconciled to the differences in her life.

"Are you happy, though? Are you glad you made the decision that you did?"

She thought about it for a moment. "Yes, I can say that, and with all honesty. Just because I'm having to adapt doesn't mean that it's bad. I loved my life here, but I'm learning to love life there, too. Kipa—oh, you should see him. He wears an apron and keeps the cottage clean and cooks for us. And I go every day to Van's cabin—that's what Väinämöinen lets me call him—and learn. We walk in the woods and he points out different varieties of trees and plants and animals, so that I can learn to identify them both in summer and winter. We talk about magic, and I think I've learned more in the past few weeks than in my lifetime."

"Does your mother come visit you?" I asked.

"Yes, she does. My father is trying to be as helpful as he can. I think the realization of what he did to me almost broke him."

"How about the ferrets?"

"They love it. Kipa's set up a room for them, and he's built an enclosed run so they can go outside if they want." She paused, then said, "I've never told you the truth about the ferrets, have I?"

I paused, glancing over at her as she settled on the loveseat in my office. "What do you mean?"

"I mean, I've never told you how I found them. Or what they truly are." She ducked her head. "I think maybe it's time. Because Väinämöinen is positive he can help them."

"Help them? What do you mean?" I put down my tablet and leaned back in my chair. We still had a few minutes. All I knew about her ferrets was that both Angel and Talia had felt odd energies from their room at one point.

Raven took a deep breath. "The truth is, they *aren't* ferrets. Back in the 1980s, I was up on Mount Rainier camping. I found three spirits trapped in a tree. Long story short, I tried to free them but set off a hex and ended up trapping them in the bodies of ferrets. I've been taking care of them ever since, trying to find a way to break the curse."

I blinked. "What?" I was about to ask why she hadn't told us, but then reminded myself that we all had secrets, and sometimes we had good reasons for hiding things.

But she seemed to read my mind. "I didn't tell you because I've always felt such a responsibility for them, and somehow, it felt dangerous to tell anybody. But now…we have so much protection in that cottage. Van himself dropped by and set up our wards."

"What happens if you can free the ferrets from their curse?"

"Then they'll move on in the spirit world, but that feels like the right thing to do. Templeton has slid into his ferret nature, though—until he's freed, he'll be full ferret. Gordon's trying to hold on to himself, and Elise manages better than the other two. She can communicate with me. But the trip through the portals seems to have shifted things so that Templeton's fully gone. His spirit is buried under the ferret nature now and there's no going back." She glanced at the clock. "We'd better get in there."

I nodded, still absorbing the fact that Raven had been babysitting three spirits for nearly forty years. She was a collector of strays, I thought. She gathered unwanted and tormented strays to her, and took them under her wing. And that seemed a beautiful thing.

As we passed Talia's and Yutani's office, they joined us. Viktor jogged down the hall from where he had been inventorying the stock room, and I poked him in the arm.

"We got our bridesmaids' dresses hemmed today."

He snorted. "I bet that was fun for Miss Evelyn. And before you ask, yes, *everybody* calls her that. She's a whiz with the needle and sewing machine, and makes all of Sheila's regalia for her magic. She's also making my tux."

The thought of Miss Evelyn ordering Viktor to hold still or she'd jab him with a pin made me laugh. Viktor gave me a long look, but said nothing as we entered the break room.

Herne was there and he gave me a quick kiss, motioning for me to sit beside him. On the other side of the table sat his father and mother—Cernunnos, who was Lord of the Forest, and Morgana, Lady of the Fae and the Sea. Cernunnos was dressed as normally for being outside of Annwn as he ever could be, wearing jeans, a pair of motorcycle boots, and a muscle shirt, with a bulky bear fur cloak over his shoulders. His dreadlocks were caught back by a thick tie, and his eyes glowed, gleaming like a cat's.

Morgana, on the other hand, was wearing a pair of white jeans with a long, cold-shoulder tunic of swirling violets and blues over the top. She had belted it with a silver belt, and her jacket was military-style, to mid-thigh. She had on knee-high leather boots with a thick platform heel, and her abundant hair was caught up in a high ponytail.

They waited for us to sit down, and Angel brought in the pizzas. As we served ourselves, no one made small talk. The tension in the room was so thick that it made it hard to breathe. Both god and goddess politely refused food, their impatience showing.

Once we were all settled, Cernunnos motioned to Herne. "Go ahead, son. Tell them what we told you."

Herne cleared his throat. I could tell that he was nervous —he glanced at his father a couple times before beginning. "Echidna is ready to go against Typhon. We're at the eve of battle. She's called him out, trying to lure him over the Puget Sound so their battle won't endanger the city. The question is, will he respond? Will he launch an attack before she can maneuver out over the water? Because she called him out, he's allowed to pick the place of combat, which is a worry."

I stared at him. "Why does he get to set any rules at all?"

"Because among the Dragonni this is considered a duel, which means that the loser will be bound by the winner's desire. If someone tried to attack Typhon without a formal declaration, all the other Dragonni who choose to follow him could demand blood payment if he lost. And if he *didn't* lose, he could go back against his opponent with all gloves off." Herne frowned. "It's complicated, but setting it within the parameter of a duel means that Typhon can't claim revenge if Echidna wins. He'd have to yield and bow to her conditions."

"So if the fight isn't defined in the beginning, then it's all gloves off and damned be collateral damage. But if it's set as a duel, that will minimize collateral damage." I was beginning to get the picture.

"Right. If he loses, he must accede to her demands. But he won't surrender. He'll fight as long as he can. Neither can die, but they can be hurt so gravely that it would take them years to recover."

Angel rubbed her temple. "What if *she* loses?"

Cernunnos lowered his chin, his eyes solemn. "Then we'll have a massive problem because he will be without mercy."

"So what do we do?" I asked.

"Be prepared. We still don't know if he knew that she was around. It seems a hard thing to hide, but who knows? Maybe if he didn't, the summons will throw a scare into him and he'll leave. I doubt it, but we can hope. *You* will all be responsible for cleaning up collateral damage as best as you can."

"What about the Dragonni Village?" The theme park had been started by the Luminous Warriors—those dragons who aligned themselves with Typhon—and it was now up and running. The mayor had cleared the way for it, oblivious to the danger. Or maybe she was getting paid off, but whatever the case, they had insinuated themselves into society and had been chipping away at the fear surrounding them.

We couldn't come out and tell the populace what the dragons were up to because…well…panic. But we had tried to convince the governments that it was dangerous to allow the dragons leeway. So far, half the officials believed us and the other half thought "dragon" equaled "treasure hoard" and their greed was winning out.

The vampires, on the other hand, had retreated far out of the dragons' reach. Typhon's father was a god of the dead, and so when Typhon had reentered this world, the dead had begun to rise and walk, spurred on by his presence. There were questions as to whether the Father of All Dragons could control the vamps, so the Vampire Nation, in its wisdom, had ordered the vampires to retreat into the underground, leaving the upper levels of the cities in case Typhon could actually wield power over them.

I sighed. "What if he wins? What if Typhon manages to kill Echidna?"

"He cannot kill her, since they're both immortal. But he might be able to defeat her." Morgana, who was not only my future mother-in-law but my goddess, held my gaze. "Then we will have work to do. And you and the members of this agency will retreat to Annwn."

With that, we all fell silent, thinking about the battle and what the future might hold for all of us.

CHAPTER TWO

AFTER WHAT SEEMED LIKE FOREVER, MORGANA FINALLY
spoke again. "I know this is a shock. Even when you know
something is barreling down the road toward you, when
it arrives it still feels new and overwhelming."

"What about my brother?" Angel set down her
notepad. "I don't want DJ at Cooper's while this happens.
What if the dragons strike there?"

"The fight will be over Seattle," Herne said. "It would
be more dangerous for DJ if he still lived here. Cooper
can keep him safe better than we can, Angel."

She looked like she wanted to argue, but then sat back
in her chair, biting her lip. "Will you make me a promise?"
she asked.

Herne was good at reading people. He leaned forward,
elbows on the table. "I promise you that if anything goes
wrong, we'll take him to Annwn and look after him."

Relief flooded her face. "I believe you," she said. Even
though she had taken an elixir to extend her life, she was
still mostly human and vulnerable. And with Rafé's death,

we had all seen how easily life was snuffed out, regardless of life expectancy.

"What do we do now? How do we prepare?" I racked my brain, trying to figure out how to prep for a battle like this. We wouldn't be fighting Typhon—that would be a suicide mission for anybody but the gods. But when Cernunnos said we were responsible for taking care of collateral damage, I had no clue what to expect.

"You get ready for incoming dead. When Typhon enters the skies, it will wake more skeletal walkers, ghouls, zombies, whatever happens to be around, and they'll respond. They'll be coming out of the graves, looking for their master." Morgana pursed her lips. "It's going to be *Night of the Living Dead* all over again."

"What about the vamps? Has somebody warned them?" Viktor asked. The half-ogre was a soft-spoken man, a gentle giant, but now the grim look on his face said he was ready to kick some undead butt.

"I have," Herne said. "I called Dormant Reins and he informed me that the vampires have retreated deep into the lower levels of the Catacombs. They'll stay there, and hopefully Typhon's presence won't reach down through that many layers. Though if the Father of All Dragons can summon the dead out of their graves…" He left the thought unfinished.

"Yes, but the dead are buried in shallow graves—the vampires will be hundreds of feet belowground. The levels in the Catacombs descend farther than anybody knows, from what I understand." I played with my stylus, tapping it on the table until Yutani reached over and grabbed hold of it.

"You'll break it if you keep that up. Just because it has

the name 'pencil' doesn't mean it *is* one," he said. He turned to Herne. "What do we do? Ember's right—if we're supposed to take care of collateral damage, shouldn't we be gathering weapons? And what time does this go down tomorrow?"

"It goes down, as you say, at sunrise. Echidna is on her way now. Typhon has received the challenge. If he doesn't show, he forfeits the battle." Cernunnos shook his head. "I'm concerned about something, however. I made my concerns about the upcoming battle known to the council of gods who have been working on this, but they didn't take it seriously."

The thought of anybody not taking Cernunnos seriously seemed incredibly stupid. Before I could ask which gods, however, Morgana spoke up.

"They're fools, my love," she said. That was one of the first times I had heard her use an endearment with Cernunnos, even though I knew they loved each other deeply.

"Why on earth wouldn't they listen to you? And what's concerning you?" Talia asked.

"Some of the gods prefer to take the optimistic route. I do not. I look at all sides of the issue." Cernunnos turned to Kipa. "Mielikki was not one of them, however. She fears the same thing I do. Perhaps it's only the gods of the forests who can see into the future."

Herne let out a long sigh, then crossed to the counter to bring back the coffee pot. "More, anyone?" He emptied the pot refilling coffee, and Angel took it from him, quickly fixing a new pot. Herne stirred cream and sugar into his cup and then said, "My father's right. There's a danger no one is looking at here. Perhaps it's because the

Wild Hunt—my father and mother included—and Mielik-ki's Arrow have worked with humans for so long that we can see the potential for betrayal and dishonor to win out."

"What I foresee happening," Cernunnos said, interrupting, "is that Typhon may lose but not honor the rules of the duel. That he will be bested and continue to fight Echidna. Or that he will lose by the rules of the game and the Luminous Warriors will continue the fight. Also, remember, Typhon can't be killed. Neither can Echidna, since they were both birthed by the Titans. So there's no endgame where either one can be destroyed. They cannot be unmade. None of the gods can."

The thought of Typhon simply refusing to accept defeat hit deep and hard. We had seen it many times in humankind, but usually there was some method of stopping the aggressor. With the dragons it wouldn't be so easy.

Another thought occurred to me. "Given the dragons are all descended from Typhon and Echidna, who are immortal, are *all* the dragons immortal? Can we even *kill* a dragon?" I wasn't all that sure of the answer.

Cernunnos sighed. "We don't really know. Nobody that I've known has ever managed to kill one. But your reasoning is logical, although I pray, faulty." He paused, then said, "There is one possible way. Even if it will not kill them, it will disable them."

I immediately knew what he was talking about. "The allentar bolts."

Morgana straightened. "You still have them, don't you?"

Herne motioned to Viktor. "Bring them out, would you?"

We had locked the allentar arrows away, keeping them hidden for the time we might need them. Six months back, Cernunnos had received them from Echidna and he had given them to us to keep for emergencies. The rare magical metal could pierce dragon scales, and could bring a dragon down out of the sky. But each bolt would be destroyed upon use, and there weren't many of them. The arrows—and for me, crossbow bolts—were thicker than the usual arrow, and so we each had twenty of them, filling the quiver. But Echidna had not said whether they could kill a dragon.

"What do we know about allentar?" I asked.

"Let me call Ginty," Herne said. "He'll know the most about it. Dwarves are the only ones who know how to craft it." He stepped away from the table to call the dwarf. Ginty McClintock owned Ginty's Waystation Bar & Grill. He was a fair man, and he acted as the mediator during parleys, especially between Saílle, queen of TirNaNog, and Névé, queen of Navane.

While Herne was on the phone, Viktor brought in both Herne's quiver of allentar arrows and my quiver of allentar bolts. He set them on the table and I withdrew one of the bolts from my quiver, shivering as it throbbed in my hands.

"This thing feels alive," I said.

"It should," Cernunnos said. "Once it was alive. Allentar is made from dragon scales."

I brushed my hand over the smooth metal of the shaft. The metal was cool under my fingertips, and the throbbing continued as I brushed my fingers onto the fletching.

There, another energy seemed to join in with the throbbing from the metal. The fletching was made of feathers, that much was obvious, but the feathers were stiff, brilliant blue and orange, and a shiver raced down my spine as I brushed my fingers over them.

"What bird are these from?"

Morgana smiled. "I thought you would feel the power in those feathers. They're from a phoenix."

I stared at her. "Really? A *phoenix*?"

"Yes. And the tips are made from the fangs of dinosaurs that have been coated with the allentar." Cernunnos held his hand out and I handed him the bolt. "These are worth more than all the gold and jewels in my vaults. These could save your life if you run into a dragon."

Herne returned then, and he stared at the arrows. "They might save our asses tomorrow. They won't work on Typhon, but if his children decide to interfere, we may need to use them." He set the bolt back down on the table and held up his phone. "Ginty is on his way. He's the only one I've told about the arrows because I don't trust anybody else not to try to steal them. They're worth a fortune. Literally."

"I take it we'll be at the site of the battle?" I didn't want him to say yes. The last thing I wanted was to be near a dragon fight, but given we might hold the key in helping Echidna to win this war—and a war it was, no doubt about it—I couldn't see any other choice. Right then, I wished that Herne and I had already married and that I had undergone the Gadawnoin ritual. Once I was a goddess, I'd be immortal. Walking into a battle between two immortal dragons didn't seem like a good recipe for coming out alive.

"Yeah, we will. Kipa—did Mielikki give you some of her arrows?"

Kipa nodded. "I've said nothing because, like you, it seemed to be wisest to keep them under wraps. But I will be there, by your side, along with the Huntress herself."

"The rest of you will also be there," Herne said. "We'll gather here and go down together. Raven, you, Viktor, and Yutani need to be ready to take on the undead that are sure to rise. If anything goes wrong, if Echidna cannot drive him into submission, then we'll implement Plan B."

"What plan is that?" I asked. This was the first time I had heard of a secret plan. And it had to be secret, otherwise Herne would have shared it with me.

Herne glanced at Viktor, then said, "If things go south, to ensure the safety of everyone in the agency, including DJ. If I give the signal, Talia will immediately notify Cooper, Ginty, Saílle and Névé, Dormant Reins, and the deputy mayor. They will then begin evacuating all necessary personnel to safe havens. If the Luminous Warriors think Typhon is losing, I don't trust them not to immediately implement their plans to enslave this world. And if he wins, the same."

"Where will everyone go?" Angel asked.

"We will journey to Annwn, and Cooper will bring his family and DJ there. Ginty will evacuate those who have sought sanctuary, and he will return to his people. I expect the dwarves will retreat to their cities in Wildemoone—a different realm. The dwarves have much to fear from the Luminous Warriors. They're grasping and greedy, and the dwarves are known for their fortunes they amass."

"What about the vampires?" Angel asked.

"Dormant Reins has plans for the vampires, though I'm not sure what they are. Saílle and Névé will probably evacuate to Annwn, though I doubt they'll be happy about it. There, they will have to step down from their reign and hand over their people to the ancient Fae Queens. As for the deputy mayor, Maria and I've held a few secret talks and if the dragons take over, she's planning to stage a coup, overthrow the mayor, and take control of the city. Mayor Neskan publicly supports the dragons, and when faced with an actual crisis, I have a feeling that she'll be useless. At least Maria Serenades understands the danger."

"There's no way to drive the dragons back to the Forgotten Kingdom, is there?" Yutani asked.

The Dragonni had been trapped in their kingdom and kept out of our realm since Typhon was first forced into stasis by the gods. But when he managed to break out, his children—both good- and ill-natured—were also freed.

I shook my head. "If there was, we would have tried it by now, I think."

"Even if Echidna can wound him deeply enough to put him back into stasis, she won't be able to seal them behind the gates to the Forgotten Kingdom again. The situation now is vastly different than the first time," Morgana said. "Apparently, the dragons had settled in their realm back then, and very few had remained here. The few that were still here returned to the Forgotten Kingdom when they heard about the battle, and Echidna was able to seal the portal, trapping them there. Her children weren't able to open it by themselves, but when their father started to wake, they were able to draw on his power. When he broke open the stasis field, it sent a shockwave through the seal to the Forgotten Kingdom."

"So, even if the gods and Echidna can return him to stasis…"

"Yes, the dragons will still be here," Morgana said. "And the Luminous Warriors will do what they can to carry out their father's plans."

"So we'll still be up shit creek without a paddle," Viktor said.

Yutani was typing away on his laptop. "One thing we have going for us, at least right now, is they haven't fully grasped how to use technology. But you know they'll find humans—or Fae—who are experts, and they'll use it to their advantage."

"We're forgetting the Celestial Wanderers and the Mountain Dreamers," Talia said. "They'll be on our side."

The Luminous Warriors followed their father's nature. Though all dragons were dangerous, the white, red, and shadow dragons were out to enslave the world with their father. The other two factions—the Celestial Warriors, the blue, silver and gold dragons—and the Mountain Dreamers, the green and black dragons—were friendly to humankind and inclined to fight their more treacherous kin.

"They may be, but to be honest, I don't want to count on them. I can only trust the Dragonni so far," Herne said. "They've said they're on our side, but we have no idea if that situation will change. And while Ashera helped save both Raven and Ember, we can't afford to be complacent."

Ashera was a blue dragon who had fought off Pandora

to help both Raven and me escape from the psychotic goddess's clutches.

Raven took a shaky breath and said, "Though I know in my heart she's on our side, Herne's right. I've learned the hard way—you can't ever place your trust fully in someone you don't know from the inside out."

I hated that we had to cast suspicion on someone who had helped save our lives, but I knew both Raven and Herne were right. We couldn't afford to take a risk. We could trust Ashera as far as we could trust her, but in the end, until we saw her go up against her brethren, we would have to count her as an ally who might change her mind at any time.

My phone rang at that moment and I glanced at the caller ID.

"Speak of the devil," I said. It was Ashera. I stepped away from the table so I could hear better. "Hello?"

"Ember, are you with Herne? I'd like for both of you to hear this." Her voice sounded almost breathless, which surprised me.

I turned back to the table. "Ashera's on the line and wants to talk to you, too, Herne." I spoke into the phone again. "Everybody's here, including Cernunnos and Morgana. I'm putting you on speaker." I punched the speaker button and set the phone down on the table, turning the volume to high. "Go ahead, Ashera."

She wasted no time. "A group of us are flying over late tonight. We'll be there for the battle in the morning, and we'll do our best to keep the Luminous Warriors from helping Typhon."

"How many of you are coming?" Herne asked.

"At least twenty-five. I don't know how many of

Typhon's brood will gather to support him, but the rest of our people are spreading out to prevent as much backlash as we can. I suggest that you contact your government and do your best to instill a curfew starting at midnight. I know it can't be worldwide, and there are places that our kind have not yet settled in, but over the past months, hundreds of dragons have returned from the Forgotten Kingdom, and while there are many who are on our side, there are too many of the Luminous Warriors. Tomorrow will be a bloody day, I'm afraid."

We all fell silent at that. In human form, the Dragonni were dangerous. In dragon form, they were deadly beyond reckoning.

"I'm sorry," she said. "I cannot express the depth of my sorrow at what Typhon is bringing to your world, and if I could change matters, I would. But I can help to boost your efforts."

I glanced at Herne. She sounded sincere, her voice cracking.

Ashera continued. "We'll be there by morning light, before the duel, and we'll do what we can to help."

"Thank you," Herne said. "We can use all the help we can get."

"Till dawn." Ashera signed off.

"I know what you'll say, but I trust her," Talia said. Beside her, Angel nodded.

"I *want* to trust her," Herne said. "But come morning, we'll find out one way or another." He tossed me one of the arrows. "Get used to the weight. Serafina will shoot these fine, but you'll have to get used to cocking them. They're tricky."

I picked up one of the bolts, testing the weight in my

hand. Once again, the energy rippled through the shaft, up my arm, and through my body. A thought crossed my mind. "How do they get the dragon scales to make this metal if dragons can't die?"

"Very carefully," a voice said, booming through the room.

At that moment, the door opened and Ginty walked in. I wondered how he'd managed to get into the office, given both the door and elevator were locked, but then I remembered—he worked on the astral at times, and his Waystation led out into a parallel universe where he kept safe those who sought Sanctuary.

We all turned as he approached the table. He inclined his head to us and gave Cernunnos and Morgana a stiff, but respectful bow. Herne moved forward to clasp Ginty's hand and clap him on the back.

"Ginty, well met. Please, take a seat." Herne moved to bring a tall stool to the table. Ginty climbed up on it, sitting at eye level with the rest of us. He was a short, burly man—well, dwarf—and as handsome as his manner.

"To answer your question, Ember," Ginty said after we were all seated again, "select adventurers managed to steal cast-off dragon scales long ago, when they were still in the world. All it takes is a small amount from one scale melted down into some ilithiniam to infuse it into allen-tar. But those scales are rare and precious because, until now, the dragons had all left this world. One scale could be infused into a dozen weapons."

"But there aren't many artifacts around, are there?"

"Of allentar? No, they're probably hidden in old tombs and broken-down castles. And when my people discovered that an arrow made from allentar could bring down a dragon out of the sky, we poured our energy into that. The great dwarven scrolls in the Hall of History back in our home realm tell of dragons raiding our holds. They knew we were wealthy beyond most others, so they targeted us. With the arrows, we had a fighting chance. And while no tale tells of killing a dragon, we wounded several so severely they began to think twice about targeting our lands." Ginty shrugged and rested his elbows on the table. "So, tomorrow Echidna flies?"

Herne nodded. "Tomorrow at dawn. Warn your people. We have no clue of what will happen."

"We'll arm ourselves, but I doubt many will descend from the mountains to join the fray. In fact, I expect an exodus for the home world. The United Coalition has not been favorable to dwarves over the years." Ginty let out a soft sigh and glanced at me. "Will you be joining the gods, or our side? You're not yet a goddess, but neither are you fully in our camp."

"We're all on one side," I said, and realized I meant every word.

CHAPTER THREE

HERNE BROKE THE MEETING SHORTLY AFTER. "GO HOME. Rest. Be back here by three A.M." He paused, then said, "If you have unfinished business, take care of it. Who knows what the day after tomorrow will bring."

As I started to leave, he motioned me over. Draping his arm around me, he kissed me. "Love, are you ready? If you want, I'll send you to Annwn."

I shook my head. "I can't stay behind when we all have dreams of the future. Viktor's getting married in a couple weeks. Angel has DJ. Talia has her own life. Raven and Kipa have a future. I won't shirk my duty. Do you *really* think I could sleep at night if I hid?"

Herne nodded. "I expected you would say as much, and I'm proud of you." He kissed me again, his lips cool against mine. "Well, love, what do you think? What will be the outcome of tomorrow?"

I shrugged. "I don't know. I don't even dare to hope. Too much rides on this. Even if Echidna injures Typhon enough so that the gods can drive him back into stasis, what of the others? The Luminous Warriors? I'm afraid they'll stick around to make life hell."

"I truly don't know, love, but whatever the case, we will face it together." He squinted, his brow narrowing. "I wish we were already married."

I knew that he really meant he wished I had gone through the Gadawnoin already. He was afraid I'd be killed. But I was still mortal and until I completed the ritual, there was nothing to be done about it. I couldn't slink off and hide in a closet.

"Do you want…one last…" I wasn't sure how to say it, suddenly feeling shy. But I knew it wasn't shyness that stopped my voice. It was the realization that there were so many things that needed to be done before the battle, and Herne was in the thick of them, being a god himself.

"I wish I could," he whispered, holding me by my shoulders as I crossed my arms. "But Cernunnos…the others need me. We're finalizing plans."

"Go then, and be safe. I'll see you back here at three." As I slowly turned away, Angel waited for me. I joined her as Herne returned to his mother and father.

ANGEL AND I DROVE HOME, barely speaking. Finally, I eased to a stop in front of our house. "If something happens to me, Mr. Rumblebutt will need a home," I said.

Instead of glibly saying that everything would be all right, she said, "Of course. I'll always keep a space for him, if it's ever needed." She bit her lip, then ducked her head. "I'm afraid, but to be honest, I'm more afraid of what happens after."

"You think the world will survive this one?" I asked, gathering my things and locking the door as we headed toward the house. It wasn't a throwaway question. Angel had the ability to predict a number of things from the future. She was an empath and part magic-born, and she had grown in power over the past couple of years.

She stopped in her tracks, spreading her legs as she craned her neck toward the sky, her eyes closed. After a moment, she slowly turned back to me. "You and I…we'll survive, I think. But the world will never be the same. Win, lose, we're at a massive crossroads. Regardless of the outcome, everything will be different. The world is step-ping into the unknown, Ember."

I slowly nodded. Often there was a riddle in her words, but this was clear. And it didn't take a seer to know that she was right. The world would move as it did, and we were just along for the ride.

I called Ronnie Archwood, my pet sitter, and asked if she could come out tonight and stay the night in the guest room. I couldn't tell her what we were facing, but I did tell her we had an important battle the next day, and that I couldn't go into it worrying about Mr. Rumblebutt's safety.

She arrived half an hour later, armed with snacks and books, and we settled her in the guest room. Angel joined me in the kitchen while Ronnie went back out to take care of a couple clients who were away for the evening.

"Why isn't Raven staying with us?" I asked.

"She and Kipa wanted to stay in her house for the

night." Angel paused. "Do you think she'll ever come back to live here for good?"

When Raven first left, she had been hesitant, both excited and yet afraid. Now, she seemed eager to get back to her studies. The fact that she was studying with one of the Force Majeure was hard to believe, even now, but she and Raj were quickly adapting to life in Kalevala, a fact that made me both relieved and sad.

"I don't know. I don't think so, to be honest." I opened the fridge. "Last meal? Just in case."

"What do we have?"

I eyed the fridge. "Leftover spaghetti. And we have a lasagna in the freezer you made a couple weeks ago in case we got busy." I shifted several packages of hamburger out of the way and pulled out the Pyrex square pan. "I'll put it in for forty minutes."

"Better make it an hour, so it bubbles in the middle." She took out lettuce and carrots and cherry tomatoes and radishes. "I'll make a salad to go with it."

While Mr. Rumblebutt wove his way around our legs, we went about the mundane business of making dinner, talking about anything and everything as we tried to ignore the fact that tomorrow morning, the dragons would rise and the world would change.

THE ALARM RANG way too early. I had some sleeping powder from Ferosyn that didn't leave me in an afterfog and both Angel and I had taken it, but still, two-thirty came early and the anxiety over what was going to happen weighed heavy on our hearts. Still tired, we dressed for battle. Meaning leather jackets, warm but not bulky jeans and tops, non-skid boots. I braided my hair back while Angel fixed hers in a bun.

"Angel…" I paused, turning to her as she made us breakfast sandwiches while I fixed her tea and my coffee.

"Don't say it. We're both coming through this." She cut the sandwiches in half and handed me two, keeping one for herself. My metabolism was faster than hers due to my heritage and I ate twice as much as she did. I also made sure I bought twice as much of the groceries.

"Yeah, I know, but…what if…" I couldn't help but think about what might happen if we were caught in the crossfire.

"Herne will never let you get hurt. He'd let the world blow up first."

"No, he wouldn't, and that's the way I'd want it. I don't want him to put me above the good of everyone else," I said, realizing I meant it. "Remember *Star Trek*? 'The needs of the many outweigh the needs of the few. Or the one.' I believe that. When we can manage the good of all, so much the better, but if it was a choice between rescuing me, or saving a city…or a world…I'm never going to ask him to pick me."

Angel nodded. "Yeah, I feel that way too. But damn it. You're asking me to look at a potential future where you don't exist. I didn't drink that elixir just to spend a thousand years without my best friend." She toyed with her sandwich. "What do *you* think will happen? What's your best guess?"

I shrugged. "I don't know, to be honest. I have no clue on this one. If we can't take Typhon down, then the world will become a far more dangerous place to live. Once the general populace witnesses the fight between Typhon and Echidna, who knows what will happen? Right now, the Luminous Warriors have been easing the populace into their corner, with their amusement park and appearing on talk shows and trying to pretend they want to become a part of society. Even those who generally spout off conspiracy theories seem snowed under by all the glamour and glitz. But that will all change after today."

Several spokes-dragons had appeared on TV, including Gyell, a dragon who had a personal vendetta against us. He had done his best to kill us and we'd managed to escape, but now he had turned beefcake to horny women—he appeared on TV with his shirt off and a smoldering look in his eyes—and he was proving to be a popular guest, and a popular representation for the dragons. I wondered what they'd think when their dream lover turned out to be sizing them up for the stewpot.

"Say Echidna manages to drive Typhon into stasis," Angel said. "Do you think the Luminous Warriors will be able to follow through even if Typhon is gone?"

I finished eating, my mind turning over everything I knew about the dragons. "What I think is that the dragons will forever change our lives, even without their father. And I wouldn't put it past certain members of the government not to work with them secretly, to save their own skins. The lid's come off Pandora's box. It's too late to close it up again."

A vast future spread out in front of me, bleak and growing bleaker. I had no clue whether it would pan out, but the trouble was—I could imagine it. And if I could imagine it, it could happen. We had seen the world enslaved before, or parts of it, but world domination had to start somewhere, and each time it had threatened, the sacrifice had come in blood and bone. And we were once again approaching a pivotal time in history where there would be no going back.

"I guess we'll have to wait." Angel pointed to her watch. "Shall we go?"

Feeling the hours splintering, crumbling around my shoulders, I picked up my backpack. I tossed in some cookies, a few water bottles, and a bunch of protein bars and some candy bars. Angel did the same.

"I'm ready. Let's go." I stopped for a moment to give Mr. Rumblebutt an extra-long cuddle and a kiss on the nose. "Stay safe, my friend," I whispered, kissing his nose as I hugged him. "I'll come back for you."

Ronnie, who was returning from tending to a few of her other clients, dashed up to the house as we were running out.

I turned to her. "If we don't come back…"

She nodded. "I'm not sure what you're facing, but he'll never be without a loving human."

My heart racing, I closed my eyes for a moment, then —seeking a calmness that seemed a million miles away—I motioned to Angel and we headed to the car. Overhead, the sky was clear, glittering with the last glimmer of stars as clouds began to roll in.

We took both cars, just in case. As we headed toward the center of town, I turned on the music. Gary Numan's "Now and Forever" echoed out of the speakers, and we glided through the night, the music a theme song to the battle waiting before us.

"Echidna is on the way. Unfortunately, given she called him out, it was his right to claim the battleground, and he demanded the air directly above the docks. The mayor has instituted a curfew—no citizens on the streets until it's over, but you know people will break it," Herne said. He was decked out in leather, his hair pulled back in a braid like mine. Everyone was there, including Kipa and Raven. Raven had brought her wand with her, which could take down a building.

"The Wand of Straha might be able to do some heavy damage to a dragon," she said.

"Is everyone ready?" Herne asked.

We all nodded in silent unison.

Herne nodded. "Talia, you stay in the van. Monitor all channels and keep me informed of anything you think I should know."

"Sure thing, boss." Talia was wearing a leather catsuit, her silver hair bound back.

"If we're all ready," Herne said, "let's get a move on. Cernunnos and Morgana will already be there, along with the group of gods who are supposed to create the stasis field when Echidna takes Typhon down. Technically, they aren't supposed to intervene, but even if Typhon wins, they'll attempt one last-ditch effort to bind him into stasis."

"Then we're not playing by the rules?" I asked.

He shook his head. "The dragons won't, so neither will we. There's too much at stake to play fair, and we're using whatever we can to prevent him from winning. When you're facing an enemy who can destroy everything you hold dear, you fight, you fight hard, you fight dirty, and you hope to hell you're stronger than your enemy."

I nodded. Both sides of my heritage understood, on a gut level, that when life or death depended on your choices, all rules went out the window. With so many lives relying on us, we didn't have any leeway. A ripple of energy raced through me, into my hand where I was holding Serafina—my pistol grip crossbow. I let the feeling swell up and steeled myself, pushing away all thoughts of abiding by parley.

When I opened my eyes, I looked through the eyes of a huntress, of a warrior.

Herne was watching me. "I can feel the shift," he said, his voice low.

I met his gaze. "I had to coax that side of me out. She's resilient and cunning and won't hesitate to do whatever is necessary." My mother's blood was Leannan Sidhe, and that side rose when I needed to charm someone, to find out information that they wouldn't otherwise tell me. But my father's blood—the Autumn's Bane people—that side of me went hunting for victory.

"Are we ready?" Herne asked.

We went round the table. Everyone was there—Talia, Yutani, Viktor, Raven, Kipa, Angel, Herne, and me, and in turn, we all chimed in.

"Then let me say this. I have hope for today, but it's not going to be easy. You're going to want to run when you see them rise. There will be other dragons there. I can only ask you to hold your ground until you see it's hopeless. If you're fighting and in danger, get out of the way if you can't hold your ground—"

My work phone jangled, cutting him off. I frowned, glancing at it. Oh lovely. Saílle, the Dark Fae queen. "I'd better take this," I said, answering. "Your Majesty, what can I do for you?"

The Fae queens didn't like me because I was tralaeth—half blood. I was half-Light and half-Dark Fae and neither side wanted to claim that I even existed, but we were long past their ability to do that.

"Ember, tell Herne the Fae militia are marching to join you, even now." Saílle paused, then added, "May we all have victory today."

Startled, I blurted out, "I thought you and Névé were headed back to Annwn."

"We will, if the tide turns. But until then, this is our home and we will fight for it." And with that, she hung up.

Still surprised, but feeling some relief, I turned to Herne. "The Fae militia will be here—Saílle and Névé are staying for the battle."

Herne straightened his shoulders, his eyes wide. "Well, I never in a million years expected to hear that. I can't say I'm not relieved. We asked the government to hold back because we have no idea what their weapons can do against the dragons and now isn't the time to find out. But the Fae militia can at least try to help mitigate some of the collateral damage."

"Just when you think you know what they're up to, those two surprise you, don't they?" Talia said. That broke the tension and we all relaxed for a moment. "Well, we should get moving. It's three-thirty. We'll arrive there in time for the fight."

And so, we gathered our weapons and packs, and headed out the door. We were taking two cars and a van that Herne had outfitted with thousands of dollars of various electronics to help us keep track of the situation.

I rode shotgun in Herne's Expedition, staring out at the darkness of the city streets. The sky was overcast and the clouds reflected the light of the snow, everything meshing together to form a fusion of gray and silver. The wind stirred a mist of falling snowflakes.

The streetlamps flickered by and we could see the swirling flakes caught in their light. The roads were clear —people were taking the curfew seriously—and every so often we would see a cop car on the side of the road, watching and waiting. They knew our cars—we had given the deputy mayor descriptions so they wouldn't try to stop us.

Herne's Expedition contained, besides me and Herne, Raven and Kipa. Yutani was driving his SUV, with Angel along. And Viktor and Talia were in the van. We headed down to the docks, where the challenge was set to happen.

We arrived at the docks shortly before four and scrambled out, parking as close to the water as we could. As we shouldered our packs and weapons and headed over toward the water's edge, the tension built. Here and there, clusters of people waited, but they were all incredibly tall with long flowing hair, and by their looks alone we could tell they were dragons, waiting in their human form.

I shivered. How many of them were on Typhon's side? How many were Echidna's warriors? It was impossible to tell.

As we passed by a group of four dragons who turned to watch us, a loud sound echoed from around the street corner, and the Fae militia appeared, marching in perfect formation. They were all carrying bows, and all decked out in leather armor. Their commander shouted a halt, and they came to a stop by the edge of the pier, waiting.

I moved closer to Herne as we approached the docks.

"There will be bloodshed," I said, glancing around us.

He nodded. "Oh, no doubt of that. I hope that—there, look." He nodded toward one of the piers. There, appearing one by one as they shimmered into visibility, were Cernunnos and Morgana, and Brighid. Beside them were other gods—Mielikki, and by her side a burly forest man whom I assumed was Tapio. More gods appeared, and while I had never seen them before, it was impossible not to recognize Artemis from Artemis's Huntresses, and Ullr and Skadi from Odin's Chase, both similar to the Wild Hunt. Others arrived, all bearing bows and arrows. And then, I felt the energy of the allentar arrows all around us. We were all here to stop Typhon and his children.

"How powerful are Typhon and Echidna? I know they're immortal and massive, but..." I turned to Herne, wondering that so many gods were involved.

"They're the children of Titans, Ember," Herne said. "Remember, the Titans birthed the gods. They don't call them the father and mother of all dragons for no reason." He paused, then pointed toward the sky. "They're here."

I turned, along with everyone else, and my entire perception about what we were facing slipped away, burned to a crisp, like paper to a match.

There, in the sky, a hole appeared—a portal. And then another, opposite it. There was a drop in pressure and a collective gasp rippled through the crowds as a huge dragon appeared out of one, with blue wings, and a blue body. *Echidna*.

A hydra, she was—a dragon with multiple heads. I hadn't expected that, and it took me by surprise. Her head was massive, with brilliant blue eyes, and ears to either side. A thick horn rose from her nose, curling with a wicked edge. Emerging from the sides of her head were dozens of smaller heads on the end of snake-like tentacles. Each head mirrored the main one, and they writhed in a sinuous dance.

Echidna brought with her a flurry of snowflakes and a whirl of mist that trailed behind her. Her wings were silent and massive, somehow holding her alight. They spread out like a bat's wings, their bony fingers branching off her shoulders to stretch the wings wide. The ribs from her main throat were long and elegant, leading down the underside of her neck, all the way along the belly to create plates of armor, then down to the tip of the tail.

Her scales shimmered, rippling over her body. Plates like a stegosaurus rose from the back of her neck, down to her wings. She was gigantic, bigger than a 747, longer than several whale lengths, more massive than the longest dinosaur we could have imagined being. She majestically glided out of the vortex and it spiraled closed behind her.

As Echidna swept around the docks, flying smoothly, another movement caught my eye. The other portal was broadening, and as it did, Echidna's twin entered.

Typhon.

The color of shadow and twilight, Typhon was a hundred-headed hydra, and he looked exactly like Echidna, save for his color and the fact that he was somewhat bigger.

They circled the docks, behemoths from a bygone age. Flashes twinkled, breaking the night from various places along the dock, and I realized there were reporters down here—or at least, curiosity-seekers, and all I could think about was the potential carnage if they didn't get out of the way.

But the sheer energy brought my attention back to the dragons as they slowly circled round one another. The tension was so thick that it felt like we were underwater, or in a sauna so saturated with moisture that the vapor had replaced the air.

I turned to Herne. "I never dreamed…"

"I told you, they were born of Titans. Compared to them, their children seem like kittens." His gaze was fastened on the pair, and he reached for an arrow. "You might want to load Serafina."

I brought out a bolt and fitted it in my crossbow. "I take it we aim for their children to prevent them from interfering. The Luminous Warriors, that is?" Then I froze. "We have company," I added softly.

Herne followed my gaze. Pandora was standing over on the docks, near a group of tall men I assumed were Luminous Warriors.

"Crap. I wonder if—" He stopped as Raven let out a low cry. She had spotted Pandora. She looked ready to panic. I worked my way over to her as she withdrew behind Kipa.

"I wondered if you saw her," I said.

Raven gazed at the goddess, looking ready to kill. "*See* her? I want to shove her into the water and hold her under until she drowns. I want to blast her with a fireball. I want to use this wand and bring her world tumbling down. Except she can't die." Raven narrowed her eyes.

I glanced over at Kipa. He was watching Raven carefully. He caught my gaze and I wanted to tell him to keep an eye on her, but he inclined his head and I realized he was already doing that. Regardless of therapy, PTSD could cause some pretty questionable behavior.

"What now?" I turned to Herne.

"Prepare yourself," he said. "It won't be long."

I crossed over to Angel, who was near Raven. She looked out-of-her-wits terrified. Raven joined us as Kipa shifted, bringing out a bow. Within moments, his Elitvartijat appeared—his elite guards. Ten men emerged from the shadows. They were constantly with him, appearing whenever he called. Sometimes they took the form of wolves, but now they appeared in human form, bows ready. Kipa led them a few yards away, where they could have clear shots.

As we waited, Typhon and Echidna continued to circle one another. And then, in the softly falling snow, Echidna lifted her massive head and let out a roar that shook the nearby docks. And with that, she aimed for Typhon.

As the dragons met in midair, I felt an odd pulse, and then another, and the next thing I knew, the world was spinning and I was spinning with it.

CHAPTER FOUR

EVERYTHING KEPT SPINNING, AND I COULDN'T TELL WHICH way was up. The world had vanished and a silver mist whipped around me. My ears ached. Echidna's roar had been deafening and I could hear nothing as I tumbled over and over in the formless mist.

The next moment, I grew terribly sleepy, and found myself fading. Was I dying? Had the two dragons rained down terror and just like that, we were all dead? Unable to think straight, I finally decided to give in to the pull. I closed my eyes, and everything went black.

"EMBER, EMBER? ARE YOU ALL RIGHT?" The words were faint at first, as if spoken from a long distance away, but then they grew stronger and clearer. "Ember, wake up."

Someone was shaking me, and I wanted to tell them to stop and leave me alone, but then I remembered I was supposed to be doing something. Something important or urgent or…

"Ember, *wake up!*" The fog began to lift as a voice I recognized as Raven's echoed through the air.

I tried to open my eyes and finally managed to pry them apart. I felt like a lump. I was lying somewhere cold, staring at the night sky. The stars looked very different. They were brighter and there were so many that I knew I wasn't in Seattle anymore. I couldn't be. And then it all came back —*Echidna and Typhon. The massive quake as they met in battle.*

Raven was kneeling beside me. Angel was sprawled next to me, unmoving. I realized I was on a patch of frozen grass. As Raven helped me sit up, I tried to clear my head.

"I'm all right," I said. I was bruised, but nothing hurt overly so, and as the dizziness faded, I managed to roll to my hands and knees. With Raven's help, I stood up. "How's Angel? Is she alive?" A cold stab of fear raced through me, but Raven soothed my fear.

"Yes, but she's unconscious."

I looked around. "Where are we?"

Raven shook her head. "I don't know. I'm not certain what happened. I woke up a little while ago and it took me a few minutes to be able to function. Then I woke you up."

I checked my pack, which was still slung over my back, and everything I had packed was still there. I also found Serafina a few yards away. The quiver of allentar arrows was still slung across my back. Luckily, I hadn't stabbed myself with them. My dagger, which had been sheathed in my thigh sheath, was still there.

"I still have my weapons. Sheesh, it's cold," I said, glancing around. "Where the hell *are* we?"

"Let's wake up Angel. Then maybe we can figure that out." Raven moved over to Angel and I joined her. Together, we brought Angel around. She wasn't hurt, but she, too, was thoroughly confused for a moment.

Finally, we were all coherent and on our feet. There was a fallen log nearby, and what looked like a thicket a few hundred yards ahead, so we moved over to sit along the log.

"What do you think happened?" Angel asked, shivering. "All I remember is them meeting in midair, and then everything shifted."

"Yeah, I think we fell into some portal or vortex that formed when they clashed." I frowned. "You know, like when antimatter and matter meet in the *Star Trek* world? Rather than exploding, it created a rift or something and…we fell through."

"Do you think the others did too?" Angel asked.

I looked around. We seemed to be alone.

As far as I could see, the meadow we were in stretched out under the frosty sky. The thicket to our right loomed large in the dark and my instincts all screamed, *Do not go into the forest at night.* I couldn't see the horizon well—it was too dark—so if there was anything like the silhouette of a city or an ocean, I couldn't see it. The dark here was darker than the dark at home.

"All I know is that I'm freezing. If we don't get warm, we could get frostbite," Angel said.

Raven motioned for us to scoot closer. "I can cast a fire spell if we can find something that will burn. The log feels soaked through, but if you can find some kindling and a few pieces of wood, I can make us a fire." She paused, then added, "I could create a light spell, but if there's anything out there, it will see us."

"If you spark a fire it will reveal our presence, as well." I stopped. "*Duh*, why didn't I think? Check your phones. Maybe we ended up in another part of the city, though I can't honestly think of any place that looks like this."

I pulled out my phone and turned it on. There were no bars and the clock had stopped. There was no service at all. Raven's and Angel's phones were the same way.

"No wi-fi anywhere, and no cellular data service either," Angel said, shoving hers in her back pocket. "I say we chance a fire. I'm so cold." She pulled her jacket tighter. "It feels like it's well below freezing."

I sighed. "Okay, let's look for some dried wood. Check the end of the tree, Angel, while I check the other end. There may be easy to reach dry wood inside of it."

I headed toward the narrow end of the trunk. It was splintered and the tree top seemed long gone. But the end was filled with dry kindling. I began to cautiously break off what pieces I could. I finally dug out my dagger, using it to gouge chunks of the tree out from the end. After a while, I had a tidy pile of dry shavings.

Angel and I built a mound—a tepee of the shavings—and then we broke as many limbs off the fallen tree as we could. Some were fairly big, others small, but they were all dry enough to burn. After about fifteen minutes, we stood back as Raven approached the kindling pile. She examined it, shifted a few twigs and then held out her hands.

"Spark," she whispered, and *spark* her hands did. The flickering embers ran off her fingers to land in the kindling and flames roared up, consuming the fuel and greedily searching for more. I began to arrange the larger pieces of wood over them, so that they would catch hold. In another five minutes, we had ourselves a merry fire. As we huddled around it, I gave one more glance at the thicket, then settled down and leaned toward the flames, enjoying the warmth that took the edge off the night.

"I'm exhausted," Angel said.

"It's impossible to tell what time it is, but why don't you both get some rest? I'll wake Raven in about two hours, and she can wake you in two more. Or whatever feels like two hours. That way, we'll have someone constantly on guard." I settled back against the log.

Raven dug through her pack and handed me a small silver square. "Mylar blankets. I thought they might come in handy if we got too cold while we were waiting." She spread one out on the ground, then opened another. She and Angel lay down between them, and using their packs for pillows, they both drifted off. I draped the third one around my shoulders and kept watch in the silent night. All through the long dark, I kept thinking about Herne and the dragons and whether we'd have a home left to return to.

MORNING CAME QUICKER than I expected. With it came the early rays of the sun. One moment it was dark as night and the next, the sky took on a pale lemon chiffon color, then strawberry as the sun rose to greet the sky. I glanced around. The sun's rays streamed over distant mountains, and as it rose into the sky, dew evaporated off the grass.

I woke Raven, yawning. "I need sleep, so even though it's morning, I need to crash for at least a couple of hours," I said. "How are you doing?"

"I'll be okay. I'll let Angel sleep longer. Even with her increased life expectancy, she's still human and she'll still get tired more quickly than you or I do." Raven stretched, wincing. "I feel like I pulled something, but it should be okay. I'll do some stretching while you're asleep."

I settled down next to Angel, who murmured something, turned over, and promptly began to snore. I closed my eyes, adjusting my head on the backpack, and promptly fell asleep.

"EMBER? WAKE UP." Raven roused me when the sun had moved higher into the sky. I glanced at my phone. Still no signal, nor any clue of how much time had passed.

Angel was sitting up, looking through her pack. She pulled out a bag of brownies.

"You brought a bag of brownies to a dragon fight?" I asked, grinning.

"Yes, and aren't you glad for it now?" She handed us each one and then set the bag between us. "Do you have any food, Raven? We should figure out what we have in case we're trapped here for a while. We might not find anything edible."

"I hope we can find water," I said. "We need that more than food." I glanced in my pack. "I have two water bottles, and I brought a bunch of protein bars and candy. And some cookies." I set out six protein bars and four candy bars, along with the water and the cookies.

"I have a dozen protein bars and two boxes of cookies," Raven said. She emptied her pack, sorting the food out from the rest of her gear. "I also have two bottles of water."

Angel produced another three bottles of water, two apples, and five sandwiches. "I brought extra sandwiches just in case the battle lasted longer than a day. At least we have enough food to last for a few days, if we ration it, but the water may prove a problem." She glanced around. "Where's our best chance to find a drink?"

"As far as I can tell, that looks like the same sun that's in our sky. But last night, the number of stars seemed to be ten times what we're used to, and brighter." I shook my head. Wherever we were, it didn't *feel* like home. The flora looked similar. The nearby forest looked very much like the forests in the Pacific Northwest, the grass was green and spotted with snow, the ground a solid dirt brown, but even with all the familiarity, I knew we were far away from Seattle. My gut told me so.

"We have snow—we can at least melt that when we need to, if nothing else." Angel bent over, examining a short mound of the white stuff. "It's clean, or it looks it."

"Which direction should we go?" Raven glanced around. "Into the forest? That might be our best chance for finding water and better shelter. While we didn't see anything last night, I'm not anxious to take the chance of staying out in the open again. Last night we were lucky and nothing bothered us. But we have no idea what—or who—might be around here."

"I hate to ask, but does anybody have any tissues or napkins?" Angel asked, glancing around. "I need to…use the facilities."

I pulled out a small box of tissue. "I've got these."

"I brought a roll of paper towels and some hand sanitizer. We can't waste water for washing hands until we find more to drink, so be efficient on the tissues and use the sanitizer to clean your hands," Raven said. "Also, if possible, hide your waste. That's one way to cover our scent, so do what you can to bury it or cover it with leaves."

Angel stepped behind a nearby bush that reminded me of a small blackberry patch and I stood, shading my eyes as I turned toward the forest. "I don't know why but that forest makes me nervous, but you're probably right, that's most likely our best chance to find fresh water. And the path leads there—"

"It might lead *from* there, but the mountains look a lot farther away and it's winter, so maybe we can find a cabin in the woods." Raven stepped onto the worn trail that cut through the tall grass. All the way around, from the distant horizon on our left and right, the land stretched out in an unending series of grasslands, rolling like waves on the ocean.

Behind us, toward the mountains that rose in a dusty silhouette, the grassland rippled along, unending. The movement was mesmerizing as the wind susurrated around us, stirring the grass like waves in a vast sea of green.

The path dipped down, creating a steep gradient as it led to the forest.

"How long do you think it will take us to reach the edge of the woodland?" I shaded my eyes, catching sight of a flock of birds flying near the forest. The forest made me uneasy, and I wanted to head for the mountains, but logically, we didn't have enough food to make it there unless we found something to eat along the way. Even if we did, the chance of finding water was better in the woods. There had to be moisture, given the snow on the grass, and forests usually housed springs and creeks.

"There's death in the forest," Raven said, biting her lip. "I can feel the spirits from here. But my guess is that the mountains are weeks away on foot. The forest—a day, if that? Whatever the case, it's a lot closer than the mountains."

I took a deep breath. "Then I suggest we start off immediately. I'd rather not be traveling in the dark."

Angel returned, scrubbing her hands with hand sanitizer. "Which way are we going?"

"Into the woods." Raven opened her pack. "We need to eat. Half of a protein bar and a couple swallows of water each? Then we get a move on."

As we measured out the food and water, I wondered what was going on back home. And a little part of me, a part I wanted to ignore, wondered if we'd ever make it home at all.

THE SUN ROSE HIGHER in the sky, and even though it was bright, the day was cold. And with the cold came humidity, building in the air. By early afternoon, we were getting close to the forest.

"Storm's coming," I said. "I can feel it. The hairs on my arms are standing up." I glanced around, and caught sight of what looked like a mass of clouds behind us. They churned, roiling through the sky. "I don't like the looks of that storm. Let's pick up the pace."

We began to hurry, as the energy around us built. We were nearing the forest when Raven asked, "What's the last thing you remember? Before we landed here?"

"Echidna and Typhon running headlong into each other in the air—when they tangled together," I said.

Angel nodded. "Me too—there was a massive sound, like thunder ripping through the air, and then…next thing I knew we were here."

I closed my eyes, thinking back. "My guess is that their clash ripped open a portal directly where we were standing. The three of us were together there, apart from everyone else."

"Speaking of thunder," Raven said, glancing over her shoulder. "The clouds are building and the wind's picked up."

"Yeah, I noticed," I said. "I don't think those are snow clouds, unless we're going to have thundersnow."

We turned around to face the oncoming storm. Rolling like gangbusters, an army of dark gray thunderheads raced through the sky, the wind whipping them our way. They had already blotted out the sun, and they stretched through the sky as far as I could see.

"Thunderheads…can you smell it?" Angel said, her eyes widening. "Ozone. Lightning's headed our way. We'd better get undercover in the forest. We're the tallest things out here on the plain and that's not a good position to be in."

The ozone crackled around us, humidity saturating the air. But the chill in the air made it clammy, and my shirt plastered to my chest in a cold sweat. Raven's hair began to frizz out. Then, before we could turn again, in the far distance behind us, lightning rolled across the horizon, leaping from cloud to cloud, and the distant echo of thunder rumbled through the air. The bolts were brilliant neon against the clouds, and my stomach lurched.

"Get to the forest. Now!" I shouted. I could call down the lightning when it was close enough, and right now I could feel the storm—a malicious force that was furious and fast. I could feel the crackling bolts down to my bones, as though it had a mind of its own. At that moment, a figure raced across the sky—large and luminous. It streaked past us like a football player trying to score a touchdown.

"Crap, a lightning elemental! Run!" I didn't know much about them except that they weren't friendly. I knew better than try to communicate with them. They'd fry my psychic sensors.

We bolted along the trail, trying not to tumble down the steep grade. As we raced toward the shelter of the trees, I darted another glance over my shoulder. The storm was driving forward, the clouds chasing us. I estimated the distance to the forest. I wasn't sure if we'd make it before the storm was directly overhead.

Angel loped, her long legs leading the pack. I came next, and Raven was a few steps behind me. Even though the Ante-Fae had more resilience and stamina than the

Fae, the fact was that I was in better shape than Raven, and I was used to running and fighting.

We raced silently, accompanied by the echoes of the thunder behind us. The sky was lighting up all around, with jagged forks of lightning slamming into the ground behind us, ripping great crevasses through the soil as though razor claws were rending into the flesh of whatever world we were in.

Feeling like I was breathing underwater, I tried to keep my breath steady but the humidity kept rising. We were almost to the edge of the forest when a solid wall of icy rain caught up to us, drenching us and turning the path we were on into one long, narrow mud puddle.

Angel reached the threshold first and didn't stop to look, but plunged beneath the cover of the trees. I followed, and Raven, a few steps after me. The moment we were inside the thicket, I motioned for them to follow me and darted off trail. The path was open to the sky for the most part, and we wanted to be beneath the cover of the trees. I found a shorter tree among the tall fir and hunkered down beside it. Angel and Raven joined me. We huddled together, trying to keep as free from the deluge as possible.

"Should I get out my Mylar blankets?" Raven asked.

I shook my head. "We don't know if they'd attract the lightning and they're better for keeping us warm at night. This tree's shorter than the others and the branches are thick, so we should be fairly safe, even if we get wet."

Another flash of lightning overhead was so bright it almost blinded me. The rumble that followed shook the ground. I closed my eyes, resting my head on my knees. Where the hell were we? And how could we get home?

Raven was crawling around the base of the tree. "There's something odd about this tree," she said. "I'm not sure what it is, but I recognize the feeling. I had it once, long ago, when I found my ferrets in the forest."

Looking puzzled, Angel scrawled over to her. "What are you looking for?"

"I don't know, but I'll—well, well, lookie here." Raven pointed to a hole slanting at an angle that led beneath the tree. It wasn't big enough to fit into, but there was a shimmer across the surface that looked suspiciously like a portal. "You don't think that's what brought us here, do you?"

I shook my head. "If it had, we'd have landed here in the forest. And it's not big enough. But I agree, it looks like some sort of portal." I eyed it suspiciously. "I wonder what's on the other side?"

"I'm not sticking my head through there to find out," Raven said. "What about a stick? We poke a stick through and see what happens."

Angel snorted. "Are you sure you want to do that, either? What if there's something on the other side that doesn't like being prodded? I don't want to be the mosquito that gets swatted." She found a broken branch covered with needles still and was using it as a makeshift umbrella.

"Angel has a point," I said. "Let's leave it alone until we can safely get out of here."

Overhead, the storm was tossing about on the wind like waves on the ocean. The lightning and thunder continued to ricochet through the sky, weaving a pattern of neon and sound. The rain thudded against the ground.

"I'm cold and soaked through to the skin," Angel said.

"Come here, let's huddle together for warmth." I motioned for them to scoot closer and we crawled as far beneath the branches as possible. At first, we tried to keep the conversation going, but we were miserable, wet, hungry, and far from home. After a while, we all drifted into silence, punctuated only by the sounds of the storm.

CHAPTER FIVE

After what seemed like a long time, I jumped at a particularly loud roll of thunder. Forcing my eyes open, I realized that I was experiencing caffeine withdrawal. My head felt fuzzy and my thoughts were all jumbled.

"Hell," I said. If I was feeling it, Raven and Angel would be too. Which meant we'd all be off our game, and chances were we wouldn't be prepared for anything we'd come up against. "You guys have a caffeine headache too? The adrenaline rush of running from the storm prevented it for a while, but it's hitting me full on."

Raven nodded. "Yeah, which explains to me why I feel like I want to sleep." She glanced up, and said, "Look—a sun break!"

As I gazed up, I saw she was right. There was a break in the clouds, and the sun shone down into the forest. I motioned for them to stay put and slowly stood, wincing as I stretched before heading out to the path. There, I glanced up at the narrow slip of sky between the dense overgrowth on either side. There were still clouds, most of them dark, but they seemed to be a bit more distant, and the sun had broken through them. Maybe the worst of the storm was passing.

I turned back to Angel and Raven. "Why don't we try to make some time while this break holds. Maybe we can dry off a little. I can't tell whether the storm is on the way out or not."

They joined me on the path. We were soaked through, despite the cover of the trees. It occurred to me that unless we got dried off, we could all freeze to death come night. "Don't work up a sweat, walk at an even pace. We need our clothes to dry as fast as they can. I'm thinking we might want to find a place to start a fire. We can scout for wood along the way."

"That might be a good idea—" Raven paused. "Wait. I hear something." She cocked her head, listening.

I closed my eyes, trying to focus on the noises around us. The wind whistled along but beneath that, I could make out a different noise as well. It sounded like some great beast shuffling along. The steps didn't shake the ground, but there was a tremor in the air, a reverberation that fluxed at a steady pace, coming from the entrance of the forest.

"What the hell?" I glanced along the path behind us. There was nothing unusual to be seen, nothing that seemed out of the ordinary. But the noise increased and I had the feeling that we were standing in the road as a massive bulldozer bore down on us.

"Come on." I led them back into the trees until we were a couple yards off the path.

A few minutes later, a ghostly image appeared on the path, looking like some massive holographic elephant.

The golden creature strode on six massive legs. While its body reminded me of an elephant, its neck stretched out like a horse's neck, and though it had a trunk and massive tusks, it had no tail. The ears reminded me of giant butterfly wings and its eyes were brilliant blue. There was something about it that settled my fear, calming me. My pulse began to slow. Behind the creature were two more just like it—though one was a lot smaller and had that babyish look all baby animals do.

"What's that?" Angel asked, her eyes wide.

"I don't know, but it's beautiful," Raven said. "I am fighting an urge to go give it a hug."

"You and me both," I said.

The energy of the translucent creatures was so gentle, so peaceful that it was all I could do to prevent myself from running out to greet them. As they passed by, flickers of what looked like lightning bolts darted around inside their massive bodies. They were headed into the depths of the forest.

The rajamahs, sister of the Water. The whisper came from near my feet, in images rather than words. Startled, I glanced down. I was standing near a puddle of water. I knelt and placed my fingers in the water, reaching out. Sure enough, a very tiny water elemental looped around my fingers, and the playful energy ricocheted through me.

Hello, my friend. Can you tell me about the rajamahs?

They come with the lightning, and wander until the energy of the storm moves on. They follow the storms. The storm is passing quickly, and so they will follow it until it dissipates.

Are they dangerous?

If you touch them, they will kill you, but through no malice. They are lightning encapsulated in form.

I paused. *Are they elementals themselves?*

No, but they are bound to the lightning just like lightning elementals are.

While I had the chance, I decided to find out what I could about where we were. *Do you know where we are? This is not our home, we're here by mistake, and we're lost. Where are we?*

The forest. You're within the forest. That is all that I know. But I will tell you, beware the Star Hounds. They're dangerous to all who walk the land. They're ravenous. And now, I must sleep, sister of the Water. May you find your home safely.

The water elemental fell silent. Elementals didn't actually sleep, but they could shut down into a meditative state that was very much like sleep.

"I found a little water elemental." I stood up, wiping my fingers and putting my glove back on. "Those creatures are called rajamahs and they're formed out of the lighting. If we try to touch them, we'd be touching a live wire that would jolt us into crispy critters. But they aren't deliberately harmful."

"Did you ask where we are?" Raven said.

"I did, but the elemental didn't know. However, it did warn me to watch out for the Star Hounds, whatever they are. Apparently they're ravenous." I glanced up at the sky. The sun break was growing larger. "I think the storm's mostly passed, given what the elemental told me about the rajamahs. We should head out. And now that we know that there's at least one dangerous predator around, keep up your guard."

We returned to the path and began to follow the path that the rajamahs had taken. I shook my hair loose, hoping it would dry faster that way and took off my coat.

While it was waterproof, I hadn't thought to zip it up, and my shirt and bra were soaked. So I stripped them off, tied them to my pack to dry, and put my coat back on. I couldn't very well take off my jeans, so I left them on, but luckily my boots were waterproof so my feet were still dry. Raven and Angel saw what I was doing and they followed suit.

As the frosty sun returned and the clouds vanished, I began to focus on our surroundings more. The forest was mostly coniferous, though interspersed with bare-branched birches and oaks and a few maples. Herne had taught me how to identify dozens of trees. For him it was an innate ability, but it had taken me some time.

The forest floor held scattered pockets of snow. It looked like it was melting, but we were a long ways from spring, it felt. The undergrowth wasn't nearly as thick as back home, though ferns and bushes crowded the tree trunks, surrounding them like tutus around a ballerina's waist.

I listened closely, trying to pick up on any animals that might be near. The birds were chirping again—they had gone silent during the storm—and I tried to identify what kind they were, but I wasn't much of a bird watcher. Once in a while the bushes nearby would rustle, indicating some creature passing through, but otherwise, the forest seemed oddly silent.

"Where do you think we are?" Raven asked, after we had been walking for probably an hour. "The forest seems to be a large one. I don't want to get lost."

"Newsflash," Angel said. "We already *are* lost."

"She's right," I said. "We have no frame of reference except for this path. Say, the creature that elemental mentioned…does the name ring a bell with either of you? *Star Hound?*" I was sure I had heard it someplace before, but for the life of me, I couldn't place it.

"It sounds familiar," Raven said. "Let me try to sort out where I've heard it."

Angel shook her head. "Not to me."

We were approaching a clearing and I cautiously stopped at the edge of it. It was like a turnout to the side of the road, open enough so that we could see that the storm seemed to have fully passed. But the sun was starting to set. I looked around the open space, noting a couple of downed logs, as well as what appeared to be a cushy mound of moss.

"Let's make camp here. We can light a fire and dry ourselves out."

They followed me into the clearing. Everything seemed safe enough, though I was still uneasy. The forest wasn't exactly welcoming, but now that we were into it, I wasn't feeling anything outright malicious. "Gather wood, and Raven, can you start a fire for us? I see some good-sized rocks, so we can make a fire ring."

While I gathered rocks to create a fire pit of sorts, Raven and Angel gathered wood. By the time we had enough fuel to last a few hours, the temperature had begun to drop.

"Raven, if you'll start the fire, Angel and I will gather some more wood. Then we'll eat something." I led Angel toward the edge of the clearing, near the back side of it. The sound of running water caught my attention. As we stepped into the thicket, we found ourselves a couple of yards from a stream that was flowing parallel to the path.

"Well, we've found water, at least." I knelt beside the

stream and plunged my hand into the icy current. "Let me see if it's safe to drink."

I closed my eyes, searching for any water spirits. At that moment, a woman rose out of the stream. She was soaked through, naked, gorgeous, and had the most flawless body I had ever seen. Her cerulean hair was one shade darker than her skin, and her eyes flashed a brilliant silver.

My Leannan Sidhe self responded to her—she was Water Fae.

"Hello," I said, wondering if she could understand me. "Can you help us?" But my words came out in a language that I didn't know, and while I knew what I had said, I couldn't understand what my speech had translated into.

She gazed at me for a moment, with one fleeting glance at Angel, then said, "I might be able to, sister of the Water." She spoke in the language that had come out of my mouth and I understood her perfectly.

I turned to Angel. "Do you understand what she's saying?"

Angel shook her head. "No, and I feel like I should get the hell out of here." She was staring at the woman with wide eyes.

I turned back, eyeing the water spirit. "Yes, I'm Leannan Sidhe—part of my heritage, at any rate. We're strangers here, lost from our homeland. Is it safe to camp in the woodland?"

She stared at me for another moment, then gracefully inclined her head. "No more dangerous than anywhere else." She grinned then, and I could see the razor-sharp teeth in her mouth. *A kelpie!* I slowly backed away, but she laughed. "I won't attack you, given we're both of the water, but tell your friend to watch herself."

The warning was clear. I turned to Angel. "Go back to the camp. Now. Don't tarry. She's a kelpie."

Angel gave me a nod and turned, carrying the filled water bottles with her. As she vanished into the trees, I turned back to the kelpie.

"Can you tell me where are we? We were catapulted through a portal and have no idea where we ended up."

She regarded me for a few moments and then said, "Very well. You're in Annwn, in the land of Caer Arianrhod."

"Caer Arianrhod?" I caught my breath. Caer Arianrhod was the land where the goddess Arianrhod dwelled and lived. The goddess of the Silver Wheel, Arianrhod's castle —Caer Sidi—was in this realm, yet also in between the worlds, in space. Arianrhod ruled over reincarnation, fate, fertility, and childbirth.

And then the kelpie's words hit me—we were in Annwn. We could find Cernunnos's palace and safely find our way home from there. "Do you know how we can find Cernunnos's palace—or Brighid's palace?"

The kelpie narrowed her eyes. "They're both far. Travel afoot will take you a long journey. And until you leave the boundaries of Caer Arianrhod, you risk being hunted by the Star Hounds."

Once again, I felt like I had heard the term before, but I still couldn't remember what they were. "What are they?"

"Arianrhod's guards. They're the predecessors of the Black Dogs, and they hunt anyone who isn't native to this land. All of us born here bear Arianrhod's mark—down to the smallest sprite. And since the dead pass through Caer Arianrhod on their way to greet Arawn, the majority who travel this realm live among the world of spirits." She yawned, then smiled again, showing those razor-sharp teeth again. It was better when she was frowning. "You tire me now. Be off, before I forget our connections."

I thanked her and turned, heading back to Raven and Angel, who had managed to build a fire. Angel had rigged up a few long sticks close enough to the flames so the heat radiated around them, but they weren't near enough to burn, and she had hung our shirts over them. She and Raven were standing close to the heat, butts toward the flicker of flames, trying to dry the rest of their clothes. I joined them, welcoming the warmth, although it made me acutely aware of how cold I actually was.

"If you hear a voice urging you to go to the stream, don't listen," I said.

"I told her already," Angel said. "I knew the kelpie was dangerous the moment we saw her. She reeks of predator."

"She is, like I am," I said softly. And it was true. Both sides of my heritage were dangerous, and I—especially with my Leannan Sidhe blood—was as deadly as the kelpie. "But I have some good news, at least. We're in Annwn. In Arianrhod's lands."

"Well, at least we know we're not in some distant realm we'll never find our way out of," Raven said. "If we can make it to Cernunnos's palace, we should be fine."

"That's what I was thinking. But first, I'm going to try to catch us some fish. We need more food than half a protein bar, and even though it's winter, there will be fish in the stream."

"You'll have to do it without me," Angel said. "I'm too afraid of being caught by the kelpie. She had a set of mean-looking teeth."

Raven sighed. "Kelpies aren't going to catch me, that I can tell you right now. But I don't want to leave Angel here alone, especially if there are Star Hounds on the loose." She shivered. "The Black Dogs are dangerous enough. I know, given my father's one. But if the Star Hounds are their ancestors, then we're in trouble."

I made sure I had my dagger, and I took Serafina with me, in case I was attacked while at the stream, though I dreaded using up the allentar arrows. That brought me back to thoughts of what was going on back home. We had been here, what…nearing two days? In that time, the entire world could have changed. And I had no clue what we'd be returning to.

As I approached the stream, the kelpie was resting on the other side of the water. The stream wasn't fully a river, but it looked deep and the current was swift. I debated on what to say, if anything. Finally, I decided that I'd have better luck if I asked for her help.

"Hey, sister of the Water, can you help me? I need to catch some fish, and I don't have a fishing rod." I wasn't sure if she would even answer, but it was worth a shot.

She stared at me for a moment, then dove beneath the surface. So much for that.

I looked around for a branch that was long and thin enough to use for a pole and found one that had broken off of a nearby fir tree. As I tried to figure out what to use for a fishing line and used my dagger to saw off the small limb, a noise made me glance over my shoulder. The kelpie was on my side of the shore now, and she placed nine trout on the ground.

"This should keep you for the night and to break the morrow's fast." Before I could thank her, she once again disappeared into the icy water.

I waited for a moment, but she didn't reappear, so I picked up the fish, which were so fresh they didn't even smell, and carried them back to the camp. They were slippery, but I managed to cradle them against my chest.

"You can't have had that much luck in such a short time!" Raven gaped at my catch.

"No. Our frenemy the kelpie gave them to me. They're freshly caught."

"You don't think they're spiked with some drug, do you?" Angel asked.

I shook my head. "No, I don't."

"Give them to me, I can clean them." Angel had a dagger of her own, though she was reluctant to use it, but now she dug into the fish with it, effortlessly cleaning them. After she was done, I ran back to the stream with them to rinse them off. When I returned, Angel fixed them on a stick to roast over the fire. The other three, she packed inside a pile of snow near us for morning. We drank as much water as we could and I carried the bottles back to the stream to fill them up again.

The smell of roasting fish made my stomach rumble as the three of us sat around the campfire. Our clothes were dry and we redressed in our shirts and bras as the evening wore on. The moon rose high—it was going to be a clear, cold night. We poked around, finding more wood, and Raven added an extra oomph to the fire with her magical flame, which amped up the warmth.

"What do you think's happening at home?" Angel asked, checking on the fish.

I shrugged, my arms wrapped around my knees as I scooted closer to the flames. "I don't know. It seems so far away right now. But at least we know where we are."

"I wonder if the dragons won," Angel murmured. "I keep thinking about DJ."

"I'm sure Cooper's keeping him safe," I said, though I knew it wasn't much help. All our loved ones would be frantic about us, and we were frantic about them. Well, most of them. The only reason I wasn't worried about Herne was that he was a god, but Talia and Viktor and Yutani could be killed. "I'm trying not to second-guess what's happening. There are so many variables."

We fell silent as the evening wore on. The hot fish in our bellies made us sleepy. I took first watch again as Angel and Raven curled up beneath the Mylar blankets. The stars wheeled overhead, and as I watched them, I thought of Annwn, and how vast of a realm it was. Would we ever find our way to Cernunnos's palace?

A sudden howl in the distance made me shiver, and I paused, wondering if it was one of the Star Hounds. I made sure Serafina was ready, and nocked an arrow, cocking the crossbow so it would be ready the moment I needed her. As the night wore on, I sat in the darkness, watching the flames, missing Herne, and Mr. Rumblebutt, and all my other friends. But mostly, I kept coming back to the question: Would we still have a home to return to, and what would the world be like when we made it home?

CHAPTER SIX

RAVEN HAD TAKEN OVER, AND I WAS DEEP IN A DREAMLESS sleep when she woke me up.

"You need to get up, Ember. I hear something."

I sat up slowly, trying to get my bearings. The fire was still burning brightly, and overhead, the moon shone down out of the cloudless sky. As I slipped from beneath the blanket, the chill of the night hit me full force and I shivered.

"What's going on?" I asked.

Raven pointed to our left, toward the tree line. "I hear something. I've heard something for the past twenty minutes, but I thought it might be the wind. Now, I'm not so sure. There doesn't seem to be a breeze."

She was correct. Neither bush nor tree were stirring, and yet when I listened, I could hear what she was talking about. It was a soft rustling, like something skulking through the bushes. I motioned to Angel's sleeping form.

"Wake her up. We don't want to be caught a woman down."

As Raven went to wake Angel, I gathered my bow and quiver, nocking an arrow and putting the safety on. We were all within range of the campfire, which made us visible targets. I tried to decide whether it was wiser to douse the flames than keep them lit. As long as we were visible, we were potential pincushions for anyone with a bow. But if we extinguished the campfire, and there *was* something out there, we'd be fighting blind when it attacked. I decided to make an executive decision. Even though it made us more vulnerable, the fire would give us an advantage should anything come out of those woods.

"What do you think it is?" Angel asked, now awake.

I shook my head. "I have no idea. Maybe an animal, hopefully something like a fox. But it could be something else, too." I kept coming back to the Star Hounds. I still didn't know enough about them to gauge whether they would be found running around the woods or not. If they were Arianrhod's guards, it stood to reason that they would be near her castle. But if there were others — not employed in her service — then they could easily be out here in the forest.

Raven poked me in the arm. "Remember, I'm carrying my wand. But I don't want to use it unless absolutely necessary. Consider it a last chance solution."

I gave her a sideways glance. The fact was, Raven was carrying a wand that could destroy buildings. "Yeah, we do not want to waste the power of that weapon. You can use that once before you have to charge it, correct?"

She nodded. "Yes, so we want to save it. I'd hate to use it and find out there was only something like a bear out there."

"Don't you think standing around talking is going to

give them more of an advantage?" Angel said. "Whatever *they* are."

She was right, but I wasn't sure what else we could do. Wandering into the forest to discover what was watching us didn't seem like the best idea, especially in the middle of the night.

"Do you *really* want to go trekking into the forest? In the dark? I don't want to use up the flashlights any more than possible."

"Do you think the kelpie might know what's out there?" Raven asked.

I snorted. "She's helped us twice, once with information and once with the fish. I'm not sure I want to push things for a third favor." Another thought occurred to me. "I wonder if this forest is part of Y'Bain."

The massive forest of Y'Bain spread across most of Annwn. The gods weren't allowed inside of it, and the woodland was filled with dangerous creatures. I had been in the forest before, and knew firsthand how easy it was to get lost in there. Even if I could get in touch with Herne, he couldn't come rescue us here. Which meant—if that was where we were—we'd have to fend for ourselves until we found our way out.

"If we are in Y'Bain, neither Herne nor Kipa can come to the rescue us."

"That's why I haven't used this," Raven said, pulling out a coin. "I remembered I had it this morning." She was holding a silver coin the size of a silver dollar, with the figure of a stag on it. "Herne gave this to me before Kipa and I left for Kalevala. I've been holding onto it. He told me if I were to hold it and think of him, he would come to help. I forgot I had it while we were still out in the open plains. But I know it won't work in this forest if we are in Y'Bain, so I've held off trying it. If I use it, and he can't come, it's a waste."

I stared at her for a moment. This was the first time I had heard that Herne was in the habit of giving away coins to summon him. "I wish you had thought of that when we first landed in Annwn."

"I wish I had, too. I carry it in a little pouch in my backpack whenever Kipa and I have to go somewhere that might prove dangerous. It's not that I don't trust Kipa, but it's always better to have two gods in your side than one." She looked crestfallen. "I let us down. I was so dazed by the transfer over here that I completely forgot."

"Don't fret," Angel said. "We all make mistakes and we all forget things. It's human nature, and it's the same with the Fae and the Ante-Fae. We're all prone to shock and surprise, and none of us ever expected to end up in Annwn when we headed out for the battle between Typhon and Echidna." She glanced over at the tree line. "Can you still hear whatever it is?"

I closed my eyes and focused on the trees. There it was, balancing on the edge of perception. I listened closer. The sounds weren't random, but rather—methodical, as though someone was pacing first to the left, then to the right. I had the sudden image of a big cat in a cage, watching its captors. The sense that we were intended prey hit me full force. I opened my eyes and spun, staring at Raven.

"It's a predator, all right. It seems impatient, as though it's waiting for an opening so it can pounce. I don't know if someone's keeping it on a leash, or if there's a reason it hasn't made its move yet, but whatever the case, we're on the radar."

"Maybe it can't act in the dark," Angel said, glancing nervously at the tree line.

"Maybe it can only attack under the cover of the forest," Raven said.

Neither prospect boded well. I glanced at the sky. Dawn was on the way, so if Angel was right and it couldn't act in the dark, we'd best be ready come first light.

"Let's sit by the fire, eat the rest of the fish, and try to be prepared." I sat down on the log that was near the firepit.

Angel yawned, then skewered the three remaining fish. She fixed them over the fire on the makeshift rotisserie. As they sizzled in the flames, I handed out bottles of water and we drank them down. Might as well get as hydrated as we could while we were near a stream.

As the first streaks of pale blue and yellow began to flicker into the sky, I noticed a decided red tinge to the dawn. " 'Red sky at night, sailor's delight. Red sky in morning, sailors take warning,' " I said. "Storm on the way." Sometimes the old wives' tales had it right, and this was one of them that I trusted.

"I hope not another thunderstorm," Raven said. "Though seeing those…what did you call them? Rajamahs? They're beautiful."

"They were, at that," I said. "As soon as the sun's up, I'll go try to get some more information out of the kelpie."

Angel handed us each a fish and they were as flavorful as the night before. The lack of enough food to fill us up tended to make what we *did* have taste so much better. I thought about breaking out a package of cookies, but we didn't know how long we'd be on the road. Hell, we didn't even know if we were headed in the right direction, and I didn't want to use up what we had. On the other hand, we needed a few carbs along with the protein, so I added another half protein bar and two cookies to each of our meals, counting on the sugar and chocolate to give us immediate fuel.

As the dawn gave way to morning, I could still faintly hear whatever was pacing in the woods, but as the sun broke through the trees, the sound vanished. I decided to make the short trek to the stream. I entered the forest and paused. The only noises I heard were the sounds of small animals and birds. I crossed through the trees until I came out on the shores of the stream. In the early morning, the whitewater tumbled over the rocks and the endless forest beyond, both making me feel isolated and yet, reminding me of home.

The kelpie was sitting on the shoreline, eating a raw fish. I grimaced, but reminded myself that it was far better than if she were eating a human arm or a leg—which kelpies routinely did when they attracted strangers into their lairs. She looked up at me, her brows narrowing.

"You're still here? I thought you would be on your way," she said between bites.

"We needed to rest. Say, do you know what's been pacing in the trees, watching us all night? Could it be one of the Star Hounds?"

The kelpie shook her head. "No, they would attack. You probably heard one of the night-watchers. The spirits of those who journey through the forest to Caer Sidi. Some of them are angry, and some very powerful. Some refuse to complete the journey and can attack, if they're strong enough. If they can't reach into the physical realm, they watch, angry that they're dead and unable to free themselves. You do know what forest you're in, don't you?"

I shook my head. "No, we were thinking Y'Bain."

"No, not Y'Bain. You're in the Foraoise na Marbh. The Forest of the Dead." She leaned back, arching her back. Her breasts lifted, round and plump, their nipples stiff in the breeze. If I had been bi, gay, or a guy, my eyes wouldn't have been on her face. She looked even more alluring now than before. "This forest rings Caer Sidi, encircling the borders of Caer Arianrhod. You're on the inner side."

My heart sank. "How wide is the forest? And how far is it from Cernunnos's palace?"

"Wide enough that it will take you weeks to traverse on foot, and then only if you keep to a steady pace. You're in northern Annwn, a long jaunt from the Forest Lord's lands."

I sat there, brooding. After a moment, I looked back at the kelpie. "What's your name?"

She hesitated, then said, "Irianie."

"I'm Ember. I'm Herne's fiancée."

That produced a reaction. First, she looked startled, then she seemed to mellow—her stance became less rigid, and she brought her knees up to her chest and wrapped her arms around them. "Then you'll become a goddess."

"Yes, I will." I let out a long sigh. "Thank you for talking to me. For helping me."

She inclined her head. "I cannot journey with you, but I can bring you more fish for your journey, and something else that might help." She dove beneath the water again and when she returned, she carried twelve more fish in a net, along with some bulbous water plants.

"Thank you."

"You may need this as well," she said, handing me a small bag that jingled. Inside were a dozen gold coins— far'ens, the money of Arawn. Each coin was worth twenty qik. "I've little use for this sparkle and I gather it's worth quite a bit."

I tucked the bag in my pack. "Thank you again. I won't forget your kindness."

"Consider it…a good will offering," Irianie said. "Which way will you travel?"

"If we travel to the mountains, we'll be heading to Caer Sidi, correct?"

She nodded.

"And it's closer than Cernunnos's palace?"

Again, a nod.

"Then I propose we start off for there. Maybe Arianrhod will be able to help us. But we'll need to watch out for the Star Hounds. Do you know if they run free or are they pretty much near her castle?"

"They're all through the Forest of the Dead, and all through the land. And there are other creatures, just as deadly. Snakes are venomous, as well, and several species of spiders, along with a few predatory animals. Caer Sidi lies at the top of a mountain. The path you came through the forest on will lead you there. But the open land will be cold and there won't be much food along the way." She handed me the bag of fish. "The plants are water-roots. They're edible but they need to be cooked. You'd best carry some wood with you. There won't be much when you cross through the grasslands."

I stood, hoisting the fish over my shoulder. "What about water?"

"This land is crisscrossed with streams and creeks. You should find water without much of a problem, even in the heart of summer."

"When Herne and I marry, I'll return to say hello. Maybe I can repay the favors you've shown me."

"I would welcome the visit," Irianie said. She watched me as I headed for the trees, but said nothing.

"So, we're not in Y'Bain. This is the Forest of the Dead. Which means your coin should work here," I said.

Raven nodded. "Should I use it now?"

"Yes, if you can. We might as well try before we set out on a long trek."

Raven pulled out the gold coin. I stopped her for a moment, holding up one of the coins Irianie had given me, but they didn't match.

"Okay, I just wanted to see." I stood back, as did Angel.

Raven took hold of the coin, closing her hand around it. She closed her eyes and focused, and murmured, "Help. Herne, please help."

The coin was in the center of her palm and, as we watched, it shimmered, pulsing once, then once again before it sat lifeless. Nothing happened.

"Well, crap. Maybe you have to be in the same realm as he is—" Angel started to say, but Raven shook her head.

"No, because he gave it to me right before I left for

Kalevala. So it has to sync into other realms. I'm not sure why it didn't work." She looked at me, as though expecting an answer.

"*I* don't know why it didn't work," I said, almost defensively. "Herne's the one who programmed the damned thing. Maybe he's still tied up in the dragon war. He can't die, so I'm not worried that he got himself killed, but maybe the war's still going on. I wonder if they're still fighting? It's been how many days?"

"Three? Four? I've lost count," Angel said. "I guess we take off and if he's detained, he'll find us wherever we are, given the coin is with Raven." After a moment, she added, "What do you think is going on back home? Do you think the dragons won?"

I shrugged. "I have no idea and I'm almost afraid to speculate. If Typhon won, it won't be good news. If he didn't, it might still be a mess. Either way, it's going to affect the way the people see the dragons. That theme park of theirs might go bust if he loses. But…the Dragonni are tricky, and I don't trust them not to carry on their father's fight behind the scenes."

"Let's smoke these fish before we leave. It will take an hour or so to cook them, and then we can wrap them in cold leaves so they last longer. I'd say we'll need to eat them up within two days, so a fish each in the morning and another at night." Angel set about gutting and spitting the fish, then she placed the spit over the fire.

"So, you want to head north, you said?" Raven was using some twine from her pack to tie bundles of kindling together. "We'll need wood. I can spark a fire off the grass, but it burns so fast that we wouldn't have the heat for long."

"Why don't we fashion a sledge or a travois that we can drag behind us to carry wood. It will slow us down, but with the weather being so cold, we can't chance being caught without some sort of heat." Angel wiped her hands on her jeans and stood up. "Let's hope that Herne is just detained and that he'll be here as soon as he can."

She was taking everything so well that I wanted to give her a medal. I started to say something but then thought back. When Mama J. had died, Angel had been a rock, taking over the care of her little brother without a single protest. When Rafé had died, she had mustered up, coping with the loss of her boyfriend better than I had expected. And now, she was dealing with being lost in a strange land with pragmatism and patience.

"All right, what do we need to build a sledge?" I looked around. "I suppose we'll need to make a sort of land raft, if you know what I mean. Small but big enough to hold a bunch of wood. Damn, I wish we had a saw."

"Look for branches we can break easily. There's a lot of downed wood in this forest, I've noticed," Raven said. "In fact, it feels like the energy of the forest is slowly evaporating. Maybe it's the ghosts."

"You think?" Angel said.

Raven nodded. "I can feel spirits here, but they feel different than the ones I'm used to. Less aware, and more…like the flickering of shadows on a wall. Because here's the thing…Arawn is the god of the dead. *I'm* his priestess. But he sends some of the souls to Arianrhod to reincarnate, and he sends heroes to Cerridwen to go through the cauldron of rebirth. And others…wander until they've paid their penance. Still others are forever caught in limbo, and some are destroyed for good. The most evil among men are slated for oblivion."

Angel and I stared at her. "Wow, I had no idea that those who follow the Celtic path go through all that after they die."

"You'd be surprised by the Finns. It's far more intense, in many ways. Over in Kalevala, I've heard the strangest legends and tales." She frowned, eyeing the forest. "What might be easiest is to find two long poles and then lash branches to either side. It would be easier than trying to make it entirely of wood. I have a length of rope in my pack we can use to bind everything together. Back in Kalevala, I never go anywhere without rope. The land is a beautiful but rugged place to live."

While the fish roasted over the fire, we gathered two branches, each about five feet long and a good inch or two in diameter, and then we used our daggers to cut long boughs filled with needles off of the trees. We lashed them to the central poles, creating a sledge, then used the rest of the rope that Raven had brought with her to create shoulder straps that we could loop over our shoulders so that we didn't have to use our hands to pull it along.

While Angel packaged up the fish as best as she could, Raven and I gathered wood and stacked it on the sledge along with the bundles of kindling that Raven had made. Since she could spark a flame with her magic, we wouldn't need to carry smoldering embers from the fire.

We were finally ready. I made one last visit to the stream to fill every water bottle we had after we drank them down, and to say good-bye to Irianie.

"Thank you." I knelt by the stream and handed her the

bottles as she filled them and returned them to me. "I'll see you again. I know I will."

"I feel it as well," she said. "Well met, Queen Ember."

I laughed. "I'm not a queen yet."

"You will be," she said. "And people would do very well to walk on your good side."

With that cryptic statement, she dove beneath the water and vanished. I returned to Angel and Raven and, with me hauling the sledge, we began to make our way back along the route we had come, toward the north, starting on the long journey to Caer Sidi.

CHAPTER SEVEN

WE CAME TO THE EDGE OF THE FOREST NEAR DUSK. WE HAD taken turns pulling the sledge behind us, and we were all shoulder-weary and sore. It was much harder than it looked in the movies. We stepped out of the forest, back into the open. I scanned the sky but could see no sign of a storm coming over the horizon. The night would be clear and it was already growing bitter cold.

I turned to the others. "Where do you want to spend the night? In the forest, or out there in the open?"

"The grassland," Raven said. "While it would be nice to have some cover one more night, at least out there we can see if anything's approaching."

Angel agreed, so we gathered a couple more armfuls of wood, piling them atop the sledge so that we wouldn't have to use our stash so quickly, and then we made our way up the sloping incline, with me hauling while Angel and Raven pushed the sledge. Once we could see the miles of grassland ahead of us, I stopped.

At that point, it occurred to me that the pathway was

wide enough for a wagon to travel on. This had to be one of Annwn's major roads. A look at the grass to either side of the road and I realized that we'd better clear an area for the fire so we didn't run the risk of sparking the wildfire of the century. The grass wasn't dried out, but that guaranteed nothing.

I pulled out my dagger. "Come on, let's build a fire ring. We may not have any stones, but we can dig a wide ditch and watch so the fire won't carry over. When we put it out…well…if there's moisture in the air, I can coax it out to drench the flames."

"Cool," Raven said. "I can create the fire, you can call water. We need to remember that if we run out."

"Well, as long as there's some humidity, I can coax it out. If it gets hot and dry, all bets are off." I began to shear blades of the tall grass down at the root while Angel pulled out a dagger she was carrying and plunged it into the earth, digging out a trench.

"How deep should I make it?" she asked, glancing up at the waning light. The sunset in the west glowed orange, and overhead, the sky was growing dark at a rapid pace.

"At least six inches deep and a foot wide."

Raven helped her as I finished cutting the grass away. I was careful to sever it at the ground, and the blades of grass, which were a good eighteen inches long, I set aside for later. We finished carving out the fire ring and then laid a bundle of kindling down and prepared enough wood to hopefully last us the night. Raven struck a spark with her magic and soon we had a small fire crackling.

As we huddled near it, the temperature took a nosedive and we wrapped ourselves in the Mylar blankets, trying to catch the heat of the flames to mirror against the reflective material.

"It's going to be a cold night," Angel said, shivering. "I wish we had a tent."

"I wish we did too, but yeah, we weren't expecting this little jaunt, were we?" I rubbed my hands together. Even in my gloves, my fingers were tingling from the chill. A wave of loneliness washed over me and I realized how much I missed my home and Mr. Rumblebutt. Was Ronnie taking care of him? Or Herne?

"I miss my kitty," I said, tears gathering in my eyes.

"And I miss Raj," Raven said. "He won't understand why I'm not home."

"I can't bear the thought of Mr. R. feeling like I abandoned him."

We were set to have a good pity-party, but it was hard to focus on anything else.

Angel came to the rescue. "I have my e-reader with me, and it has a long charge on it since I only use it for reading. Why don't we read a book while we're resting? We can take turns reading through a couple chapters. If we parcel it out, we should be able to get a month out of it before it dies. I have several books downloaded so we don't actually need a signal."

I perked up. Angel and I had the same taste in books—murder mysteries with a touch of romance. Raven also was eager to join in. So Angel picked one none of us had read—*A Kiss of Bones* by Erian Lancsher, a Fae author, and we started to read aloud, the cold black of night surrounding us, and the only glimmers in the darkness were the flames of the fire and the backlight of the e-reader.

RAVEN WAS ON WATCH FIRST, and so I snuggled up next to Angel and tried to sleep. It was colder out in the open than it had been in the forest and overhead, the stars shone down with a brutal intensity. I stared at the constellations, or what I thought might be constellations, unable to sleep. Had Herne gotten the message from Raven's coin? What could be happening? Was he involved in the fight and unable to get away? Or did he somehow not hear the summons? It was then that I realized how much hope I had put on the chance that he could rescue us.

If he didn't know where we were, we were going to have to manage it ourselves. If we could get our asses up to Arianrhod's castle, she might help us. As to prayer, I hadn't even given it a thought, but now I found myself wondering if I prayed to Morgana or Cernunnos—or if Raven prayed to Arawn or Cerridwen—shouldn't they be able to hear us better since we were in their realm? Slipping from beneath the blanket, I crept over to where Raven was watching the fire, keeping it stoked.

"Hey," I whispered, settling down beside her.

"What are you doing up?"

"I couldn't sleep," I said. "I was thinking about the gods. What if we prayed to our gods? They hear us when we're home, what about here? We're in Annwn, shouldn't reception be better since this is their home realm?"

"Hmm," Raven said. "Maybe you're right. I usually don't think about praying for help. I only pray when I'm trying to get in touch with them to ask if there's anything I should be doing."

"I don't pray at all," I said. "It seems so odd to do so, when I can usually pick up a phone and text Morgana."

Raven laughed. "It is odd, when you think about it. The concept of prayer. I guess they can hear us because we're their priestesses. But…the phone? Have you tried texting here?"

I shook my head. "I'm not sure how they get our messages, but…" I pulled out my phone and looked at it. "It's out of juice. I can't recharge it without electricity. So it's pretty much a thin paperweight ri—" I paused, straightening. Alarm bells were ringing in my head. "Raven, something's watching us. I can feel it. The hairs on my—"

"Yeah, I can feel it too," she said. "I'm trying to pinpoint the direction." After a moment, she added, "Whatever it is, it's hiding in the grass behind us." She kept her voice low and even.

My back rippled with tension. There was something out there that was stalking us. The Autumn's Bane blood from my father told me that. Born with predator blood, I could sense when another predator was around.

"It's stalking us," I whispered. "I have a bad feeling about this. Get your spells ready." I made sure Serafina was locked and loaded with one of the allentar bolts, then cautiously knelt beside Angel to wake her up.

"Hey, get up," I said, my words soft as I shook her shoulder.

She woke hard, but after her initial gasp, she sat up, shaking her head. "What's—"

"Shush," I said, leaning close. "We've got a visitor across the trail, watching us. I'm not sure what it is, but it's in hunting mode."

Angel slid out from beneath the blanket and followed me back to the fire. Once there, we waited, back to back, staring into the darkness. While I sensed the menace coming from in the grass across the trail, we didn't want to leave anything to fate. Better to keep an eye out in all directions rather than get a nasty surprise.

I hated the feeling of being stalked. If an attack was coming, I wanted it out in the open. I had been stalked by an ex-boyfriend by the name of Ray Fontaine for months. Finally, Herne had helped me take care of him but during the time he was stalking me, the knowledge that he was out there watching me had left me wanting to beat the crap out of him.

"Look," Raven whispered. She was watching across the trail.

I turned, and sure enough, there was something moving in the grass. It was impossible to tell what was there, but an inky spot in the darkness warned that we were, indeed, being observed.

Angel gasped as she turned. "It's after us," she said. "I can feel it from here." She was an empath and I trusted her feelings implicitly.

"Dangerous?"

"Worse. Malevolent. Get ready because it's on the way —and I think there's more than one." Her voice quavered as she pulled out her dagger. Angel was learning to fight, and doing well, but she wasn't cut out for anything hard core. Not yet.

"Get behind Raven and me," I said.

She didn't put up false bravery, but quickly moved behind Raven and me, and picked up a flaming stick from the fire. "This will probably be a better weapon for me than the blade," she said, sliding the dagger back in its sheath.

I trained Serafina on the figures moving toward us. Every nerve in my body was screaming "Shoot! Shoot!" but I knew better than to send a bolt into the dark. They needed to be close enough so that I couldn't miss. I was a good shot, but I wasn't Herne, who never missed his mark.

Raven was murmuring an incantation, building up her spell. The Wand of Straha was hanging by her side, but that much firepower was better left for more than a road-side skirmish, especially since it was one use only, after which she'd have to recharge it. Flames began to flicker from her fingers, but they looked more powerful than I remembered from before. They crackled green and yellow, rather than the usual orange-red, and the hair on my arms stood up as I averted my gaze. The wisps were mesmerizing, and I needed to concentrate on what was happening, not on watching the dancing flames.

The figures were now on the path and we could see them better. There were two of them, bipedal, tall and muscular, but they were blacker than night, as though they were pieces of the void encapsulated in form, and they reminded me of the figures of the Egyptian gods who were half man, half beast.

"Black dogs, but more than black dogs," Raven whispered, staring at them.

"Crap. *Star Hounds*." I leveled Serafina, aiming at the nearest, and squeezed the trigger. The bolt soared, shimmering in the night. The allentar took on a violet glow as it winged toward its mark. My target paused for a moment, then shook its head and tried to jump to the side. But my bolt hit square center in its chest. If its heart was where a man's would be, then I managed to hit it.

The Star Hound shrieked and the silhouette of its body began to flicker, like a TV gone staticky. It howled but it continued to lope toward me, as the bolt disintegrated.

The other Star Hound growled, rumbling through the night, and went down on all fours, rushing toward Raven. She thrust her hands forward, launching her spell, and a spray of the green fire jetted out in a long stream, engulfing the Star Hound.

It let out a howl as the flames took hold. Instead of dying away, they clung to its body, their ethereal fire spreading to envelop the beast. The creature dropped to the ground, rolling as it tried to extinguish the flames.

Meanwhile, I nocked another arrow in the crossbow and sent it singing toward the first Star Hound, who was mere yards away. The bolt found its mark again, and this time, the Star Hound went down on its knees, convulsing as the magical metal worked its magic.

Raven quickly called up another spell and this time, she launched herself toward the Star Hound who was almost at my feet, slapping her hands against the void of its body. Her scream mingled with the howl of the creature and I was close enough to see that Raven was hurt. I knocked her away from the Star Hound even as a ball of fire began to glow in its chest.

As I held her, rolling away from the creature, the fist-sized orb of fire exploded, and the Star Hound went limp and collapsed.

Angel shouted, pointing at the other creature. It was back on its feet, but staggering toward us, and I quickly locked another bolt in Serafina and fired. Again, I hit the mark, and the Star Hound staggered. Once again, it collapsed as the arrow vanished. I wasn't sure if it was dead or just wounded, so I yanked out my dagger and raced over to the Star Hound. I skidded to my knees by it, reaching down to hold it firm against the ground.

That was a big mistake.

"Holy fuck!" I yanked my hand away. My fingers felt like they might freeze and fall off, and I realized why Raven had screamed.

I was about to draw my dagger across its neck when the Star Hound shattered into tiny shards. The other hound did the same, and I scrambled back as the wind swept in and picked up the pieces, carrying them away toward the north.

"What the hell?" Angel said, turning to Raven. "Ember, Raven's hands are hurt."

I hurried over. The sensation that we were being watched was gone. We were safe for the moment.

By the fireside, Raven held out her hands. The skin was blistered and peeling, as though she'd had hypothermia. I examined her fingers closely. She could still bend them, though it hurt her to do so.

"You're lucky. If you'd held onto the Star Hound much longer, you might have lost a few of your fingers. As it is, the skin's peeling. This is going to hurt for a while. Why weren't you wearing gloves?"

"Same reason you weren't—it's not easy to fight in them, and I sure as hell can't cast a spell with them on," she said, wincing. "What should I do? I don't want them getting infected."

"I have some first-aid salve that Ferosyn made for me

awhile back. I always carry it with me. Most human antibiotic creams don't work on the Fae. Question is, will it work on one of the Ante-Fae?" I dug through my pack, looking for the little jar.

"It should. We're different, but your race did come from mine," she said, holding out her hands again. "I'm willing to give it a try."

I rubbed the salve across her hands, trying to be as gentle as I could.

She sucked in a sharp breath, holding it for a moment before letting it stream from between her teeth. "Your touch hurts, but the salve feels good."

I stared at her hands. The blistered skin was regaining the color it should have, and already looked better.

"The salve has a numbing quality for pain. It should help, but you probably shouldn't go conjuring fire like that. At least not for a few days. Though if we need it..."

"If we need my spells, I'll cast them regardless of the pain," she said. "So, we know what the Star Hounds are. At least we know what we're going up against if they show up again."

"It's obvious they won't be shy about attacking, if we come across any others. Even though the first arrow hurt that one pretty bad, it was still coming for us."

Angel sighed, sitting down by the fire. "I got a glimpse of their natures while they were attacking. I think they're programmed to attack. From what I could sense, they were totally fixated on killing us. There was no other intent there."

"I wonder why. I mean, do they do that to all the creatures here, or only those who don't belong to the land of Caer Arianrhod?" Raven said.

"I'd guess the latter, rather than the former, but I don't know. Arianrhod's not a bloodthirsty goddess, but she's removed from humankind—more so than the other gods." With the gods, sometimes there was no way of knowing what their natures were. I glanced at the frosty sky. "We should try to get more sleep. I'll keep watch. Raven, you and Angel get some rest."

And so I took my place by the fire, tense and feeling like I'd drunk an entire pot of coffee. It was amazing what a good adrenaline rush could do.

CHAPTER EIGHT

By morning, I was bleary eyed again, but I pulled out some of the remaining fish—we had enough for about another day and a half—and Angel handed us each two cookies. Breakfast wasn't filling, but it was a mix of protein and carbs—and the cookies were a treat compared to the fish. Even though they remained fresh in the snow-packed bag, the unseasoned trout were beginning to get monotonous.

The temperatures seemed to be rising to just above freezing during the day, but at night, they plunged into the frosty range. The constant cold was making us tired and I was worried we'd start making stupid mistakes.

We ate breakfast and drank some water. Preventing dehydration was paramount. But since the patches of mounded snow looked clean, I took two of the empty water bottles and packed them full of snow to melt. It wouldn't be a lot of water, but every bit helped and we could continue to fill them as we went along, because there was still enough snow to do so.

"All right, let's set off again. I took a gander down the road and it looks like there's a slight rise in the grassland ahead, where the trail starts to curve. I thought we were seeing flat land, but with the way the grass out here ripples, it's kind of like being on the shore and watching the ocean and not realizing you're looking at a tsunami rolling in." I pointed to the curve in the road where it turned toward the right and then seemed to disappear.

"I wonder how far we are from the mountains," Angel said. "Didn't you say the kelpie told you that Caer Sidi was at the top of a mountain?"

I nodded. "She did." I stared ahead at the misty silhouettes rising from the horizon. My gauge of distance wasn't always accurate. "I have no clue. It could be several weeks, so we're going to have to find food along the way. I'm not used to flatlands."

"Me either," Raven said. "I guess we'd better get going. We have to make the food hold out as long as possible, and after the fish is gone tomorrow, we're back on rationed cookies and protein bars. We need to find protein, so I'm thinking watch for birds or deer or any creatures that we might be able to eat. With the snow increasing as we near the mountains, we'll be able to melt enough to have water."

We made sure the fire was out and, with Angel dragging the bundle of wood, we set out on the road again, heading toward the mountains. As we plodded along, I found myself thinking of home. Even though we were in Annwn, my hopes of finding our way safely to Cernunnos's palace, or Brighid's castle, or at least Arianrhod's castle, felt like they were flagging. I was trying to be optimistic, but when we were cold and hungry and alone, it was hard to maintain a positive outlook.

Angel suddenly stopped and pointed at the sky. "Look."

I followed her direction. There, in the distance to the west, great clouds loomed and they were coming in fast. They didn't look like the thunderheads of the first day, but I caught the scent of ozone on the wind. These were snow clouds.

"It's going to snow." I looked around. We had been walking steadily for what seemed like several hours, and now I realized that, off the path to either side, the snow was becoming fairly uniform. No more piles here and there, but rather, patches. We were headed north, and it was winter.

"We should find a place to take a break," Raven said. "Though at least walking keeps us warmer."

We were nearing the bend in the road, and now I could see that the grasslands were swelling up the side of a hill. Small in terms of the mountains at home, the hill was still of significant size. We could make it up the slope, but it wouldn't be a quick jaunt.

"I think I want to go up on that hill and see what's on the other side," I said. "It won't take me too long. It's a hike, but not too exerting and it could help cut some miles off our journey."

"Why don't we all go?" Angel said. "Then, if the other side is an easy descent, we won't waste time. I wonder if the path continues to curve to the right." She paused, then added, "What if it curves east? What if we have to go cross-country if the path doesn't lead north?"

That hadn't occurred to me. Traveling cross-country could be dangerous. If there were any villages near, chances are they'd be along the road rather than out in the middle of nowhere.

"I guess we'll figure out what to do when and if that happens."

I took over the sledge—I was the strongest—and we started up the hill. The slope wasn't terribly steep, but after a while, dragging the wood began to prove too heavy for me, so Raven looped one side of the rope over her shoulders and, together, we dragged it behind us. We didn't dare lose our wood supply. Angel slipped behind the sledge to push and working together, we managed to reach the summit, which provided a flat mesa from which we could look in all directions.

The first thing we saw when we looked below was that the road, indeed, curved to the east from the bend, and didn't appear to curve north again as far as we could see. But relief spread through me as I saw a village at the base of the hill. Beyond the village, to the north, a copse extended north toward the mountains. Actually, it was *more* than a copse. I shaded my eyes, realizing that the forest thickened the farther north it went, spreading to the east as well.

"All right, let's hope they're friendly," I said. "We need help and maybe they'll be willing to extend a hand. At least we have the coins the kelpie gave us."

Shouldering the rope of the sledge again, Raven and I cautiously began the descent with Angel guiding the sledge from the back as she kept it from lurching forward to slam into Raven and me. As we picked our way down the hill, the clouds socked in around us, covering the sky, and snow began to fall, at first with a hiss and a sputter, and then in big, fat flakes that froze the moment they hit the ground. By the time we were at the bottom of the hill, a good inch had already accumulated on the ground.

The village was compact, but seemed a decent size. I estimated there were probably five hundred to six hundred people living here given the number of houses in the surrounding area. The village reminded me of Eselwithe—the village near Cernunnos's palace.

Most of the houses were built of wood, and rather than thatched roofs, they had wooden shingles. Every house had a chimney rising from it, and the smell of woodsmoke rose from the town, making me long to be inside by the fire. There seemed to be a central thorough-fare—the trail ran through it from what we could see—and it was lined with shops and what looked like an inn.

"Oh, thank gods. Let's get down there. I think that large building to the right might be an inn," I said, pointing to a large structure that had a stable behind it.

"Let's move." Angel's teeth were chattering and her hair was covered with snow. "I'm freezing."

We increased our pace and finally reached the main road again. There weren't many people out and about, and what there were, I recognized as mostly Elves, with a few Fae among them. They stopped to stare at us and I realized that we were wearing clothing that didn't fit the area. We were obviously outsiders.

When we reached the inn, I wondered if we'd be able to communicate. I didn't speak Elvish, but I spoke both Turneth and Nuva—the dialects of Dark and Light Fae. Though the dialects were probably different back home, given both languages had their roots in Annwn, someone should be able to understand me.

The inn was two stories tall and stretched the length of about three of the cottages that we had passed. Stained-glass windows lined the front, beautiful and yet thick enough to protect from the winter weather. The door was ornately carved, and showed no signs of ax marks or anything indicating violence.

We tied up the sledge outside and entered the building.

Contrary to many inns, we didn't immediately enter the dining hall. Instead, the setup reminded me of a hotel from back home. There was a reception counter, and behind it, a bulky man who looked midlife. He was writing on a handmade note pad—I recognized the style from being in Cernunnos's palace many times—and when he looked up, he did a double take.

Focusing on me, he spoke in Turneth. "May I help you?"

I nodded. "We're not from around here. There are three of us. We need a room and food, and some information."

"Two people per room, unless you care to pay for the extra bunk."

"We'll pay." I pulled out the bag of coins.

"Then that will be one far'en, twelve qiks."

I handed him two coins and he counted out the change.

"How far are we from Caer Sidi?"

He frowned, then pointed to a map on the wall. "We're right here," he said, pointing to a village.

I leaned in closer and read the name. We were in Bream. Then, he drew his finger north to a castle in the center of a mountain range. Caer Sidi. But as I scanned the map, I realized that the road we were on, the one leading east, led beyond the mountains away from the lands of Caer Arianrhod, directly toward Y'Bain. And to the south of Y'Bain, I caught sight of a welcome notation: Cernunnos's Palace. It was farther than Caer Sidi, but the route looked safer.

"Do you have any caravans leaving for the east?" I asked.

He frowned. "Well, there's one coming through that's headed toward Thirsty Gulch. They get in tomorrow. I can book you passage on it."

I followed the trail on the map. Thirsty Gulch was south of Cernunnos's Palace. "How much do they charge? And how long will it take before they reach Cernunnos's Palace?" I pointed to the map.

He nodded. "One far'en per person, and the journey to Thirsty Gulch takes five days by caravan unless something goes wrong, so…three days to reach the Forest Lord's palace, thereabouts."

I counted the coins in my pouch. We had ten fa'rens and eight qiks left, which meant we'd have enough for the passage and for food. "You say they arrive tomorrow?"

"Yes, in the early morning. They'll head out around noon, after they take on new provisions. Are you interested? I can sell you tickets now."

"Please. And make sure we wake early." I handed him three more far'ens and he gave me three slips of paper with printing on them that stated we had booked purchase to Thirsty Gulch on the Avoteen Caravan. After that, I gave him another six qiks and he gave us the key for our room, along with tickets to the dining hall, which was behind a thick wooden door.

As we entered the dining hall, I felt exhausted. The trip had been dangerous and tiring and frightening, and to suddenly see a massive fireplace crackling with heat and smell the abundance of food in the air was almost more than I could handle.

The dining hall was spacious, with the fireplace on one end, along with matching sofas. An elk head watched over the fireplace, so lifelike that it made me think of Herne. There were two paintings, one on either side of the mantel, one a rustic setting that was more landscape in nature, and the other was a depiction of what I recognized as one of the ancient battles the Fae Courts had waged.

The seating options included several long tables with chairs around them—each one seating eight people—and then another table with a bench on either side. The counter was manned by a waitress, who took our tickets and pointed us to the buffet, which was manned by another waitress. We picked up serving trays—wooden—and dishes along the way.

There were two entrees—stew and what looked like a casserole—and then rolls, vegetables, cheese, and fruit to choose from. The casserole was some sort of beef and potatoes option, and I selected that, then filled my plate with several rolls, a thick wedge of cheese, and an apple. Angel opted for the stew. Raven matched my own choices. We sat down near the end of the empty table, and I shivered. The cold had thoroughly penetrated, chilling me to the bone.

I scooped up a spoonful of the casserole and closed my

eyes, the savory taste of gravy making me aware of just how hungry I really was. Grateful for the protection from the storm and the food, I paused, wanting to weep. The past few days came crashing down and I sat there, staring at my dish, almost unable to move.

"Are you all right?" Angel asked.

I nodded, trying to get hold of my feelings. "I'm overwhelmed, I think."

Raven reached for my hand with her left, then took Angel's hand in her right. Angel and I joined hands and we sat there, a triangle, connected and weary and heartsore. After a few minutes, the tears retreated and we fell to, eating like we were starved.

The food was good and plentiful, with seconds included, and Raven and Angel and I remained silent as we ate, focusing on recharging. We were all exhausted and cold and on edge, but at least we weren't hungry anymore. After we finished, we moved over to the massive fireplace and sat near it, warming ourselves.

"We're going to make it. I wonder if they've been looking for us," I said.

"Of course they are. I still wonder why Herne's coin didn't work." Raven shrugged. "Do you think it's possible that the battle between Echidna and Typhon is still going on?"

"I can't imagine it taking so long," Angel said.

"Both dragons are immortal, remember. If they're evenly matched, even with the help of the gods and the interference of the Luminous Warriors, it could take more time than we think." I noticed there was another map on the wall next to the fireplace. I wandered over to it. "You know, there are other lands on here besides

Annwn—other realms. It looks like Annwn connects to a number of realms."

"Such as?" Angel asked. Both she and Raven joined me.

"Such as...the Forgotten Kingdom—the realm of the dragons. It's north of Annwn. Here." I pointed to a spot at the northernmost tip of the map. "And east of the Forgotten Kingdom lies Kalevala, Raven!"

Kalevala was the realm where the Finnish gods hearkened from. North of Kalevala was Pohjola. To the east of Kalevala was Asgard, the realm of the Norse. Below Kalevala and Asgard was a massive realm I'd never heard of—Wildemoone. Peeking out west of Annwn was Olympus.

"What happens when you come to where one realm ends and another begins? Is it like borders? Does the world you're in just stop and vanish?" Angel asked.

"I don't know, to be honest," I said. "But I'm fairly certain all these realms are within one world. Almost like there's a huge world over here, just like there is at home, and the 'realms' are actually countries within this world. Or maybe you can see the other lands but have to step through a portal to get there? Like an invisible force field?" I turned to Raven. "Have you been to Pohjola? Is it in the same realm as Kalevala?"

She nodded. "Yes, so there's no need to cross through a portal from Kalevala to arrive there, though you can use them as shortcuts. Teleporters, in a sense." She paused, then said, "I think you're right. This is all one massive world, connected to our homeworld by portals. All different countries, on the same planet. Except for the Forgotten Kingdom, which was cut off by the same force field that also kept Typhon constrained. Now, I'll bet you can get there by going on foot."

I stared at the map. Raven was right—I knew it. We were in a massive world, so to speak, that ran parallel to the one we were born in. And how many more existed?

Raven yawned. "I'm sorry, but can we go to bed? I know it's barely twilight, but I'm tired. It's been a rough past few days. I need to sleep."

With the help of a housekeeper, I led the way to the back of the dining hall where a staircase led up to the guest rooms. We unlocked ours—room number six—and inside found three narrow but comfortable-looking beds. A fire burned brightly in the fireplace, and a plate of pastries and hand pies waited on a small table to the right. There was a bathing chamber, and I paid the girl an extra six qiks for hot water for the three of us.

"Go ahead and bathe first," I told Raven. "You were hurt, and you seem more tired than Angel and me."

After one of the maids filled the tub with hot water, then added enough cold to make it bearable, Raven climbed in the tub while Angel and I lounged on the beds. It wasn't the most comfortable mattress in the world, but it sure beat sleeping on the ground.

"So, three days until we can go home." I leaned back against the headboard. "That means we'll have been gone almost a week."

"Anything could have happened in that time," Angel said.

I nodded. "I don't want to think about what's going on if things went wrong. I love my home, and I can't imagine..." I stopped myself. Visions of dragons raking the city with their fiery breath intruded. The last thing I wanted to do was carry those images into my sleep. "Let's read to each other again," I said.

Angel pulled out her e-reader. "Do you want to start?"

I nodded. "You can take a bath after Raven. I'll go last." And so I started in, once again immersing us in a story of another time and another place as I sought to blot out the worries stirring up a storm in the back of my mind.

CHAPTER NINE

THE MAID WOKE US EARLY, AS WE HAD ASKED, AND BROUGHT our clothes to us, cleaned and dried. For fifteen qiks, she had taken care of them and now they felt warm from hanging near the fire, and they were clean and even pressed.

I wiped the sleep out of my eyes. I had slept deeper than I had in a while, and though the bed was too soft for my liking, it had gone a long ways to making me comfortable.

We washed up, and I blessed hot water once again—it felt wonderful to be clean. Once again, it had only cost a few qiks to entice the maid to bring up basins of hot water so that we could take sponge baths. Raven opened the window—it was hard to see through the stained glass —and glanced out.

"Holy crap, the snow's piling up. I hope the caravan can manage it." She motioned for me to join her. The snow was falling—fat flakes drifting to the ground, where they built into a thick carpet. It was beautiful, but also daunting.

"I hope so too," I muttered. "What should we do for breakfast? Eat here, or eat out of our provisions? We have most of a couple packages of cookies left and a protein bar or two."

"Does the caravan ticket include food?" Raven asked.

"I don't know. I just figured we could buy something, but I'll run down and ask." I dashed down the stairs and through the dining hall to the door leading into the reception area. The innkeeper was there, with a cheerful smile.

"Can you tell me if the caravan ticket provides food, or do we need to bring our own?"

He pulled out a thick pad of paper and flipped through till he found the page he wanted. "The Avoteen Caravan offers provisions along the way for ten qiks per day, per person, for two meals a day." Pausing, he glanced across the counter at me. "I would caution you, they charge a pretty price. I can supply you with food for less."

Thirty qiks, for unknown food in an unknown amount. That was one and a half far'ens. "How much would you charge for two loaves of bread, a round of cheese, and... oh...say, three apples?" It wasn't a feast but with the remainder of our cookies, we wouldn't go hungry.

"Twelve qiks, and I'll throw in a day-old pie." He grinned, his eyes glinting.

"Deal. Can you package it up for us?" I handed him a far'en and he gave me back eight qiks. We still had almost half the coins the kelpie had given me.

"Gladly. Do you want any breakfast? I'll toss in another loaf of bread and fresh butter for free." He leaned on the counter. "You're one of the most pleasant-looking group of visitors we've had in months. Day in, day out, it's rough and weary travelers."

I gave him a winsome smile, using whatever it took to get us a better deal. We had eaten all the pastries and hand pies that had been provided in our room the previous evening. "Sure, thank you." I waited while he vanished into the dining hall and then returned with a filled burlap bag.

"Here you go. Bread, butter, cheese, and apples. Also a pie." He handed it to me.

As I accepted it, I thought that—once I was Herne's wife, and a goddess—I'd come back here and do something nice for the inn owner. "Thank you. When's the caravan get here?"

"It's due in any time. It might be late due to the snow, but the Avoteen Caravan almost always makes it through unless there's a blizzard or a flood." He paused as the door opened and a flurry of snow blew in as a broad-shouldered man dressed in furs entered. It was hard to tell if he was human—he reminded me of Viktor, a half-ogre—but he was big and burly with a scar on his forehead and the darkest brown eyes I'd ever seen.

He saluted the innkeeper. "Sala, well met. It's blowing up a storm out there. My men want to load up as soon as possible. We need to head out quickly because there's a bigger storm behind us—a real blizzard—and we don't want to get caught in it." The man spoke in Turneth and it was easy for me to understand him.

The innkeeper nodded. "They can go around back. There are several crates waiting. You'll be picking up three passengers. This is one of them—what's your name?"

"Ember," I said, turning to the burly man.

"Ember, meet Kraka, the owner of the Avoteen Caravan."

I nodded to him. "My friends and I are traveling to Cernunnos's Palace. I'll go get them. When do we leave?"

"As soon as we pack up the freight. Get aboard now. There's a heated carriage waiting." He barely glanced at me, but turned back to Sala. "You should warn the village about the blizzard. Send out messengers. Nobody should be caught away from home when it comes through. I'd park and wait it out, but we have precious cargo that's headed to Thirsty Gulch and it can't wait."

I dashed upstairs. Angel and Raven were dressed and ready.

"We need to get to the caravan. I have food for our breakfast, as well as the next few days. It's going to be a dicey ride. There's a blizzard coming. But the caravan owner says the coach we'll be riding in is heated, so there's that."

We gathered up our things and headed down. I approached Kraka again. "We have a sledge of firewood outside. You want us to bring it?"

He thought for a moment, then nodded. "It can't hurt to have some extra wood. Here, let's get it aboard." Turning back to Sala, he said, "Fix me a breakfast to go, would you?"

Sala nodded, then waved at us as we followed the caravan owner out the door. "Come again when you can, ladies. Nice to meet you."

Outside, it was icy cold, and the wind whipping the

snow in furious waves, sending it swirling in circles. I gazed up at the sky. There seemed to be no end to the flakes, and they were thick and furious in their descent.

We led Kraka to the sledge. He stared at it a moment, then said, "Who made this?"

"We did," I said. "We're lost and on our way to Cernunnos's Palace. I'm engaged to his son." Usually namedropping rubbed me the wrong way, but it might provide us with some protection on the journey. I had no idea who else was riding on the caravan, but if mentioning a god might make people more afraid to try anything, then so much the better.

It seemed to do the trick. "His *son*? Isn't his son over on Earth?"

So Sala knew about the Wild Hunt.

"Yes, and that's where we're from. This is my friend Angel, and this is Raven. We all work with the Wild Hunt."

"I thought you looked out of place. I'll have my men load the wood. Do you want the rope back as well?"

I nodded. "Yes. Thank you."

"Follow me, then." Kraka led us over to a string of covered wagons and carts. We weren't talking *Little House on the Prairie*, but similar in nature. The Avoteen Caravan consisted of ten wagons. Six looked to be cargo wagons, with no real covering save for tarps that were lashed down. Two, in the rear, were spartan carriages, and had the name of the caravan painted on them.

The other two were obviously meant for passengers, and reminded me of vardo wagons—the Romani wagons you saw in old movies. They had hard outer exteriors and were painted dark blue with elaborate designs in gold, red, and green. Against the snow, they were a stark contrast. They were covered with detailed embellishments that looked like runes. There was a stepstool in front of one of them, and the door was surprisingly wide. Both carriages were each about the length of two cars, and about the width of a school bus.

"That's yours. The other contains a lord, his concubine, and several servants. I advise you to leave them alone when we make camp. They're…unsavory types. Stick to yourselves, and if you have trouble, come to me," Kraka said.

I nodded. "Thank you." We handed him our tickets and he took them, shooing us into the carriage.

The interior of the carriage was lit with soft glowing lights—lightning flits that were created out of lightning. The gentle globes floated softly in the air. They wouldn't burn down anything and the wind wouldn't blow them out like it did lantern candles.

The carriage had four cushioned benches that could be used to sit or sleep on, and there was a blanket on the end of each one. I wondered what happened when the caravan had more people than it did benches, but then thought— of course, they'd make camp. However, making camp in the middle of a massive snowstorm seemed dangerous, and I hoped we'd be able to keep moving. The horses looked up to the job—massive, like draft horses, but they looked like they could run faster.

Kraka poked his head in. "I don't expect any more passengers, but we might pick up a stray along the way if they're caught out in this storm. If we have to make camp, since you're the fiancée of a god, you'll have this carriage for your own, unless we stumble over anybody too old, pregnant, or injured."

I nodded. "That's fine. We'll do fine either way. So, about three days to reach Cernunnos's Palace?"

He nodded. "We travel from dawn till past dusk. If you have to use the facilities, there's a private screen and a chamber pot back there. We'll stop twice—once at noon, once in the late afternoon—to give the horses a break and to empty the pots and clean up." He folded up the step-stool and placed it inside the door. "We're ready. Your wood is being stored on one of the cargo wagons. This carriage is heated, so no building any fires." He looked square at Raven. "I know you're one of the Ante-Fae and that you carry fire in your belly—no lighting anything on fire, understand?"

I translated for her and she laughed.

"Tell him I promise to behave."

When I told Kraka what she said, he snorted. "As if one of her kind *ever* behaves themselves. You travel with interesting friends, Lady Ember." And with that, he slammed the door shut.

There was a window to the left side of each bench, so we spread out, watching as the caravan began to move. The horses picked up pace and the swirl of snow beat against the glass, turning the outside world into a kaleidoscope in white.

I opened the bag of food and pulled out the pie. "Pie for breakfast? Or do you want bread and butter? We have cheese, too, and apples, plus the cookies we have left." I saw that Sala had added six extra apples to our stash.

"Pie. The other foods will keep better," Angel said.

I brought out the pie, which smelled of apple and cinnamon and sugar. It was bigger than the pies at home and deep-dish, so I used my dagger—wiping it first—to slice the pie into six wedges, two for each of us. We had no plates, so we improvised. We still had plenty of paper towels, so I doubled them and handed Raven and Angel their shares of the pie. As we ate, the caravan rocked gently along and the snow picked up.

"Three days of sitting here traveling, huh?" Angel said. "Want to read more of the book?"

I nodded. "Yeah, watching out the window's going to get old." I kept thinking of Mr. Rumblebutt. "I hope somebody's feeding Mr. R.," I whispered. "I'm worried."

"At least I know Raj is home with Curikan," Raven said.

"How are things going now? With you and your father?" I finished off my pie and wiped my fingers. "Does he like living in Kalevala?"

Raven and her father had had a major blowout in December, and he had turned on her and essentially gotten her labeled a pariah in the Ante-Fae community. The whole mess had been nasty and heartbreaking, and I was shocked when she accepted him back into her life after he realized what a stupid thing he had done.

"All right. Curikan is happy over there. He's got a long ways to go to ever make up for what he did to me, but he's trying." She shrugged. "My mother's visited a couple times. She says it suits me."

"What do you think?" Angel asked.

"I think…it suits me, too. I never thought I'd like being away from a major city, but we're living in Tapiola—Mielikki's woodland—and it's so peaceful and beautiful. We've been meeting a lot of her metsan haltija—the Finnish forest folk. They're a noble people. The väki of the forest is far more powerful than I ever dreamed."

"Väki?" I asked.

"The...how to phrase it—*spirit? Essence?* Väinämöinen is teaching me to use the tulen väki—the essential powers of fire. I have to be careful, though, because when I practice my magic, it's easy to offend the väki of the forest if I get too near the trees or plants. He's a wonderful teacher, and he can be stern to the point of scaring me, but he's also funny. He and Kipa get along. In fact, he reminds me of...oh...a grandfatherly Kipa."

Her face was glowing, and I realized that there was something different about her. We hadn't had time to catch up before the battle, and on the road from the Forest of Death, we'd been too exhausted and afraid to talk much. But now I realized that Raven was growing, and she seemed more mature than she had.

Angel stared at her for a moment. "Are you coming back to live on the Eastside after the training and internship?"

Raven paused, then cracked a faint smile. "I will come back to visit, but I feel at home in Kalevala. I don't belong in Annwn, and while I love the Seattle area, I feel like I'm in my element now. I fit in over in Kalevala. Even wearing the clothes that I do, I fit. Raj misses television, but we've found ways to circumvent that. And he's getting more exercise, which is good for him."

"So you're saying...no?" I asked, though I wasn't that surprised. I'd had a feeling when we saw Raven off to the realm of Kalevala that she was leaving us for good. Oh, we'd see her again but...not on an everyday basis.

"I'm happy there. I'm ostracized from my people, but the Banra-Sheagh can't rule the Ante-Fae who are out of her reach. Vixen and Apollo and all my other friends have to make up their own mind about being Exosan, but at least I won't be adding to their worries this way." She paused, then said, "Kipa and I wanted to tell you this together, but I'm going to tell you in private because the two of you are so close. He's asked me to marry him. We'll stay in Kalevala, where he can run with his wolves freely."

"You're getting married?" Angel shouted, slipping out of her seat to hug Raven.

I joined them for a group hug. "When?"

"Not till after I finish my training and internship, but then yes, we'll get married. I'm to become a goddess of fire over there. I'll be going through the Gadawnoin, too, Ember, so you can give me pointers!" She beamed, grinning.

"When did he ask? What did he say?" Angel asked.

"We were lounging in front of the fire, talking about a trip to meet his stepmother. His father is Ukko, Lord of the Finnish gods, and his stepmother is Rauni—the mother of the pantheon."

I blinked. "Who's his mother?"

"Kuu, goddess of the moon, but she's skittish and left Kipa to Rauni's care. We don't even know if Kuu remembers giving birth to him." She shrugged. "Rauni and Ukko brought him up and he treats Rauni like his own mother."

"How does that even work? I know Hera was jealous as hell when Zeus went out catting around," I said.

"Rauni apparently gave Ukko permission to father a child for Kuu. Kuu didn't have a mate and wanted a baby. But the moment she gave birth to Kipa, she was done with being a mother, I guess. Kipa told me that Kuu is so focused on the cycles of time, and the sky, that she loses track of anything soil-bound."

The Finnish gods sounded very different than the Celtic ones, and I could see Raven fitting into their world.

"Anyway, so you two were talking about taking a trip and—"

"And then he told me he had something to ask. He said that when he left home to travel to Earth, Rauni told him she wanted to see him wed and settled because he was a wild child. He promised he would, but he never told them about his relationship with Venla, because she had no desire to become a goddess. She didn't want to live forever."

"Who's Venla?" I asked.

Raven blinked. "I forgot you didn't know. Long ago, Kipa fell in love with a human and he stayed with her until the day she died. She had been beaten by her stepfather, who tried to rape her, and then cast out because she fought him off. The beating injured her uterus, but she healed up and was living in the forest when Kipa found her."

I stared at her. Kipa was growing more and more complex with every word. I had thought of him as a player, helpful and fun, but irresponsible. But now I was learning he had a side that made him so much more than that.

"After that, he asked me if I liked living in Kalevala. When I told him how much I loved it, he asked me if I'd be willing to make my home there, with him, and marry him. And I said yes." She gave us a gentle smile. "Yes, Kipa's a wild child like his mother, but I can match him in that, and we're both passionate. We love each other. I never dreamed I'd marry a god—which means I have to become a goddess—but here we are."

Angel sighed happily, clasping one of Raven's hands. "Congratulations!"

"Well, we have two years till we get married, but in the meantime, I'll continue to train and by the time I go through the ritual, my powers will be much stronger. Väinämöinen warned me that if I chose that path, I can never become one of the Force Majeure, and I thought for a while about it. But the fact is, I might never become one anyway. Training with him doesn't guarantee me a spot on the list. And there are already twenty-one of them and nobody seems to be showing any sign of dying."

There were twenty-one members of the Force Majeure at any one time, and attrition rate was achieved through only through death. Given all the magicians, witches, and sorcerers in the organization were at least a thousand years old, it would be a long time before Raven even stood a chance of making it.

"True that," I said.

"I gather each member picks an acolyte and trains them for years...like understudies. But I'm not patient enough to wait for that and I don't think being in the Force Majeure would suit my temperament. So when Kipa asked me to marry him, I knew that was the right path." She motioned to our benches. "Move it, I want to stretch out my legs. I'm still tired from the past few days."

We reluctantly returned to our benches and after speculating what our weddings would be like, we continued reading the mystery. After a while, the rocking of the caravan made me sleepy, and I wasn't the only one yawning. So we bundled down in the early afternoon for a nap, waking for dinner. The caravan continued to travel along, but outside the storm was getting worse, and I wondered how they would keep on the path come dusk. But my question answered itself.

When night fell, shortly before we stopped to make camp, I glanced out the window and saw a trail of blue lights marking the sides of the path. I wasn't sure if they were lightning flits or what, but they glowed so bright that they were impossible to miss, and they were spaced out every hundred yards or so. They lined the road, and so the caravan managed to stay on track until the movement eased and we pulled off to the other side.

Kraka knocked on our door before popping his head inside. "We'll be making camp here. Come out while we empty your chamber pot. You missed this afternoon."

The chamber pot was like a portable toilet, and it was on wheels. After we exited the carriage into the chill of the night, Kraka called one of his men to attend to it for us.

"The fiancée of a god will not empty her own chamber pot on my caravan," he said.

I realized he was currying favor for the future, but that was fine with me. "Thank you," I said. "I'll tell Herne what good care you've taken of us."

"Thank you, milady. Now return to your carriage. There's a lock on the inner door. I suggest you use it. While my men are trustworthy, as I said, the other passengers aren't to be trusted. While my men keep watch, we can't guarantee something won't happen. If you're locked in, so much the better. I noticed you have weaponry."

"We do, and if for some reason the Star Hounds attack —they attacked us a few nights back—then call us. We can fight."

"I believe you," he said. "Now go and sleep well."

After his man brought the now-empty chamber pot back to us, I shut the door and locked it. "We should still keep watch," I said. "I trust Kraka, but I don't want to be caught unprepared."

And so we kept watch, with Angel taking first shift, Raven the second, and me the third. All through the night the howling of the wind kept up a steady pace, and I prayed we'd be able to continue come morning, given how fast and thick the snow was falling.

CHAPTER TEN

THE SECOND AND THIRD DAY OF THE TRIP WERE BORING, but we made good time. We didn't pick up anyone else, and stopped at only one village along the way for more cargo. Whoever was in the other carriage kept to themselves and, as nosy as I could be, I decided to take Kraka's advice and leave well enough alone. We finished the book we were reading, and another, and were about to start on a third when, near late afternoon on the third day, the caravan stopped.

Kraka knocked on our door and I opened it. "We're near the palace. Eselwithe village is right up ahead, and Eselwithe is at the base of the Forest Lord's lands."

I knew that village—and so did Raven and Angel. We'd been there often enough.

"Can you take us into Eselwithe? Walking in this snow could be dangerous. Though the storm has let up, I don't trust us to not get lost."

"We'll let you off at the edge. We're not scheduled to stop in town so it would be disruptive for the caravan to trundle through." He glanced at the sky. "Get your things together—it won't be long before we're there."

We gathered our things as the caravan began to move again, finishing off the last of the bread and cheese and cookies. By the time we were ready, the caravan stopped. Outside of the window, we could see the houses of the village.

"Should we make for the portal itself?" Angel asked.

I frowned, then shook my head. "My gut tells me to go to the palace."

"All right, but let's try to find someone to guide us. The landscape looks so different with so much snow." Raven frowned. "It snows a lot in Kalevala too. And even though it's another realm, we still get the effects that Finland does with the sun—the land of the midnight sun, you know."

"I thought that was Norway," I said.

"I thought it referred to Alaska," Angel countered.

"There's more than one land up that high toward the Arctic Circle. The reference can be made about all of them," Raven said. "Okay, let's get moving."

I gave Kraka our wood, and he gave us back our rope. We said good-bye and I promised to recommend his caravan to Herne and Cernunnos. As they headed out, Raven, Angel, and I entered Eselwithe.

There were few people on the streets, but we stopped in at the Trader's Day Post—a shop that catered to travelers. They hired out guides and horses, along with leading other trips. I approached the counter. An Elf looked up, breaking into a smile.

"Lady Ember! You grace us with your presence." He scrambled to stand at awkward attention.

Given I'd never been in the Trader's Day Post before, I

wasn't sure how he knew who I was, but then it occurred to me. The village belonged to Cernunnos. Chances were my engagement to Herne had been announced, and Cernunnos and Morgana weren't shy about using Earth-side technology like printing up posters. They could have easily sent out fliers about our upcoming wedding.

"Thank you," I said, wanting to ask him how he knew about it, but I decided to leave that for another time. "My friends and I need a guide to the palace. We got lost in Caer Arianrhod and made our way here from there. I don't trust our navigational abilities."

"Of course. In fact, I have horses you can ride. Given you're Herne's consort, of course there's no charge. I'll have a guide lead you to the palace here in a moment." He paused. "Would you like blankets to drape over your head so the snow doesn't chill you too much?"

I nodded, pulling out my coin sack. "Yes, but I insist on paying you. Here, take what we have left." I started to take the coins out of the sack, but he shook his head.

"No, milady. There will never be a charge for Herne's fiancée or her friends." He quickly moved to the side and motioned to a man lounging near the woodstove. "I have a job for you. Deliver these women to the palace. Don't tarry, and make certain they get there safely or your life is forfeit."

The man jumped up, nodding. "I'll ready the horses," he said. "I'll return when they're saddled."

We gathered by the stove to wait. I wanted to do something in return for the shopkeeper's generosity, so I found several trinkets—a couple belt buckles that were hand engraved—for Viktor and Yutani, and a beautiful handwoven scarf for Talia. This time, I insisted on paying for them—it was one far'en and five qiks.

The guide reappeared a short while later. "We're ready, milady."

We followed him out into the snowstorm, where instead of horses, we found a carriage. The guide beamed. "I thought we didn't have any available, but look what I found."

Relieved—I wasn't looking forward to riding a horse through the snow—we clambered aboard and he shut the door, making certain we had blankets tucked over our laps first.

I leaned back, exhausted. The past five days had been grueling and the thought of going home was so appealing that tears welled up in my eyes. I missed my cat and Herne and our home and everything familiar. We had seen more of Annwn than I cared to, at least in this manner.

"Tired?" Angel asked.

I nodded. "Yeah. I imagine we all are."

Raven nodded. "I miss Raj and Kipa."

"Let's hope Echidna won," Angel said. "If not, who knows what we'll be going home to."

"Yeah." I didn't want to think about what might happen if Typhon won, and I had managed to stave off most of the thoughts in that direction since we landed in Caer Arianrhod. But now that we were close to going home, they came charging back like gangbusters. I sighed. "I suppose we should talk about what happens in case…in case we aren't on the winning side."

"You mean, if Typhon won?" Raven said. "What I want

to know is since they're both immortal, how can either one win?"

"They may be immortal, but remember, the gods can be hurt. They can be maimed, and they can be knocked unconscious. And during that time, they can be bound. When the pair clashed, remember, it was strong enough to open a vortex and throw us here." I leaned forward to look out the window. "Let's just hope Echidna was able to bind Typhon."

SOMETIME LATER, we could see Cernunnos's palace looming large under the silvery sky. The massive stand of oaks that housed the Forest Lord's palace was covered with snow, a magical sight as lights filtered out from the myriad rooms and chambers within the tree palace. The trees all sprang from one central trunk, trunks calving off from the central core. Roots wound together to form the staircases that curved up the trunks, leading to different rooms and chambers. The steps looked like they'd been cleared, but all in all, the snow made the palace more magical in every way.

The guide let us out near the main set of steps leading up into the palace, where four guards watched over all who entered. They took one look at me and bowed. While I'd been to the palace a number of times, it was still made me nonplussed that I was recognized in Annwn. I gave them a smile and asked to be taken to Cernunnos.

"Very well, milady," one of the guards said, giving me a long look.

I glanced down and realized that Angel, Raven, and I

all looked pretty rough-and-tumble. Even though we'd had our clothes washed back at the inn, our days on the road had taken their toll. None of us were wearing makeup, our hair hadn't seen a brush in days, and our clothes were wrinkled beyond the help of an iron.

"We've been on the road," I said, feeling self-conscious.

"Very good, milady," the guard said, then led us over to one of the elevators at the base of the tree. They worked on a pulley system and as we began to ascend, I realized I was grateful that we didn't have to climb the hundreds of stairs to reach the main level of the palace.

Once we were inside, my heart lifted at the familiar surroundings. We followed the guards through the hallway till we came to the throne room.

The throne room was vast, with the ceiling so tall that it was difficult to even see. But the stalactites jutting down from overhead glimmered from the inclusions of quartz, lighting up to form an ambient glow. I knew they could become brighter, but for now they provided a comforting backdrop of light.

The walls were woven from interlaced trunks, roots, and branches, lignified into a stone-state. The throne in the center was also formed of the same interlocking roots and branches, and it rose up from the ground, reached by a short staircase. Various gems glimmered from the nooks and crannies created by the root system.

I let out a sigh, relieved to see the Forest Lord atop his throne.

Cernunnos towered on the throne, bare chested with a bearskin cape around his neck, fastened with a golden brooch of Celtic knotwork. His muscles rippled, glowing in the soft light, and his hair was caught up in dozens of thin braids that hung down to his thighs. He wore blue jeans—he had developed a love of them from our world —and a headdress of horns and feathers. He was gloriously handsome, but with a feral look that never failed to make me jump. His smile was sensuous and slightly cruel. He wasn't malicious, but I had seen his ruthless side.

He pivoted and, seeing us walking toward him, leapt off the throne, landing on the floor. "Ember! You're alive!" The next moment, I found myself caught up in an embrace so tight I could barely breathe as he swept me up and spun me around. Then, giving me another tight hug, he set me down again and stepped back. "We thought the three of you might be gone for good."

As I caught my breath from the sudden dance, Raven said, "We ended up in Caer Arianrhod." She paused, then frowned. "I always thought it was up in the heavens, not in Annwn."

"How did you get out of there? And it's both—it's a multidimensional realm. Arianrhod's castle, Caer Sidi, exists in both the stars and in Annwn." Cernunnos frowned. "How did you get here?"

I shook my head. "With a lot of luck. We walked for several days—we landed near the Forest of Death. Then, three days ago we caught a caravan in the village of Bream. The caravan dropped us off down in Eselwithe an hour or so ago. They were headed for some place called Thirsty Gulch."

Cernunnos scanned all three of us, shaking his head. "You're lucky you made it out of Arianrhod's realm without running into her—"

"Star Hounds?" Raven asked. "We met them—at least

two of them. Overall, I'd say our biggest problem was the weather."

"You ran into a pair of Star Hounds and you're alive? My admiration grows," Cernunnos said. "Now, we have to contact Herne and the others. They've been searching everywhere, trying to find you. Morgana told them you were alive—she could feel your life force, but couldn't figure out what happened."

"When Echidna and Typhon slammed into each other, it created a portal right where we were standing—" I paused. "Speaking of...what happened?"

Cernunnos's expression dimmed. "That's a difficult question to answer."

My heart sank. "Don't tell me Typhon won?"

"Not exactly...but neither did Echidna." He motioned for one of the guards. "Prepare the portal. I will be taking the girls home myself." He stood. "We'll talk about it when we get over to your side of the pond, so to speak. For now, let's get you home and ease Herne's and Kipa's hearts." He bundled us toward the door, following the guard.

I expected to go outside again to one of the portals, but Cernunnos ushered us up to a private platform where a portal crackled and popped, situated between the upper branches of two oak trees next to the main palace. There was a narrow bridge over to the portal, and a platform built between the two oaks so that we wouldn't have to step out into thin air and risk falling before we made it into the vortex.

"Come, this leads directly to the portal in the park next to Herne's house." He motioned for us to go first.

I practically ran across the planked bridge, leaping into the vortex, I was so anxious to get home. The next moment, I stumbled—still in mid-leap—into the arms of Orla, the portal keeper.

He steadied me, breaking out in a wide smile. "You're alive!"

"Yes, we are. And I have to see Herne—do you know if he's home?"

"I don't know, miss," Orla said as Raven appeared, and then Angel and Cernunnos.

"Thank you," I said, hugging him. We were in the woods near Carkeek Park, the part that buttressed up against Herne's backyard. Though the path was slick, I didn't care. I began to careen down it and a few minutes later, I opened the gate and ran around to the front door, followed by Angel, Raven, and Cernunnos. I tried the knob. *Locked.* Pulling out my keys, I fumbled through them for the one to Herne's front door, and then, unlocking it, burst in.

"Herne? Herne!" I called, but there was no answer. Instead, a loud mew echoed from the bedroom and out ran Mr. Rumblebutt, leaping into my arms as he frantically licked my face.

"Oh, Mr. Rumblebutt, I'm sorry I was gone so long!" I snuggled him, burying my face in his fur. "I missed you. I missed you so much," I said, realizing I was crying.

Angel fussed over him too, while Cernunnos did a quick search of the house.

"He must be at work."

"I'd call him but our phones are out of juice and Herne doesn't have a landline," I said, biting my lip.

"I'll call him," Cernunnos said. "You three go wash up and have something to eat." He pulled out his phone.

Torn between wanting to stick around to talk to

Herne and desperately wanting to take a shower, I finally decided that I really wanted to be clean and change clothes. I had a stash of clothes here, and even though neither Raven nor Angel were my size, I found a loose sundress that would fit Raven, and a lounging gown that Angel could wear.

"Come on. There's also a shower in the guest bath. You two go ahead first," I said.

Angel shook her head. "You go. I'll see what's in the fridge and make up something for lunch. Something besides bread and cheese, as good as it was."

While Raven and I headed off to shower, Angel headed to the kitchen. As I stepped under the wonderfully warm spray of water, I tried not to think about what Cernunnos had said about the dragons. I didn't want to know, but all the time I was soaping up, my mind kept trying to open up the can of worms that I had a feeling was waiting for us.

CHAPTER ELEVEN

ANGEL HAD FOUND SOME GROUND BEEF AND A TRAY OF freshly grilled hamburgers waited for us. She had also made a pan of brownies. As Raven and I sat at the table, Raven wearing my sundress and me in fresh jeans and a turtleneck, Cernunnos joined us, politely refusing the food. He waited till Angel returned—wearing my lounging gown, belted at the waist with the tie to my robe.

"Herne's on his way home, along with the rest of the Wild Hunt," he said, then paused, looking concerned. "I also notified Morgana that you're back and she's on her way as well. We have to discuss the dragon situation now that you're accounted for. We already have, among ourselves, but you have to know what we're facing."

"It sounds grim," Raven said.

"It *is* grim," Cernunnos said. "I'm not going to lie. None of us expected this outcome, and it's going to be problematic. More than problematic."

"I feel like we're eating our last supper," I said.

"Not exactly, but…there are decisions to be made and one, in particular, involves you, Ember." But he wouldn't say anything else till the rest of the crew got there.

"EMBER!" Herne's voice echoed from the hall. He slammed into the room, followed by Kipa and the others. "Love!" The relief on his face was apparent, and he swept me up in his arms, even as Kipa did the same to Raven. Talia hugged Angel, and behind her, Viktor and Yutani crowded in. Between the hugging and kissing, Morgana showed up.

My heart was pounding as Herne covered me with kisses, his eyes glistening. "I thought I lost you," he said. "I thought we lost all of you."

"We were lost," I answered, my head against his chest. "I missed you so much."

After we finished our lunch, Herne guided us all into the living room. I sat on his lap in the recliner, while Kipa and Raven snuggled on one end of the sofa. Angel and Talia joined them, while Yutani and Viktor sat in the love seat. Mr. Rumblebutt jumped on Angel's lap, and Cernunnos and Morgana sat on two of the ottomans.

"So, start by telling us where you went and what happened." Herne scooted over so I could sit beside him in the oversized chair. I slid off his lap and took a deep breath.

"Well, we ended up in Arianrhod's realm." With Raven's and Angel's help, I told them about our journey, including the kelpie, the Star Hounds, and Sala—the helpful innkeeper in Bream. "What I don't understand is on my first visit to Annwn, I saw Caer Arianrhod up in the sky—"

"It's simultaneously there and also soil-bound. Arianrhod inhabits several realms at once, and it's all very… interdimensional. Don't even try to figure it out—it will confuse the hell out of you because she lives outside the confines of time and space." Morgana shook her head. "I'm amazed you managed to take on the Star Hounds."

"Without the allentar arrows, we wouldn't have survived." I paused, then asked the question that was heavily on my mind. "Now, the dragons?"

Herne took a deep breath. "Nothing is settled. Well, that's not true. Some things are, but… You said you vanished when they first collided in midair?"

I nodded. "Yes."

"Then you missed the battle. They fought for hours, severing heads—which will grow back, but it was a bloody mess. We—the gods, I mean—were trying to hold back the Luminous Warriors. As we expected, they ignored the agreement and took to the air to help their father against their mother." He paused, then stood and went over to the television and turned it on. He turned on the DVR and then fast forwarded through what looked like a news program. The film was a choppy and dark segment, but I could see the dragons fighting in the air. It was horrible—the sounds reverberated even at a low volume, and whoever had shot the film had obviously been on the move because the images bounced up and down.

But we could see the two Titans rolling in the air, wrestling and snapping at each other. Echidna was stupendously beautiful, and Typhon, just as gorgeous save

for the dark miasma that clung to him. Their heads—
hundreds of them—writhed in a sinuous dance, all aimed
at destruction. They were entangled, so much so that I
thought it a wonder either dragon could even attempt to
break free. It reminded me of a snake ball, when snakes
mated, except they were clawing and ripping at one
another. Blood flew everywhere.

Then, more roars echoed as a flurry of smaller
dragons arose, taking flight, and the sky was filled with
snow and blood as they began to clash with the gods. I
recognized several of the gods flying into the air, going to
battle against the dragons. One, muscled beyond descrip-
tion, wearing furs and carrying a shield and a massive
hammer, launched against one of the Luminous Warriors.
Thor. That has to be Thor, I thought. He struck at the heart
of one of the dragons with Mjolnir and the dragon began
to tumble out of the sky.

Elsewhere, the gods were doing their best to keep the
lesser dragons out of the main fray, but it dawned on me
as I watched, there would be no winning. The dragons
were immortal. The gods were immortal. They could
fight forever and no one come out the victor.

The footage went on and on, and we watched for two
solid hours as the bloody battle continued. Then, whoever
was shooting the footage screamed and the next moment,
the film stopped.

"What happened?" Raven asked.

"We aren't sure. Someone picked up the camera but
whoever was filming hasn't come forward. There was a
lot of collateral damage," Herne said, his expression
somber. "Pike Place Market looks like a bomb went off.
The entire downtown area looks like a war zone. The

building our office is in was heavily damaged, as well as most of the buildings along that block."

That brought it home. I caught my breath. "How many people died?"

"At least two hundred. And another two hundred unaccounted for. Downtown Seattle is a pile of rubble."

"And the dragons?" Angel asked.

"Echidna and Typhon managed to wound each other heavily. The gods were able to build the stasis field but… we couldn't untangle them. We had to imprison Echidna along with Typhon, in stasis." Morgana squeezed her eyes shut and hung her head. "We didn't want to, but there was no choice. At the end, Echidna shouted for us to 'seal the door'…and so we did. They'll be fighting for eternity in there."

I caught my breath. Echidna had sacrificed herself. Tears welled up as I thought about her sacrifice. "I don't know what to say," I whispered.

"There isn't anything you can say," Morgana answered.

"Then Typhon's no longer a threat?" Raven asked.

"No, but his children are. And a number of the dragons who were on Echidna's side are angry at us and at the human world. Some of them have returned to the Forgotten Kingdom, but the Luminous Warriors haven't," Morgana said.

Cernunnos cleared his throat. "They've retreated to the land they bought, and we don't know what they're up to. We've managed to convince the government that nuclear weapons wouldn't faze the dragons, so they aren't counterattacking. But reports are trickling in from other countries that the Luminous Warriors are attacking rural areas, destroying villages and towns, and claiming the land. They seem intent on carrying through their father's plan."

So, Typhon was no longer a threat, but his children were. "And just like that, the world changes," I said. "What about TirNaNog and Navane?"

"Saílle and Névé have played it close to the chest, but they have been upping their militias. Everything is in turmoil, and there's no sure footing anymore." Herne shook his head.

I thought about the whole mess. "What do we do?"

"We can't fight the dragons effectively, and they seem determined to stay here. We haven't made firm plans yet, but the first thing we're going to do is make sure that you pass through the Gadawnoin as soon as possible." Morgana turned to me. "Herne's attention was divided the past few days, worrying that you were dead. It's time for the ritual. I know you expected to have more time, but you must be safe in order for Herne to focus his attention where it's needed."

I stared at her, taking in what she was saying. Even though part of me was screaming, "So soon?" I knew she was right. I planned on marrying Herne, and if me being immortal would help him focus his energy, then I would undergo the ritual.

"All right," I said, my voice barely registering even in my own ears.

"You don't object?" Herne asked, straightening. "You're okay with that?"

"Of course. I'm not about to leave you, and I agree with your mother. I don't want you to worry about me. So…yes." I took a deep breath. "How long does the ritual last?"

"It depends on the person. I can only tell you that you need to rest up for a day or so. Today's Tuesday. We'll set the ritual for the weekend, I believe. In the meantime, you stay out of sight. We can't chance the dragons coming after you in revenge."

Kipa turned to Raven. "We're not going back to the house on the Eastside, either. You're safer here."

"What about afterward? What about the Wild Hunt?" I asked.

"And my brother—what about DJ and Cooper's family?" Angel spoke up.

"Don't worry, Angel. We've already moved Cooper's family—and your brother—over to Annwn," Herne said. "The coming days are far too precarious to let them stay here. Chances are they'd be okay, but until we know what the dragons are planning, we won't take any chances."

Angel nodded, looking relieved. "I'd like to see them soon."

"You will," Cernunnos said. "They're staying in the palace for now. I would have told you while we were there but we needed to discuss everything and I knew you'd want to visit with them, so I decided to wait. You can see them in a couple of days."

"As to the Wild Hunt," Herne said, "if—and that's a big *if*—we stay here, we'll have to find a new space for the office and probably go undercover. Luckily, we have a backup of all our files in the cloud. We're printing everything off now, in case we have to leave for Annwn without warning. Viktor sorted through the rubble for all the weapons he could find."

I thought of the office where Angel and I had spent

almost two years learning a new way of life, of how we had made new friends and become part of something much larger than ourselves. And now it was gone. Everything was shifting again. Feeling melancholy and nostalgic for a world that was vanishing, I stared at my hands.

"How's Charlie?" Angel asked.

"I got in touch with him two nights ago through a private connection," Herne answered. "The vampires have done a lot of research, and have discovered that the dragons can't control them like we feared. But given the state of affairs, they're leery of coming topside again. The stock market crashed after the fight—it's in ruins. Several world economies have been wiped out." He gave me a bleak look. "Everything's hunky-dory if you're a rock. Or a slug."

"So Charlie won't be coming back?"

"He can't. Dormant Reins isn't allowing any of the vampires topside. They've got enough bloodwhores down there with them to last for a long time, and they also have a massive stash of animal blood from what I understand." Herne's phone rang. "Hold on," he said, looking at it. "The deputy mayor's calling."

He moved off to one side. I yawned, stretching. "I'm so achy from the days on the road. I thought I was in shape but damn, this was an eye-opener. I feel like I could sleep a week."

"Me too," Raven said, following my cue. She yawned so loudly it startled Mr. Rumblebutt, who raced out of the room. "I miss Raj," she said, leaning back.

"We'll go home soon," Kipa promised. "Your father is good with him, you know that."

"I know," she said, leaning against him. "I told them, by the way."

"Told them?" Kipa asked, then broke out in a smile. "You did? I was hoping you might."

"Don't trust my commitment?" Raven teased him.

"What are you two talking about?" Viktor asked.

"We're engaged. We won't be married for a couple of years, but we made it official," Raven said. "I'll be following Ember's lead and going through the Gadawnoin."

"You'll be going through it long before the marriage," Kipa added. "After what happened—with you vanishing? I can't take a chance on you dying."

I glanced over at Angel, who was sitting there silently. She was smiling, but I had the feeling she wasn't as calm about the whole matter as she let on. With both Raven and me going through the ritual to become deified, it left her out. And we had to do something to remedy that.

Morgana stood. "Ember, I'd like to talk to you privately."

I nodded, following her to Herne's office. She shut the door behind us.

Morgana was wearing a suede jacket and linen trousers, with a sky blue blouse. Her hair was gathered back in a ridiculously intricate chignon, with tendrils curling down around her face. Even dressed in modern clothes, she was obviously not of this world.

She motioned for me to sit on the sofa, and then sat beside me. "I've made a decision. Tomorrow morning, we'll leave for Annwn. You and I. Today's Tuesday, so we'll start the preparations for the ritual on Thursday, after you've had a day to rest, and then Saturday, you will go through the Gadawnoin. Once you've come through, we can plan your wedding for when you like."

I swallowed my fear. It felt like we had been engaged for a long time, though it had only been around six months. But Herne was my match, and I couldn't imagine being without him. The Gadawnoin had loomed far ahead, something that I was heading for, but that had remained nebulous and ephemeral. Now, though, it was solid and firm. My heart began to pound. The ritual, much like the Cruharach, could propel me into my future, or it could destroy me.

"Will Raven be with me, since she's engaged?"

"No, her goddess will put her through her paces. Something is weighing on your mind. What is it?" Morgana asked.

I sighed. "It hit me, while we were out there. Raven's marrying Kipa. Both she and I will be ascending to goddesshood. But Angel is our third. I feel like..."

"Like you're leaving her behind?" Morgana examined my face, holding my gaze.

I nodded. "Yeah. And I can't do that. She's had the potion of life...but this is a much bigger step." I bit my lip, then blurted out, "I know this is highly irregular, but isn't there a way—isn't there something that we can do or some reason we can find to bring her through the ritual, too?"

Morgana blinked. "You want Angel to become a goddess? It's not like we hand out invitations like party favors, you know."

Blushing, I stared at the floor. "I know," I said, lowering my voice. "I realize that. But elevating her to goddesshood would only benefit the gods. She has so much to give."

Morgana opened Herne's desk drawer and pulled out a pack of breath mints, popping one into her mouth. "So, you think she would make a good addition? Well, so do I, but it's not up to me. Unless she's marrying into the pantheon, her ascension would have to be approved by the Triamvinate. And they're a tough trio to sway."

The Triamvinate were the three cornerstones on which the Celtic pantheon of gods was forged. Consisting of Danu, the mother of the pantheon, the Dagda, the father of the gods, and Eiru, who was the land incarnate, they held sway over the entire realm of Annwn. And their word was law.

"Can you talk to them?" I asked. "I know it's a lot to ask, but..."

"But...where Angel goes, you go. I swear, the two of you have to have lived past lives together, to be as tight as you are." Morgana relented, smiling. "Very well. I'll discuss it with them, but I make no promises. And do you even know if she's interested? On the off chance that I talk to them and they approve your request, they'll expect her to accept. I want you to discuss this with her before I plead her case. They owe me a favor, and I don't want to use that marker for no reason."

"I will," I promised. "And now, can you tell me what I should do to prepare for the Gadawnoin?"

"Rest. Hydrate. And think over your fears and why they are there. For that is one aspect I am allowed to tell you—you *will* be facing your fears." She stood. "Let's return to the others and find out what the deputy mayor had to say to Herne."

I followed her back into the living room. So much was happening, and all I wanted to do was crawl into my own bed, in my own house, and pull the covers over my head.

HERNE WAS WAITING for us to return. "Okay, I talked to Maria Serenades. The news isn't good. About an hour ago, a group of the Luminous Warriors demanded a meeting with all government officials from the United Coalition. This will happen tomorrow morning."

"We need to call Ashera and find out if she knows what this is about," I said. "Can I borrow someone's phone, since mine is still charging."

Herne handed me his phone and I headed over to the table while they continued to talk. I called Ashera and waited. She answered on the fourth ring.

"Herne?"

"No, it's Ember. My phone…never mind—I haven't had my phone available for a couple days, so I'm using Herne's. Do you mind if I put you on speaker?"

"Go ahead. I'm glad you called. I tried to phone you but there was no answer and I was sent straight to voice mail. I suppose you've heard by now that the Luminous Warriors have approached the United Coalition?"

"Yes, just now. What's going on? Do you know?"

Ashera sighed. "Yes, unfortunately, our agents do know what's going on. The Luminous Warriors are going to wrest control of the UC. They're demanding a ruling place on the council and if they don't get it, they'll start destroying cities and towns. The government knows there's not much they can do. And we—the Celestial

Wanderers and the Mountain Dreamers—can try to fight them on this, but it would be an unending battle, given we're immortal. We'd end up destroying what we were trying to protect. We could do what they are doing and demand a voice on the council, but that would lead to a stalemate, as well. We could withdraw to the Forgotten Kingdom—"

"If you do that, you leave Earth to the mercy of the Luminous Warriors. You told us they plan to make our world their own private lunchbox. I had hoped they would honor the agreement Echidna and Typhon made." I had a headache now, full blown and pounding away.

"The Luminous Warriors *have* no honor. I will be honest, some of the dragons are returning to the Forgotten Kingdom. We can't leave the Hedge Dragons to tend to it forever—they're younglings and it's far too dangerous to leave them all alone."

"Hedge Dragons?" It was the first I'd heard of them.

Ashera lowered her voice. "We don't talk about them much, outside of our own kind. They're a species of dragon formed from the connection between elemental magic and some of our own DNA. They aren't immortal, but they do carry the magic of the elements. They're young, though—so incredibly young compared to us, and they are under the protection of the Celestial Wanderers and Mountain Dreamers. The Luminous Warriors hate them and would kill them all if they had their way."

"I had no clue...there's so much in this universe that I don't know about." I paused, then added, "So, are all of you leaving?" It made me incredibly sad and scared to think of the world left to the machinations of the Luminous Warriors.

"No. But those of us staying are going to have to establish our own stronghold in order to throw a scare into the Luminous Warriors. We may be able to keep things in a checks-and-balances state for a while, but eventually, things are going to get rough and we want to be around to help where we can."

I silently stared at the others.

Talia spoke up, loud enough so Ashera could hear. "So we're at war, but this time, with dragons."

"I'm afraid you're right," Morgana said.

Ashera paused, then said, "I'm sorry about your offices being destroyed."

"You didn't do it," Herne said.

"No, but somebody had to say it." She sighed.

Cernunnos motioned for me to hand him the phone. "Ashera? I'll have a messenger come by your place. You'll know who he's from, trust me. He'll bring you information on how to reach us once we return to Annwn. May the spirit of Echidna be with you."

"And may you journey safely through the realms," Ashera said, ending the call.

Cernunnos hung up and handed Herne back his phone. "I'll have the portal keeper over on Bainbridge take her a message. She can meet us in Annwn. Because for now, that's where we're going. There's not much we can do here, not at this point. Saílle and Névé know how to get in touch with us."

I yawned. "I'm so tired. I want to sleep."

"You'll sleep more safely in the palace," Herne said. "We haven't had a chance to tell you about the Fire Eaters. The Luminous Warriors have managed to assemble enough thugs and malcontents among the humans and the Otherkin community into roaming bands of toughs. They're combing the streets for enemies to the new regime. The National Guard has its hands tied. They can't go up against the dragons and they know it. The dragons have shown enough force in the past two days, razing monuments and buildings, that the United Coalition has knuckled under. I think they're all in shock, to be honest. So these ruffians are—"

"Brownshirts," I said, my heart dropping.

"What?"

"Hitler's brownshirts. The *Braunhemden*. Essentially the Luminous Warriors are militarizing groups of people to do their dirty work for them."

Herne's expression chilled. "Yeah, that. Right now, our best bet is to withdraw to Annwn and decide what to do. We can talk with other leaders of other realms. The dragons could do what they're doing here, anywhere."

Angel, Raven, and I stared at each other. We had been away for five days and the world had gone to hell. In some ways, it was worse than coming home to find absolute chaos. At least then, we could try to make some sort of order out of things. But while some buildings had fallen, and there had been casualties, life sounded like it was going on as though nothing at all had happened, at least for most people. And that was more surreal than the total anarchy.

"So, does everyone have their luggage?" Morgana asked.

Viktor, Talia, and Yutani nodded.

"My dogs are in my car. I'll go get them," Talia said.

"I'll crate Mr. Rumblebutt in his carrier," Herne said, hurrying toward the bedroom.

"I have to pack," I said, heartsick over the fact that we couldn't go home. I loved my house, and while I knew that—once I married Herne—I wouldn't be living there, I had hoped to give it to Angel, and to visit her there.

"You're already packed—at least for now. I asked Talia to pack for you," Morgana said. "You too, Angel. Come now, let's go before the cold settles further. There will be carriages waiting on the other side." She shooed us toward the door.

Herne returned, carrying Mr. Rumblebutt in his crate, and hoisting a pack over his back. "Some last-minute additions. I sent over a buttload of cat food and litter, so we're fine on that account. At least for now."

I took one last look at Herne's house. I loved his place as much as I loved my own. I didn't want to live in somebody else's palace. But right now, retreating and regrouping seemed like the best option. And if I was to start preparations for the ritual, I'd need rest.

We trudged out to the backyard and headed up the trail that wound through the trees. As the snow fell in little whirls and swirls, Mr. Rumblebutt yowled a couple times, then fell silent. Ten minutes later we were at the portal, and the next moment, we were in Annwn, right near the palace at the base of two portal trees I didn't recognize. Without a single word, a company of guards assembled and—guarding the lot of us on all sides—they led us into the tree palace, to our new home.

143

CHAPTER TWELVE

MORGANA SETTLED US INTO OUR SUITE OF ROOMS, LEAVING her maids behind to help us. They had already unpacked for us, and there was a tray of pastries and savory treats on the table. Angel and Talia's room was to the left, Raven and Kipa were staying to the right. Yutani had a room down the hall, and Viktor and Sheila were staying together. Except for Angel, who was visiting her brother and Cooper's family in rooms farther along the wing of the palace, we all gathered in Herne's and my rooms, and the mood was anything but excited.

After the servants had brought jugs of ale, bottles of wine, and a bucket of milk, they vanished out the door, leaving us to ourselves.

I dropped on the bed, groaning as I leaned back to lie on the pillows. "What say we take this up again over breakfast? I'm so exhausted, I can't think."

"Sounds good to me," Raven said, slapping Kipa on the knee. "Come on, Wolf Boy, take me to bed."

He grinned. "Gladly, love. At least we know we'll be safe here." He led her out of the room. Talia and Yutani also withdrew, followed by Sheila and Viktor. That left Herne and me.

I turned to him, feeling oddly out of place. But then, the entire past week I had—very aptly—felt out of place.

"So, tomorrow I rest, and then…"

"And then prepare for the ritual," he said, motioning for me to join him in bed. I stripped off my clothes, sliding beneath the heavy quilts. I settled into the crook of his arm, resting my head on his shoulder as his scent filled my heart, making me feel ever safe and secure.

"So, here we are," he whispered. "You're trembling. Are you scared?"

"I'm afraid of so many things right now," I whispered as Mr. Rumblebutt leapt up on the bed and curled up at our feet. "I'm afraid of what's going to happen next. Back home. I'm afraid the world I grew up in, as flawed as it can be, will never be the same. It will never go back to being a world free from the Dragonni."

"You're right," Herne said. "It will never be the same. And I hate to tell you this, but before it's over, it's going to get worse. Ashera and her comrades will try to help out, but one thing we've discovered over the past months—the Luminous Warriors are stronger than their Celestial Wanderers kin. The Mountain Dreamers maintain a slight edge when it comes to strength. This will be the cold war to end all cold wars."

I stared glumly at the wall. The flames in the fireplace crackled and popped, casting a glow around the room. Herne had turned off the lanterns when the others had left, and outside, the snow was falling thickly. The night was far darker than most I remembered except from when we'd been in Arianrhod's lands.

"Everything feels so wild here," I said, snuggling closer. "Tell me the truth. Are we here for good? Will this be our new home?"

Herne hesitated for a moment, then said, "I think… perhaps so. We can go back over to Earth when you've gone through the ritual, but we can't stop the dragons. The Wild Hunt was formed to put a harness on Saílle and Névé, not for anything else. All the other cases we took on were incidental. Yes, we helped a lot of people, but now, there won't be much use for us any longer. Saílle and Névé may talk about beefing up their militias, but I happen to know they're looking at moving their cities."

"But what will they do about the home cities—the ones here in Annwn?" I couldn't see their egos taking a back-seat when it came to leadership, and the Fae Queens of the great walled territories of TirNaNog and Navane here in Annwn were sure to give them the brushoff.

"There are other realms bordering Annwn. I suspect they'll move their cities there. I know of one that buttresses up against the borders of our land. There are no real Fae cities there…so it's prime territory." He paused. "You mentioned a map you saw at the inn?"

"Yes. A great map with Pohjola and Annwn and Kalevala and other countries—realms—on it."

"Do you remember seeing a realm called Wildemoone?" he asked.

I nodded. "Yes, I do."

"That's where I suspect the Fae Queens will move their cities to." He burrowed under the covers, pulling them up to his chin. "I was so afraid you were dead, but my mother said you still lived. She just couldn't find you. Sometimes crossing through the portals makes it difficult to locate someone, even if you have a connection with them. Which is one reason the coin I gave Raven didn't work. I hadn't even thought about that possibility when I gave it to her." He paused. "I'm proud of you—of all three of you. You managed to survive a journey that would have killed many. But I never want to worry about your life again."

"After Saturday, you won't have to," I murmured. "If I pass through the Gadawnoin."

"Then let us hope you make it, or I'll follow you into the underworld to bring you back." Then, as tired as I was, I responded to his hands as he began to run them over my breasts. I needed him—needed to feel alive and vibrant and that something…anything…was still the same. As he slid inside me, I was able to let the fear and the worry go, and for the next hour, all I knew was that I was in the arms of my beloved Lord of the Hunt, and that we were together.

THE NEXT MORNING, I woke late, to a servant girl bringing in my breakfast on a tray. As she prepared my bath, I ate waffles and sausage, applesauce and coffee. Herne must have brought over a supply. I knew he had imported coffee plants the year before, as well, insisting that Annwn had to have its own source.

The girl paused as I finished my meal. "Milady, may I talk to you?"

I blinked. Most of the servants did their jobs and

pretty much ignored everyone. "Of course. What's your name?"

"Livie, milady. Livie of the Moors."

I nodded. I had no idea whether the "Moors" she was referring to was a patch of land in Annwn or a people, but she looked Elfin so I suspected the former. "What can I do for you?"

"Milady, when you have wed his lordship, you'll be needing a lady's maid, and I have been trained in that capacity. I'd be ever grateful if you'd consider me for the job. I wouldn't be so forward to ask, except my family is expecting another child and it would be nice if I could give my mother some of my wages to help out." She blushed, dipping her head. "I don't mean to be forward—"

"No, it's fine. I'll talk to Herne. I'm not sure of the procedure here, so I can't promise anything, but I'll remember, Livie. And thank you, for even being interested." I gave her a wide smile, realizing that my life was going to change in a number of ways that I hadn't thought through. Being a goddess meant having servants, and given I was marrying the Lord of the Hunt, meant even more than that.

She took the tray and excused herself as I padded across the carpeted tapestry covering the chamber, over to the bathroom, which was behind a half-wall. I slipped into the water, closing my eyes as the warmth began to warm my bones. I was still chilled from our journey in Arianrhod's land, and the palace, while beautiful, was drafty as hell. As I lathered up, humming aimlessly, Angel's voice echoed through the room.

"Ember, are you here?"

"Come in. I'm over in the bath." I realized this was a

good chance to talk to her about what Morgana and I had discussed. We'd have to have the conversation at some point.

She peeked around the screen, then pulled a chair over next to the tub.

"Did you see your brother?"

A broad smile spread across her face. "He's so tall, he's growing so fast. We had a wonderful talk. As much as I hate to admit it, DJ's in good hands with Cooper and his family, even with all that's going on. He's handling puberty as a shifter so much better than he would have living with me."

"How does he feel about being here?" I asked, scrubbing at a mark on my arm till I realized it was a bruise and not dirt.

"He's happy—he always wanted to visit Annwn, ever since I told him about it. But he doesn't know that he's here for good yet." Her expression fell. "I do, however. I know in my gut that we're here to stay."

"Listen," I said, scooting forward in the tub. "I have something to ask you. I can't promise anything, but I have to ask you this or I'll always regret it."

She frowned. "What?"

"I talked to Morgana last night," I said, trying to figure out the best way to phrase what I was about to ask. "How would you feel about…" I paused. How the hell was I going to put this?

"What? You sound afraid." Angel frowned, a concerned look on her face.

I steeled myself and took a long breath, letting it out slowly. "How would you feel about undergoing the Gadawnoin and becoming a goddess, too?"

The look on her face told me she wasn't expecting *that*. She stared at me for a moment, then began to sputter. "What the hell? I can't become a goddess—I'm human! Well, mostly. And I'm not engaged to a god. How the… Have you talked to Morgana about this?"

I cleared my throat. "You don't have to be engaged to a god to go through the ritual. And Morgana was one of the magic-born…and I think part human…before she ascended. She told me that she could call in some favors and perhaps make it happen, but that you had to agree to it before she tries."

Angel looked troubled. "Why do you want me to do this?"

I hung my head. "You and I…we go back. We go back farther than this life. Morgana thinks so, and so do I, now that I've thought about it. We belong together. Oh, not romantically—I know you're not geared that way and neither am I, but we have a soul-connection. I don't want to lose that. And when I go through the ritual…"

A light dawned in her eyes. "Even though I've taken the potion to extend my life, I will never be immortal."

"And I will, and because I will, we won't be able to go around the Wheel again to come back together." Without warning, I burst into tears. "Angel, we need each other. Maybe I'm clingy, but the day we met, even though we started out in a fight, it felt like we were already old friends, coming together after a long separation."

She nodded. "I know what you mean. Is there someone we can ask about this? I'm curious now what our connections are."

I stood up. "Hand me the towel, please." As I dried off, she sorted through my wardrobe. Servants had put away all our clothes, and I had to figure out how everything was organized now.

"Here, this okay?" She held out a pair of jeans and a turtleneck. "It's cold today."

"That's fine." I slid into my clothes, then zipped up a pair of ankle boots. "Morgana's still around, I think." I paused. "Though I have no clue where to find her."

"She was in the dining hall when I passed by." She stared at me for a moment, then held out her arms. I hugged her. "You've been more of a sister to me than anyone I could ever imagine," she whispered.

"And you…you saved my sanity," I whispered back.

We headed into the hall, arm in arm.

CHAPTER THIRTEEN

THE TREE PALACE WAS BUSTLING, WITH SERVANTS HURRYING through the passages. The windows showed a winter wonderland. The cliché was the only phrase that really fit. We stared out over the sparkling snow that covered every surface. It was magical here, with the lightning flits reflecting off the glimmer of the snow, and it all aligned for a dazzling display that was almost too brilliant to look at.

"It wouldn't be so bad, living here," Angel said. "Not one person has given me a nasty look."

"Why would they—" And then I stopped. Even in this day and age, back home there was always some fucknut spewing out racial slurs, and Angel was no stranger to being on the receiving end.

"I'm glad for that," I said. "You know, it is beautiful here. I guess I'm a little like Raj. I'll miss movies and TV, but there are so many things we could do here to replace them."

"If they can figure out a way to use their cellphones

here, they should be able to figure out a way to rig up a DVD player. We can ask," Angel said, laughing. She threaded her arm through mine, and we walked arm in arm into the dining hall.

Morgana was sitting at one of the tables in the corner, alone. She was skimming over what looked like a report, and we approached quietly, waiting for her to notice us. It wasn't polite to interrupt a goddess when she was busy.

After a moment, without looking up, she said, "Sit down. I'm running through some numbers here." As we settled in, she waved toward one of the servants. "I assume you want coffee?"

"Yes!" I said.

Angel snorted. "Tea for me."

"What are you doing?" I asked.

"Examining the fish that my water boys caught last month." She beamed at me. "They're living up to my expectations."

"*Water boys*? What's a water boy?" Angel asked.

Morgana laughed. "Oh, that's what I call my Meré. I have an entire city of them under my rule near my castle. The mermen provide fish for my subjects, and the women gather kelp and weave it into cloth for us."

I hadn't thought about anyone actually living *in* Morgana's castle except for her priestesses. Now, it struck me that there was an entire world of people and lands and existences that I had never thought of.

"So, what can I do for you?" she asked, setting her reports aside.

"I told Angel...I talked to her..." I suddenly felt embarrassed, though I couldn't say why.

"About becoming a goddess?" she said.

Angel nodded. "Yeah. I didn't even know it was something that might be possible for me. I'm not sure what I
think. But we also wanted to ask—do you know what our
connection is? Ember and me?"

Morgana stared at us, then finally, she nodded. "I do. I
know where you two began—or rather—where your relationship first began."

"Can you tell us?" I asked.

"No," she said, "but I can show you. If you truly want
to know. Be aware—not all of it's comfortable. Do you
still want to know?"

I glanced at Angel and she nodded. I turned back to
Morgana. "Yes, we do."

"Then let's return to your room," she said to me. "Even
here, some things are best talked about under the cover of
privacy."

We headed back to my rooms. I had a feeling we were
at another crossroads—that this would effect yet another
change in our lives that we'd never return from.

Angel and I settled comfortably on the bed, under a light
blanket in case we got cold. Morgana was sitting next to
us, in a rocking chair.

"Now, both of you drink the tincture I gave you and
then lie back and close your eyes. You'll relive a scene out
of the first life you lived together, and you'll understand
then, how this all began. How you both began your
connection. You've come down through life after life…
always connecting when you most needed one another."

I sniffed the tiny vial she had given me. It smelled like

violets. After a hesitation, I upended it, swallowing the slightly pungent drops. Angel did the same. We lay back down, pulling the blanket up.

"Take each other's hands, now. And hold on."

I reached out for Angel's hand. Her skin was soft in mine, dark against the paleness of my own skin. But we fit together—we were two sides of a puzzle, I thought. Then, quieting my mind, I closed my eyes and listened as Morgana began to weave her spell.

> *Round and round, time spins back,*
> *To days long faded into the mists,*
> *Follow now the fog-born track,*
> *Into a time where magic kissed*
> *The soil, and filled the air,*
> *Where tricksters ruled and mayhem*
> > *reigned,*
> *Find yourselves, then come home again.*

As her voice faded, everything felt like it was spinning. Like Dorothy heading to Oz, I felt as though I were being lifted out of the bed and, still holding Angel's hand, we went catapulting through the air. In midair, Angel reached out for my other hand and we went spinning round and round like the blades of a windmill caught in a gale. As we flew, the land below us began to change and then, I grew very sleepy. I yawned and Angel followed suit. I closed my eyes and everything faded.

EMBER:

I woke up, startling out of my sleep. At first, I couldn't place where I was, but then I remembered. Alluete and I had decided to go fishing, and we had chosen the banks of the Dorwhistle River as our destination. We had eaten our lunch, and prepared our fishing rods and then…and then I couldn't remember what had happened.

Groaning, I stood and looked around. I felt like I'd been given a sedative.

"Alluete? Are you around?" I wondered where she had gone to. There was no sign of her, and a chill raced up my back as I stared at the water. It was whitewater season and too many people had drowned here, trying to brave the water that rode high and fast with the early spring runoff. The whitecaps foamed and roared along. The river was good for fishing, but one misstep and it meant death.

I was used to water like this. I'd grown up along the shores of a lake that constantly churned, that was so big it might as well have been an ocean. Before we had come out, Alluete assured me that she was used to tromping through the woods and that she'd be careful. But she was human, and my mother had warned me about hanging out with humans. They were more fragile than we were, and they weren't as connected with the elements.

"Alluete? Alluete? Where are you?" My worry increased as I stood up and looked around, trying to find her. *Still no sign of her.* Even her lunch had disappeared.

Frantic now, I was convinced she had somehow fallen into the river and got caught by the current. I hustled over to the banks of the massive waterway, watching as the water careened along, splashing against the edge, right at the top of its banks. Another warm day and the runoff from the mountains would send the river into flood stage, and it would cover the lower lands of the forest. Maybe fishing hadn't been such a good idea.

Wondering what the hell I was going to do, I glanced farther down the river where a glint caught my eye. It looked like either something jeweled or metallic was caught in a natural beaver dam, about two hundred yards away. Alluete had been wearing a silver bracelet—could that be it? I debated less than a second. I couldn't chance ignoring it. I had to find out.

I raced along the bank, terrified that she might be dead. What would I tell her family? They'd hold me responsible, because they didn't like the fact that their only marriage-eligible daughter was hanging out with the grubby Fae girl from the wrong side of the market. In fact, her parents didn't want anything to do with the Fae, but they begrudgingly let their daughter spend time with me because she fancied having a Fae friend and what Alluete wanted, Alluete got.

As for me, I knew that her family begrudgingly bought all their honey and mead for their store from my mother, because ours were the best bees in the land, and my mother was adept with brewing. We were dependent on their customers for a living. My father was dead, and my oldest brother was a drunk, so it was up to me to help as best as I could.

I reached the edge of the beaver dam, immediately scouting for a branch that was long enough and sturdy enough to act as a walking stick.

The dam was massive, stretching halfway across the river, and I wondered how many beavers lived in the lodge, which was probably built into the side of the banks. The water swirled in back of it, diverting to the right. It bubbled around the opening, cascading through with a roar that drowned out most other sounds.

The glint had been coming from near the end of the dam, halfway across the river, so I cautiously began to pick my way over the branches and rocks, using the walking stick to balance myself. At one point, the rocks and sticks shifted under my feet and if it weren't for my stick, I would have tumbled into the river.

I froze, shaking. I could swim, but even the best swimmers couldn't face these currents during whitewater season. Taking a deep breath, I started on again.

As I reached the endpoint, near the halfway mark in the river, I caught sight of the glint again, in the water right behind the dam. Kneeling to see what it was, a wave of relief slid over me when I saw that it was a bucket. For a moment, I wondered if it might be Alluete's lunch bucket, so I fished it out and peeked inside. The bucket had a rusty bottom, with a few holes in it. Alluete's lunch bucket had been new and clean. So much for it being a clue to where she was.

Tossing the bucket aside, I started to turn, to head back to shore.

"Silly, what are you doing out on the beaver dam?"

Startled, I whirled around. Alluete was standing on the shore, bucket in hand, laughing at me. I tried to catch my balance but the branch slipped out of my hand and I spread my arms, trying to hold myself steady. The sticks and rocks on the end of the beaver dam chose that moment to slide, and I went tumbling into the churning current.

I screamed as the water sucked me down, and I tried to kick my way to the surface. As I came up for air, the rush of water carried me over the mini-falls that the beavers had created and tumbled me along, over the rocks. I screamed again, trying to propel myself toward the opposite shore—but I couldn't fight the rapids.

For the first time, I realized I might actually die. I could only struggle so long before the cold of the water and the fatigue of my muscles would overwhelm me. Thinking of my mother and my home, I began to cry, and tried to relax, tried to let the water keep me afloat as I careened down the river.

ANGEL:

She woke from her long sleep. Something was wrong —something was terribly wrong. A wave of fear washed through her, propelling her out of her slumber. As she shook her head, looking around, she saw that it was midday, and she rose out of her lair by the side of the river, squinting in the sun. The light beat down with a steady glow and Myris stretched and yawned, basking for a moment in the warmth. Then, curious as to what had brought her out of her long sleep, the naiad sat on the edge of the river as she scanned the waterway.

Myris closed her eyes, focusing on the fear that raced through the water. It was caught in the waves and bubbles, churning in the whitecaps that frothed at the edges of the current. Then she pinpointed the emotion— tumbling through the water from upstream. As she probed further, she caught sight of a young woman caught in the river's rush to the sea.

She dove deep, swimming along as her feet trans-

formed into fins and her hair streamed around her like
tentacles. She usually ignored victims caught up by the
river but today, the compulsion to save this girl was so
strong she couldn't ignore it. Myris took her orders from
the Water Mother and they were clear and strong: *Save
this one. Catch her and bring her to shore.*

Myris positioned herself mid-point in the river, and
called to the water to give her strength. She wove a net,
forcing the water into a barrier of woven bubbles and
froth, freezing it into immobility around her. And so
when the girl rushed toward her, the water stilled and
Myris was able to slide her arms under the girl's arms and
swim backward to shore.

She dragged the girl up on the shore beside her and
listened for breath. There was none, so Myris quickly
pressed her lips to the girl's lips and kissed her, breathing
air into her lungs, pressing on her chest to force the water
out. And as she gave the breath of life, she also breathed
the breath of water into the girl, and so bound the girl to
the Water Mother.

After a moment, the girl took a tentative breath on her
own, and opened her eyes. "What…where…"

"You were in the water. I brought you out. What's your
name?"

"Iya," the Fae girl said, and then she took Myris's hand
and raised it to her lips. "You saved me, and I am forever
in your debt."

Myris felt a stirring. There was a familiar connection
as the girl touched her. Myris had lived alone since her
mother deemed her old enough to leave the nest, and she
had swum far and wide, searching for a territory to call
her own. But now, she realized how lonely she was, and as

Iya kissed her hand, a dam inside her heart broke, and she began to cry.

Ember

I stared at the water nymph. Naiads were rare among the Fae. They were from the Light Fae family, as was I, but they were bound to nature more than I was. But now, as I gazed at the river, I felt the need to sit on the bank and watch the world go by. I loved the water—I always had—but even though I had almost drowned, it occurred to me that I didn't like life in town, and that I wanted nothing more than to live in the woodlands, in a cabin of my own, and spend my days walking in the forest, with the roar of the water lulling me to sleep at night.

I was still holding the naiad's hand, reluctant to let go. There was something about her that felt familiar and comforting. "What's your name?"

"Myris," the naiad said, watching the river. "You owe me no debt. I follow what the Water Mother tells me to do." Then, shyly, she added, "I'm glad she told me to save you." She paused, then added, "I'm lonely. I never knew it, but now…I do. I'm lonely out here."

Something about her tone pierced my heart and tears welled up in my eyes. "I understand. I've grown up around so many people, but I'm lonely too. I've always felt like I was searching for something, for *someone*, but I didn't know why or who."

A memory came back to me, from when I was around five. "My mother told me once, when I was young, that we were all born with half of us missing. She said that if we

ever found our other half—the half that made us whole—
we would know, even without words. And if we found
our other half, to never let go. That a twin soul is a bond
deeper than love, deeper than friendship. And nothing—
not marriage, not other friends, not careers, would ever
sever that bond if we could but find it."

Myris squeezed my hand. "My mother told me the
same thing, shortly before I left the nest." She cocked her
head and gave me a dazzling smile. "And you…"

"You are my twin soul," I said, finishing the sentence
for her.

That day, I moved to the riverside, and called on a few
friends to help me build a small one-room cabin. I had
found my twin soul and I'd never walk away from her.
And that day, we made a blood oath to the Water Mother
that neither marriage, nor other friendships, nor death
itself would ever separate us again.

CHAPTER FOURTEEN

THE ROOM CAME INTO FOCUS AS I OPENED MY EYES,
yawning. I was still holding Angel's hand. I gave her a
little shake and she opened her eyes. As we sat up, an odd
sense of time displacement swept over me, but I shook my
head to clear away the cobwebs, and scooted so I was
sitting back against the headboard.

"And so, you see. Do you understand your connection
now?" Morgana asked.

Angel let out a slow breath. "I was a naiad once?"

Morgana smiled. "Yes, and you answered to Great
Mother Ocean."

"We're twin souls…" I tried to take in the news. I
hadn't thought much about the concept of twin souls
before. I hadn't been sure if I even believed in the theory,
but the emotions of that meeting were still ringing inside
me and every doubt swept away. "Angel is my other half—
my twin soul. When were we divided?"

"That goes back in time beyond my ken. But I
suspected you were connected in this way. When a soul

divides for the first time, it's usually through some trauma. While that soul can never become 'whole' again, when it meets its other half, there's a sense of completion and the search for what is lost ends." Morgana shrugged. "Now, you see why I offered to plead your case with the Triamvinate."

"I understand now. Before I met Ember, even though I was very young, I always felt like something was missing from my life. I didn't know what, but I knew it wasn't a *thing*…it was something entirely different. Mama J. used to tell me to quit worrying. That I'd find what I was looking for." Angel bit her lip. "How many lives have we lived together?"

"I don't know for sure," Morgana said. "But my suspicions were confirmed when Ember told me how afraid she was of losing you when she becomes a goddess. It made sense—once she's immortal, she stops reincarnating. And—knock wood it won't be for a very long time—when you pass and return, that may fray the connection."

"And if I ascend to deityhood?"

"Then you will forever remain connected." Morgana motioned for us to get up. She turned to Angel. "Think about it, then let me know if you would like me to plead your case."

Angel reached out for my hand. I took it, wanting to beg her to say yes. I couldn't lose her—especially knowing that if I did, it would probably be forever, but it had to be Angel's choice.

"I'll think about it," she murmured.

Morgana stood. "Good. You have time. Just don't get yourself killed before then." With a smile, she withdrew from the room.

I glanced at Angel. "Well, at least we understand."

Angel nodded. "I—" She paused as the door opened and Herne entered the room.

"Get dressed. Viktor and Sheila are having an impromptu wedding."

"What?" I jumped up. "But—"

"But nothing. They can't get married back home, not with what's going on. So we decided the hell with it. Lady Brighid is in the palace to talk to Cernunnos and Morgana. I approached her and asked if she would officiate. She's happy to, but we have to hurry. She can't stay long."

I stared at the closet. "What will we wear? The bridesmaids' dresses weren't ready yet, so they're back on Earth."

At that moment, a woman appeared by the door. "The Lady Brighid sent me to fetch Lady Ember and Lady Angel. I've come to take you to the seamstress."

Raven was standing behind her. "Apparently we're getting dolled up, thanks to Cernunnos's court."

"Seamstress? How is she going to make three dresses in such a short time?" Angel asked.

"She won't. I'm sure there are a number of dresses available and they'll find ones that fit the three of you. Go now, Talia's waiting there, as well," Herne said, waving us off.

Feeling like I'd been thrown into an ocean of emotions, I grabbed Angel's hand and, together with Raven, we followed the servant down the hall, into a chamber where a crew of seamstresses worked away. I wasn't sure whether they served Morgana or Cernunnos or both. They were all in a flurry, with racks of dresses everywhere. We could have been in a store, for the size of the place. Sheila was there, looking equally dazed.

"Congratulations!" I said, waving to her as one of the Elfin women pointed toward a spot near her work table and told me to strip. "Are you thrilled?"

Sheila's gaze darted around the room as she said, "Yes, but also in a state of shock. Everything that's gone on in the past week or so has left me feeling caught in a tailspin. I don't know how to deal with all of the changes."

Angel's laugh rippled through the room. "Let them be. Walk through them with as much equilibrium as you can. That's what I'm doing."

"Do you mind that your wedding's so rushed?" Raven asked.

Sheila shrugged, wincing as the seamstress barked an order for her to hold still.

It occurred to me that Sheila didn't speak the language. "She wants you to hold still," I said, translating the "request."

"Yeah, well, she can stop poking me with pins," Sheila countered. "I suppose I should be grateful I'm getting married in a wedding dress at all." She was wearing a beautiful gown that reminded me of a Celtic renaissance fair dress. It was the color of pale pink rosebuds, with a knotwork trim and a long sash that rode easy on her hips. The seamstress was tucking it here and there with a few stitches. Another woman was weaving a wreath of red roses and white carnations for Sheila's hair, which had been brushed to a glossy sheen.

The seamstress attending me held up a simple but beautiful sheath in a muted sage color. It had an empire waist. As she slid it over my head, I caught sight of Talia, who was wearing something similar, in the same color. Within less than twenty minutes, Angel, Talia, Raven, and I were decked out in similar gowns that complemented Sheila's wedding dress.

Sheila looked spectacular, and the rose-and-carnation wreath sat atop her head.

"I'm sorry your family can't make it," I said.

She shook her head. "Most of my family is scattered to the four corners of the Earth. We've never been close. Viktor and I have that in common. I've asked Talia to be my maid of honor, and I'm so grateful the three of you are willing to be my bridesmaids."

"We're happy to be included," Angel said. "Viktor means a lot to us—we're just grateful you found each other. You're our friend too, now."

When we were ready, the woman in charge of everything handed Sheila a huge bouquet to match her wreath, then handed Talia, Raven, Angel, and me smaller bouquets of white carnations and fern fronds. We were led out of the frenzied sewing center and through the labyrinth of hallways to the throne room.

A red carpet had been rolled out and a portable archway had been erected, marble columns holding up the arch. Decorated with ivy vines, white carnations, and red roses, the columns and archway were draped with a pale pink length of material.

Cernunnos, Morgana, and the Lady Brighid were standing near the archway, talking together. To one side of the arch, Viktor waited, wearing black trousers, a green tunic with a white sash, and black boots.

The half-ogre beamed as he caught sight of Sheila.

Herne, Yutani, and Kipa were standing beside him, dressed in similar outfits, acting as Viktor's groomsmen.

Morgana caught sight of us and hustled over. She was wearing a pale green gown, gossamer and sparkling. Brighid was dressed in a long velvet green gown, and even Cernunnos was wearing ceremonial garb.

"Well, are we ready?" Morgana asked.

Sheila nodded. "I am. I'm just… I wasn't expecting this. I guess I thought our wedding would have to be put off."

"No need for that," Morgana said, grinning. "In fact, though the wedding's rushed, given that Brighid only has so much time before she has to leave for home, the celebration will continue through the afternoon and the night. I have the staff setting up a feast in one of the adjacent ballrooms, and you can meet a number of the members of Cernunnos's court, and also my court. They're used to coming here for holidays. And now that Ember will soon be joining our family, she and Herne will have to establish a hold of their own. We may just pile the holidays on their plate."

I froze. *A hold of our own?* For some reason, I had expected that we would end up living with Cernunnos, but now I realized that Herne probably already had his own home here in Annwn. This was his *father's* palace.

"If you're ready, then let's get you married," Morgana said, hugging Sheila. "Congratulations, and I hope you and Viktor will be happy. You seem well suited."

And with that, she organized us, with Talia, Angel, Raven, and me standing in front of Sheila.

Sheila leaned forward to whisper to me, "I feel like a war bride. You know, how they would rush to marry their soldiers before the men shipped out."

"In a way, you *are* a war bride," I whispered back. "Only we're at war with the dragons this time."

"Right," Sheila said, then fell silent as a flautist began to play from near the archway. The music was light and delicate, romantic and yet magical.

Talia headed toward the arch, one step at a time, with Angel following her, and me after Angel, and then Raven coming last. Behind Raven, Sheila began to walk down the aisle, her eyes on the arch where Viktor waited for her. There were no other guests there, but it didn't seem to matter. Angel, Talia, Raven, and I split off to the left side, standing near Morgana.

Viktor held his hand out and Sheila took it as they stepped in front of Brighid, who stood beneath the arch. Morgana crossed to them and wrapped a braided cord around their wrists, gently knotting it once.

Brighid stepped forward, placing her hand atop the knotted cord. "Marriage is a sacrament entered into for love, for fealty, in honor and dignity. Love crosses boundaries of race, lineage, and sex, and so I joyfully unite those who come to this crossroads freely, of their own consent, without guile or agenda, without malice or greed."

She looked at Viktor, her eyes reflecting the light of the lightning flits that fluttered around the room. "Do you, Viktor, pledge your love and devotion, your life and all acts of sacrifice and generosity, to Sheila, and do you promise to be her wedded mate, bound by the will of the gods, for as long as love shall last?"

Viktor turned to Sheila, still holding her hand. "I do."

Brighid turned to Sheila. "And do you, Sheila, pledge your love and devotion, your life and all acts of sacrifice and generosity, to Viktor, and do you promise to be his wedded mate, bound by the will of the gods, for as long as love shall last?"

"I do." Her voice was a soft murmur.

"Then to each question, assert your answer, together. Will you hold and trust your mate in both health and in sickness?"

In unison, Sheila and Viktor pledged their assent. "I do."

As Brighid went through the rest of her litany, they answered "I do" to each question.

"Do you promise to support one another, to help when the other stumbles, to celebrate when the other soars, to comfort during mourning, to rejoice during joyful days?…Do you promise to honor your mate, to help when needed, even as you stand independent in your own self?…Do you promise to protect and provide for one another, to share the burdens as well as the joys?…"

As the ceremony continued, I fell into a light trance, mesmerized by Brighid's voice. What I wouldn't give to hear her sing, I thought. And then, I began to wonder about my own wedding. I knew it would be lavish— Morgana and Cernunnos had made that clear. And I realized that every question being put to Sheila and Viktor were ones I would answer myself, that I would be happy to pledge myself to. A weight fell away—that last worry about whether I was ready to marry Herne.

"Hear me now, as you stand witness to this union. I, Brighid of the Fiery Arrow, do join you, Sheila, and you, Viktor, in marriage, as long as your love shall last. If you choose to part, you give oath to do so honorably and with respect for the journey you have taken together. If you stay together till your dying days, then you may choose to continue forth into the Summerlands together, still united." She began to unwind the handfasting cord. "I now pronounce you married—husband and wife under the sight of the gods."

After Brighid gently folded the cord, she handed it to a servant who wrapped it in a silk case and placed it on the altar table behind the goddess. The flautists took up again, a merry tune this time, and Viktor pulled Sheila into his arms and kissed her. Flustered, she laughed and waved her bouquet.

"Time to party!" Viktor roared. "Come, bride, let us raise a toast to the gods." He turned back to Brighid. "Thank you, Lady Brighid, for making this possible and for gracing our wedding day. We'll forever be grateful and never forget it."

Sheila thanked her next, and Brighid leaned down to kiss them both on the cheek. "My pleasure, but now I must run. Have fun at your celebration. And don't forget to take your handfasting cord with you. Keep it safe, for it's a charm to protect your household."

As she went on to make her good-byes to Cernunnos and Morgana, the rest of us crowded around the happy couple. Viktor and Sheila were blushing, both looking incredibly happy, and I realized that even the most beautiful garden party in our yard wouldn't have been any more special. They had been married by a goddess they both honored, in a ceremony that was as sacred as the very hall in which we stood.

Brighid made her farewells. The rest of us followed Morgana to a small banquet hall where food was piled on the center table—everything from roast chicken to a slab of beef so big that it looked like they'd sacrificed an entire cow. Fruits spilled over the edges of china bowls, and loaves of bread and pastries towered on wide trays. A tureen of potatoes and another of gravy sat beside the beef, and on the other end of the table, a three-tier wedding cake that looked straight out of some high-end bakery waited for the knife.

"What on earth happens to the extra food?" Angel asked. Her mother had opened her diner to the hungry as a soup kitchen after hours.

"Oh, none of it goes to waste. Our servants get what's left over from the banquets, as well as their own dinners, and what they don't eat is given out to the poor." Morgana handed Sheila a jewel-encrusted dagger. "A gift from Cernunnos and me. This is for your family carving board. Every couple who marries in our lands is given a family carving knife—perhaps not as dear as this one, but one they can keep for the life of their union. It symbolizes good luck and good fortune to come."

Sheila and Viktor joined hands over the hilt of the dagger, the blade slicing through the cake to cut the first piece. As they shared bites of what I recognized as carrot cake, we all clapped and cheered, and then we got down to a serious dinner. The flautist had followed us in, and he and his fellow bandmates began to play—reels and jigs and a lively blend of Celtic tunes as we stuffed ourselves silly.

I thought about Sheila and Viktor. They had made the best of a bad situation. Sure, we were forced to change by circumstance, but true adaptation—shifting one's perception to look for opportunities when bad things happened—that was a matter of choice.

Herne came up and wrapped his arms around my waist.

"That will be us, in a short time," he whispered.

"First I have to pass the Gadawnoin," I whispered back.

"You will. I have no fear on that."

But even with his trust, a part of me was afraid that I wouldn't be up to the challenge. Even though I suspected it was fear talking, I also knew that there was a very real—even if small—chance that the future would vanish with my attempt. And that led to thoughts of the dragons back home on Earth, and what was going on in the country now.

Trying to block out thoughts of the future, I focused instead on the present, and on how happy Sheila and Viktor were. I threw myself into the dancing and merriment. That worked up until late in the night when we broke up the party and once again, the future felt like it was rushing toward me like an out of control semitruck on an icy, steep hill.

CHAPTER FIFTEEN

THE NEXT MORNING, HERNE WOKE ME BRIGHT AND EARLY, poking me in the ribs till I squinted my eyes open. "Get up, love. My mother wants you in the learning center pronto. You can eat breakfast there."

I grumbled, trying to pull the covers up over my shoulders again, but he yanked them off. Shivering, thanks to the cool air of the palace, I grudgingly sat up and reached for my robe.

"Why so early?"

"I'm not sure what she wants. Maybe to prepare you for the ritual?"

I had drunk a little too much mead the night before but now, I remembered. It was Thursday and I was in for two days of ritual preparation. I wondered how many trances and magical tests I'd have to navigate.

"I hope it doesn't matter that I tied one on last night," I mumbled.

He snorted. "As long as you can take good notes and listen to the tutor, you should be fine."

Tutor? Notes? What the hell?

"What do you mean? What am I going to be taking notes on?" I frowned, trying to acclimate myself to the chill of the room. "Can you light the fireplace? It's cold in here."

"A little chill is bracing to the blood, but yes, I will light the fire. However, you have barely thirty minutes before Morgana sends out a search party to drag your ass to class. As to what you'll be taking notes on—all the things you need to know when you pass through the Gadawnoin. There are rules and regulations and decorum and...oh, so many things that those of us born to the gods learn as we grow up. Of course, you'll continue to attend classes with your tutor after the ritual, but these are the most important things."

"*How to Be a Goddess for Dummies?*"

"Well, yes, for lack of a better phrase." He pushed me toward the shower. "Hurry up, love. Mother doesn't joke around when it comes to things like this."

I stopped in my tracks, feeling overwhelmed. "I can't believe this is happening so fast." I paused as Mr. Rumble-butt wove around my legs, mewing. He was hungry. "Mr. R. needs his breakfast."

"I'll feed him for you. And I know that right now, it's all so difficult to take in, but I think that we—the gods—made a huge mistake. We believed the dragons would honor their promises."

"What did they promise, exactly?" I washed my face and took a quick sponge bath in the cool water of the basin before looking through my closet. "Remember, the rest of us weren't privy to the terms that you agreed on." I didn't feel like being pushed. I wasn't sure why I was so reluctant, but I had the suspicion that being hungover had something to do with it.

Herne sighed. "The Luminous Warriors had promised to abide by the win. If Echidna was able to injure Typhon enough to drive him into stasis, they would return to the Forgotten Kingdom and never bother our world again."

"She didn't, though. She ended up in there with him. Didn't that nullify her victory?"

He shook his head. "Not as far as we were concerned. She drove him into stasis, so her victory should hold. But the Luminous Warriors don't accept that. They maintain that he drove her into stasis and got caught with her. We know he sustained more injuries than she did. That was obvious to all the gods. But the Warriors refuse to concede."

"And given they're immortal, like the gods…"

"There's not much we can do to them. Zeus has already decreed them anathema in Olympus. Neither Typhon nor any member of the Luminous Warriors may ever appear in Olympus again, or he will appeal to Gaia and ask her to level their race."

I frowned. "Why doesn't he do that anyway? If Gaia was one of the original Titans, can't she just take away Typhon's powers?"

"Yes, but now we run into a tricky road."

"I don't understand," I said.

"Gaia's volatile. When she's roused to action, she may not stop with Typhon. Think about this: when she slumbers, her dreaming causes most of the quakes and volcanic eruptions and tsunamis and hurricanes. Can you imagine what she might decide to do if she consciously steps in to take matters into her own hands? The world lives on a precarious balance beam. What if Gaia decided to not only punish the dragons for what they're doing, but people for what's happened to her forests and her animals?" Herne shook his head. "No, appealing to her is a last resort."

"I see," I said. I was beginning to get the picture that if the gods truly decided to intervene in the world in any *major* way, the world would be toast. "All right, I'll get my ass down to the classroom." I paused at the door. "By the way, at our wedding, I want a say in my dress. That was pretty yesterday, but not my style."

"You know my mother's having your dress made," Herne said, grinning.

"I know, but that's our 'state' wedding. At the private ceremony we talked about, *I'm* choosing what to wear."

"Of course, love, as it should be," he said, waving me on.

Wearing a pair of jeans and a V-neck sweater, I hurried to the classroom. It was small and cozy, with a table and two chairs, a sideboard covered with pastries, fruit, eggs, sausage links, and a massive coffee pot, and a bookshelf filled with tomes.

I glanced around. Nobody else was there yet, so I took a plate and piled on the food. Eggs, a dozen sausage links, a bunch of grapes, and two hand pies, along with a steaming mug of coffee. As I sat down and dug in, the door opened and a tall woman—an Elf—walked in. She was wearing a pair of glasses, something I wasn't used to seeing, and she carried what looked like a briefcase with her.

"Hello, I'm Ember Kearney." I wiped off my hand and held it out to her.

She shook my hand, then set her briefcase on the table and unlocked it. "I'm Elta. Please, finish your breakfast as we talk. Don't rush on my account. We have a long road ahead of us and much to cover, and today, we'll barely skim the surface. But we'll get there," she said, with a smile brighter than I felt. "I'm your tutor for decorum, customs, and the most important things you will need to know when you pass the Gadawnoin."

"Will I have other tutors?" I asked.

"Of course. Once you are through the Gadawnoin you will learn much more, and when you marry Lord Herne, you will train with members of his own staff. I trained Lady Morgana when she was facing this trial, and she asked me to train you."

That was when I realized that the woman sitting across me was thousands of years old. Morgana had gone through the Gadawnoin when Cernunnos asked her to marry him. And that had been a long, long time ago. So long, in fact, that it was almost incomprehensible.

Elta handed me a long list of names. As I glanced through them, I recognized Cernunnos, Morgana, Brighid, and several others. I knew of Cerridwen, the Morrígan, the Dagda, Danu, and Eiru. But a lot of the names were a mystery to me.

"I assume these are the names of the gods?"

"Yes. There are a number of lesser gods that you probably have never heard of. You will be required to know all of them. Not for the Gadawnoin, but as time goes on."

"What happens if I can't remember them all?" I wondered if I'd be punished like a naughty schoolchild.

"You'll be socially disgraced, that's what." She motioned for me to open another book.

I did, gently folding back pages. It was written in Turneth, so I could understand it, and it was titled *The History of the Celtic Pantheon*. The book had to be four inches thick, and it was the size of a coffee table book in height and width. The print was small, but readable. Elta motioned for me to turn to the table of contents. I did, grimacing when I saw that it had to have over hundred chapters in it.

"Let me guess. This is my textbook?"

"Well, the first of many. You will be studying with me for at least five years. That's how long it took the Lady Morgana to learn all the rudimentary information. And we are talking almost every day, at least four hours a day. You'll notice that the book is divided into five different sections, each with twenty chapters. I expect you to read the first chapter by the end of next week. After the Gadawnoin, you will immerse yourself in your studies."

Before I could say a word she handed me three more books. The second book was a volume on customs and decorum when meeting gods who were either superior or inferior to yourself. I cringed at the thought, but I was moving into a caste system and I needed to just accept that thought. It wasn't like the Fae Courts didn't have their own caste system. The third book was a volume on activities and skills I was expected to learn. Among them were dancing, how to hold a scepter or wand, how to approach a throne and take my seat on it, and other activities I never thought I'd be reading about. And the fourth book went into the geography of Annwn, and of the other realms in the world. I recognized a map similar to the one in the inn we had stayed in.

I shook my head. "I feel overwhelmed."

"Of course it's overwhelming. You're not just changing addresses, you are moving into a sphere that most mortals never even imagine. If you thought things were chaotic within the realm of the gods, you were mistaken. In this realm, we follow hierarchy and protocol."

She sat down beside me, crossing one leg over the other and leaning on the back of the chair with her arm, staring at me. After a moment, I began to feel uncomfortable. I wanted to inch away from her, to scoot my chair back, but I had the feeling this was a test of sorts.

"Well, I see you have some instincts," she said, not explaining what those were. "All right, your homework assignments: read the first chapter in your history book, and also the first chapters of these three books as well. So that's four chapters you are to have read by the end of next week. Take notes and study the material. There will be quizzes and tests. That should give you time to rest up a day or two from the Gadawnoin."

"I thought this session was to teach me how to survive this ritual," I said.

"No one can tell you how to do that. Only those who have been through the ritual ever know what truly goes on, and they aren't allowed to speak about it. I will tell you this: once you have been through the Gadawnoin, you're never to discuss it except with someone else who has been through it. You're not to talk about it, to explain what happened, or anything of the sort. If you do, the gods will punish you. Your life would be forfeit whether or not you are immortal, and don't ask me how because I don't know. Do you understand?" Elta stared at me sternly over her glasses, which were resting on her nose by now.

I sighed, as my stomach rumbled. "I'm hungry." Even though I had just eaten.

"We'll break for lunch," she said. "But be back in an hour."

AFTER I RETURNED FROM LUNCH, which I spent with Angel since I couldn't find Herne, Elta and I plunged into an intensive study of how the hierarchy worked among Cernunnos's and Morgana's palaces. It was then that I also realized just how incredibly complex the world on Annwn was, and especially, the realm of the gods. Finally, after ten solid hours of study, with another half-hour break in the afternoon, Elta let me go.

"I will next see you after the Gadawnoin. Read your chapters and take notes." She paused, placing a hand on my arm. "I believe you will come through this and in all my years, I've never been wrong."

"How many people have you seen ascend to deity-hood?" I asked.

She shrugged. "A few. Morgana, and a few before her. Go now, and we'll talk later."

I headed back to my rooms, my head exploding with facts and figures. It had been a number of years since I had been in college, and I had been a good student, but this was different. I was cramming to enter a world that was alien to me. I hadn't considered how intensive the study would be. I hadn't thought about *anything* like that.

As I entered the bedroom, Herne was there, reading over some information. He looked up. "How did the day go, love?"

I stared at him. "You never told me I'd be headed back to school." I held up the pile of books. "Look at all of this. How long will I be studying?"

He laughed, setting aside the forms he'd been looking at. "For at least four or five years. Consider it…oh… getting a master's degree. Or getting a second bachelor's degree, this time in entering goddesshood."

Shaking my head, I set the books on the table and crawled onto the bed beside him, resting in his arms. "I hope you appreciate what I'm doing to be with you." I laughed, running my hand over his cheek. "I love you, you know."

"I know. And I love you. And that's why you're doing this—so we can be together. I won't keep you as a mistress. If I did, you could stay mortal, but I want you to be my wife—I want us to be together, in all ways." He kissed me, then sat upright. "Viktor and Sheila are off on their honeymoon."

"Where are they going? Surely not back home, given what's going on with the dragons?"

"No." He sobered. "They dare not. I sent them to a nearby lake, where an inn overlooks the view. It's beautiful, they'll be waited on hand and foot, and it will make up for them having to drastically alter their wedding plans."

I wrapped my arms around my knees, bringing them up to my chest. "Do we have any word on what's going on back home?"

"Unfortunately, yes." He went from sober to grim. "Ashera contacted us. The United Coalition has yielded to the Luminous Warriors. Though the organization still stands in name, the dragons are now calling the shots. They threatened to level New York City, Los Angeles, and Seattle if the UC didn't give them their way. And they demonstrated their ability to do that by strafing several smaller towns to the ground. Not even a tornado could have caused as much damage as they did. Thirty thousand dead, between the three towns. The Luminous Warriors have done this throughout the world. Their plan must have been in the works all along."

"What happened to trying to gain power through conniving—the theme park?" My heart sank as I thought of all the lives destroyed.

"That ended when Echidna called out Typhon. The Luminous Warriors—and Typhon—truly didn't realize we had found her and that she had agreed to help. Unfortunately, they have no honor, and so they made alternative plans should Typhon fall." Herne sounded weary, and I caught the glint of tears in his eyes.

"What about our friends? What about Ginty? Did he escape?"

"Ginty will hold to his post. He can smuggle a number of people out through the Waystation, so he's doing what he can to help important members of the Otherkin societies escape. Hopefully the dragons haven't paid much attention to him. I know he's changed the name of the bar in hopes of keeping them in the dark. It's now 'Wendy's Bar & Grill' and Wendy is frontrunning it." Herne bit his lip. "There are a lot of our friends over there who won't be able to leave. We're going to have to accept that fact.

But you'll be happy to know that Merilee is over here, now. And Raven managed to persuade Llew and Jordan to follow her to Kalevala. In fact, Vixen and Apollo and Trinity have also left—they went to Wildemoone."

"I wish we could be there, helping out." I wanted to go home, but I also realized that right now, that wasn't possible. I paused, then added. "I want you to promise me something. If I don't make it through the ritual, you'll take care of Mr. Rumblebutt for me."

"Of course," Herne said. "You'll pass through it, but I know it's important for you to rest easy on the subject." He jumped off the bed. "So, tomorrow, you'll spend in meditation. That gives us tonight together. Because the ritual will start at midnight tomorrow night, and will last for twenty-four hours." He pulled a bell cord. "I'm going to order our dinner and then…I want to spend the night making love to you."

Feeling like the condemned woman about to partake of her last supper, I nodded. In some ways, it would be much easier if we were going about things as normal—it wouldn't leave me with such a feeling of foreboding. I knew that most of the anxiety was probably just in my mind, but it was affecting my nerves and my stomach and everything else.

"I'd rather go for a walk in the snow first and then eat in front of a fire with our friends. I hope you don't mind. The making love part we'll do alone, of course." I laughed, feeling some relief from the stress.

"Then that's what we'll do," he said as the servant girl entered. "Would you please tell Yutani, Talia, and Angel that we'll meet them in the blue dining chamber in an hour?"

She curtseyed. "Of course, Lord Herne," she said. "Will there be anything else?"

"Ask them to dress for dinner. Also, alert the cook that we'll want dinner in an hour."

"Very good, milord." The girl turned to leave.

As she closed the door behind her, Herne crossed to the closet. "Come, let's go for a walk and then we'll dress for dinner. That's one thing you'll have to get used to when we're in our palace. We *always* dress for dinner. You can set the standards at your own personal hold, as you like."

*Our palace, his palace, my palace…*it felt like I was in some surreal movie. Now that things were moving faster, now that I was facing the ritual, shit was getting real.

As I shrugged into my jacket, I spied that my closet had gotten a boost. Not only were my clothes hanging there, but an entire new wardrobe as well. Including several fancy long gowns that looked straight out of a fantasy novel. Assuming that dressing for dinner meant formal, I picked one of the less ostentatious ones—a green gown with a fitted bodice and an A-line skirt—and laid it across the bed for when we returned. Herne pointed to a jewelry armoire. It was filled with jewels and gems, and I sorted through the bling until I found a simple beaded jade necklace that matched the dress, along with matching earrings. As I glanced in the mirror, I caught a glimpse of my future. Not sure whether I was excited, afraid, anxious, or a combination of all of them, I let out a long breath as we headed outside.

CHAPTER SIXTEEN

THE NEXT MORNING, I WAS HUSTLED DOWN TO THE SAME fitting chamber where we had been dressed for Viktor's wedding. The seamstress had used my measurements to make my outfit for the Gadawnoin: a simple pair of trousers—dark blue—with an equally simple tunic the silvery-blue of deep water, and a silver belt. I was given a black leather sheath for my sword—Brighid's Flame—and it attached to the belt. Then, the seamstress draped a black cloak around my shoulders and fastened it with a Celtic knotwork brooch also made out of silver. She stood back, nodding.

"It fits."

"Is this it?" I asked.

She shook her head. "There is another outfit you will need, but I must blindfold you. You can't see it yet."

Feeling like I was in some kinky Cinderella film, I allowed her to blindfold me after I stripped out of the tunic and trousers. Though I couldn't see, it was obvious that I was trying on a long gown. Fitted in the bodice, the silky material draped down to cling to my hips, then spread out near my knees. *A mermaid gown*, I thought. It had to be.

The seamstresses began to talk to each other, but they spoke in Elvish and I couldn't understand what they were saying. After a few minutes of them pinning this part and that part, they removed the gown. But before they removed the blindfold, they made me try on a pair of shoes. They felt like ballet flats. After that, the blindfold came off and they had me try on a pair of boots that went with the tunic. Both pair of shoes fit and were comfortable.

"All right, you're good to go. Return here at ten P.M. Not a second later," the seamstress said, handing me back my own jeans and turtleneck.

I nodded, my stomach flipping. So the Gadawnoin had two changes of clothing. That was all I knew, except for what Morgana had told me about having to face my fears. As I left the sewing hall, I looked around, but there were hundreds of gowns here, and I had no clue which one of them—if any—had been the one I'd tried on.

Herne was waiting for me back in the bedroom. "You've been fitted for the ritual?"

I nodded. "Yes. What now?"

"Now, you spend the day in meditation and rest. My mother will take over." He paused, trailing his fingers along my cheek. "I wish I could come with you. I wish I could be the one to guide you, but I'm not allowed. I love you, Ember. Remember that—hold the thought close to your heart. I hope it gives you strength." He leaned down, pulling me into his arms, kissing me like there was no tomorrow.

I leaned against him, letting him hold me, asking myself again if I wanted to go through with the ritual. I loved Herne, but could I be content loving him as a mistress? But would that be fair to him? As long as I was mortal, his focus would be split. If we were in battle, he would worry about me, if I got sick, he would worry about me. It was something I was used to—worrying over others—but at some point, that worry would interfere with something important and he'd be forced to make a choice. But something beyond Herne felt like it was prompting me—something deeper, older.

"What are you thinking about?" he whispered.

"Why I'm doing this. I have the odd feeling that even if I hadn't met you, somehow, this day would have arrived. I'm not arrogant enough to think that I'm one of the 'chosen,' if you know what I mean. I never expected to be chosen by the gods to become one of their own, but I've had a growing feeling over the past few months that this would have been inevitable. And I don't know why."

"That's because there's usually some hand of fate playing into this. There's something you're meant to do, that you can only do as a goddess. You'll be a goddess of the forest and the Hunt as well as of the Fae." He kissed me again. "I wouldn't have asked you to marry me if I didn't have the same feeling—that you needed to become one of the gods."

"I want Angel to go through the Gadawnoin. We're twin souls. Your mother helped us figure that out day before yesterday." In all the flurry of preparations, I had forgotten to tell him. "We're not sure when we first divided, but Morgana took us back to the first time we met."

"That doesn't surprise me either. If you're earth and water, she must be fire and air. Twin souls will always carry two elements in their makeup." He sighed as someone knocked on the door. "Then we must try to make sure she is allowed to go through the ritual. I'll talk to her if you like."

I nodded. "I don't want to put undue pressure on her, but I don't ever want to lose her. I guess I understand how you feel. Once I become a goddess, I'll be terrified of losing my bestie. My other half, I guess you could say." Another thought crept over me. "What about Mr. Rumblebutt?"

"Stop worrying," he whispered, breaking off to answer the door.

Morgana strode in, sweeping past him. "It's time for you to enter private meditation," she said. "Come with me."

I turned to Herne, desperate for one last kiss. "Will I see you again before the ritual?"

He shook his head. "Yes, my love." He pulled me into his arms again, kissing me, holding me so tight that I could barely breathe. "Find what you need to find, my love," he whispered, looking deep into my eyes. "Be strong, love of my life. My wife to be."

I nodded, memorizing his face, the depth of his crystal blue eyes, the creases around his temples, the love that surrounded me when he held me. "I'll do my best. I love you, Herne. I'm doing this for us."

"Do this for yourself, as well, love." Reluctantly, he let go as Morgana tapped me on the arm. "Remember—I give you everything I have, every ounce of love that's within me."

I paused, turning to Morgana. "Let me hold Mr. Rumblebutt again, please."

She nodded, standing back as I gathered him up in my arms, holding him close.

"Little guy, I'll try to come back. I'll try to make it through this." I wanted to weep, but instead I buried my head in his fur and breathed in his dusty, comforting scent. He began to purr, and I rubbed my face against his side, praying that I'd return to Herne, to Mr. Rumblebutt, to all my friends. But I didn't know who I was praying to, and I realized that very soon, if I made it through the Gadawnoin, *I'd* be the one people were praying to. With that sobering thought, I handed Mr. R. to Herne and followed Morgana out into the hallway.

MORGANA LED me into a chamber so cavernous that I felt like I was outdoors. I could even see the sky, but in here, there was no winter.

"Is this another realm?"

"Yes, actually, it is. You will stay in this clearing until I return for you. You are to meditate." She motioned to the ring of open grass, surrounded on all sides by trees. In fact, I realized that I couldn't see the door anymore.

"What on? What about?"

"Whatever comes to mind," she said. Then, pausing, she took my hands in hers and a rush of power raced through me. "Listen to me. You have everything it takes to make it through this ritual. Your destiny leads to this moment. There are forces much bigger than even the gods, and they decide our paths for all of us. Perhaps reach out to contact the force that led you to this moment. You'll know it if you sense it." She pointed to a patch of ground cushioned with moss. "I suggest you rest there. I'll return for you when it's time to go through the ritual."

I took a deep breath and walked over to the log near the open spot. There, draped across it, were my tunic and trousers, and sitting beside them, the boots and a pair of socks. My sword, Brighid's Flame, was there, as well as Serafina, my crossbow, and a quiver of bolts. Frowning, I turned back to ask Morgana if I should change, but she had vanished.

Curious, I sat down on the log, contemplating what to do next. She had suggested resting on the patch of grass but my instincts urged me to change clothes first. Deciding to follow my gut, I stripped quickly out of the turtleneck and jeans and put on the tunic and trousers, fitting Brighid's Flame into the leather sheath. I pulled on the socks and boots, setting the sandals I had been wearing to one side.

"Now what?" I asked aloud.

Meditate, the wind whispered.

"Okay, if you say so." I lay down on the ground, my sword and bow near me, and folded up my jeans and turtleneck to provide a pillow.

The entire past week had been an exercise in coping with the unexpected. I fretted over the fact that our lives had been so unceremoniously interrupted.

But were they? The wind seemed to have a mind of its own today, and it seemed to be reading *my* mind.

"What do you mean?"

War is never convenient. What made you think that it

would spare you the chaos that attends it? Do you think anybody's ever fully prepared for war? Other than the soldiers, of course.

I thought about it. Soldiers, warriors—they were trained for battle. They were prepared for it. But civilians? Were they ever *really* ready? Were they ready for the sudden intrusion of bloodshed and fighting that spilled into their cities? Were they prepared for sneak attacks? For broken treaties and shattered promises? What war had ever politely enquired whether this was an opportune time for it to break out? To engulf the populace in its chaos?

"I guess you're right. It feels like everything was so disrupted but…that's what war does."

Yes, that's what war does—that's what war is. War isn't convenient, it doesn't take holidays, it doesn't acknowledge the disruption it causes. War is an entity that blusters in, kicks sand in the face of the weakling, and beats on the vulnerable. War's a bully, war often fights for the love of fighting, and when it possesses a people, a nation, a country, it forces itself into every situation, every life. War leaves no one untouched when it visits.

I thought about how quickly things had deteriorated with the dragons. But whoever I was talking with had it right. There was never a *good* time for those conquered. And life didn't work that way—it didn't offer you a choice for the best time to deal with invaders. Plans went awry, plans changed. The Luminous Warriors hadn't known about us finding Echidna, so when she rose to challenge Typhon, they abandoned their attempts to slide in undercover and they had launched an all-out assault. They were smart, flexible, deadly, and arrogant. And that combination made them dangerous enemies.

I tried to focus. We were safe from the dragons here in Annwn. At least I thought we were.

"Are we?" I said aloud.

Safety is an illusion, no matter where you are. The dragons can travel where they like now, except for Echidna and Typhon. But there are enemies out there that make the Luminous Warriors look like children.

"That's not very reassuring," I murmured.

I'm not here to reassure you.

"Who are you?"

That's for you to figure out, if you want. Now, meditate.

I closed my eyes, letting myself drift. Whoever it was, whether it was simply the spirit of the wind or something else, I didn't feel threatened. After a few minutes I relaxed and before I knew it, I was drifting into a haze that was either sleep or a deep, deep trance.

I WAS STANDING ON A HILL, staring out over a frozen wasteland. In the distance, mountains rose to blot out the sky and they were so tall that it was impossible to see their tops—they faded into the night sky. I shivered, glancing around.

No one else was there, not that I could see, and as I stared at the mountains, I realized that I needed to ascend to the top. I began to cross the white field that lay between me and the mountains, but the moment I set foot on the snow-covered plain, I heard the baying of dogs somewhere nearby. In my heart, I knew they were the Star Hounds of Arianrhod, and that they were onto my scent. I began to run, scrambling as my feet slid out from under me. The howls grew louder as I managed to get on my feet again. I slipped and slid my way across the field, all the while darting glances over my shoulder, straining to see if the Star Hounds were close behind. I let out a strangled scream for help, but there was no one to hear me, and I pushed myself on, struggling to keep ahead of the sounds of my pursuers.

Each time I seemed to be gaining a lead, the howling and snapping of great jaws would catch up and I was sure that they were on my heels, but I'd chance another glimpse over my shoulder only to see nothing in pursuit.

I raced as hard as I could, going down time after time to land on my ass, scrambling up again and setting off, until finally, I caught glimpse of the shore. I realized the white field was the frozen surface of a lake and I was almost to the other side. But when I reached the opposite shore and stumbled onto the rocky plain that led up into the foothills, I could see no path. There were hundreds of rocks scaling the slopes, covering the foothills like a blanket. An alluvial deposit, I thought.

As I hopped and skipped over the rocks, they shifted under my feet and I slowed down, worried that I could too easily turn an ankle. I came to a straggly pine and knelt beside it. As I looked around, I saw that I was near the top of the tree line. The altitude of this place must be incredibly high.

I climbed the slope, still trying to ignore the baying hounds behind me. Several times, my foot slipped on an icy patch and I pressed myself flat, holding on as I caught my breath. The gradient was so steep that all I could think about was falling.

When I reached the top, I pulled myself over and

rolled onto my back, out of breath. Even if the Star Hounds were ten feet behind me, I couldn't make myself stand up—not yet. I rested, listening to the howls and yips, but they sounded distant. After a moment, I rolled up and looked out over the valley below. It stretched as far as I could see, a rolling plain of white, until it met the forest wild on the other side. A green glow emanated from the forest—peridot green, the green of sunlight on leaves, of the shafts of light piercing the tangle of under-growth. It was the light of life, not the dangerous green of purification and death.

Shivering—the wind was very much awake and active —I folded my knees to my chest, watching over the expanse below. I had no idea where I was going, but the urge to fade into the mountains loomed large. As I glanced up at the sky over the mountains, I saw the Silver Wheel of Arianrhod. This time I knew it was the core energy for her realm, though it also manifested here in Annwn.

After a few moments, I picked myself up, knowing only that I needed to keep going. I looked around for a path but there were none in sight.

"What now?"

What do you think you should do? came the answer.

"I think I need to reach the top of those mountains."

Why?

I thought for a moment. Why did I feel the push to move on? What would happen if I turned and walked the other direction? Would the Star Hounds get me? Would I wander forever, never finding my goal? What *was* my goal? What did I think I might find at the top of the mountain?

"I don't know," I finally said. "It seems that I should follow the path because..."

Because why?

The voice wasn't making this very easy. So I thought some more. I had never made the conscious decision this was the right direction—I had let instinct lead me on. But was it truly instinct? Or had fear goaded me into running? Fear of facing the Star Hounds, fear of facing...whatever I might face back in the forest.

"I don't know. Maybe fear drove me here."

What do you think you'll find at the top of the mountain?

I let out a slow, shaky breath. "Maybe a road to Arian-rhod's castle because...maybe she has the answers."

The answers to what question?

I wanted to tell the voice to shut up, but I forced myself to listen, to consider what it was saying to me. And it dawned on me that I didn't *have* a question. I was running from fear, but maybe I was also running because I believed that answers had to come from outside of myself. Maybe what I needed was to just sit quietly and listen.

I took a shaky breath, folding my legs cross-legged and resting my hands on my knees, curling my thumbs and middle fingers to touch one another. Inhaling deeply, I winced as the cold night air bit into my lungs. Then, as I slowly streamed it out, I focused on my thoughts.

Was there any question I *needed* answered? And if there was, was the answer already inside me? What was I searching for here? What did I need to know? As the moments ticked by, it occurred to me that what I really wanted was approval.

I'm searching for proof of my own authority.

Ever since I had gone to work for the Wild Hunt, I had deferred to the will of Morgana, Cernunnos, and Herne. I had accepted them as my authorities, and by doing so, had sublimated my trust in myself.

"I can't do that anymore," I whispered. "When I'm a goddess, I'm going to have to make the rules, not always follow them. Yes, there are things I need to learn but I will be one of the rule-makers rather than the petitioners."

And in that moment, I realized that I had been headed toward Caer Arianrhod in hope of finding approval—the approval that I was worthy of becoming a goddess.

If you aren't confident in your choice, you'll never make it through the Gadawnoin. You must trust yourself. You must trust that this opportunity would never be offered to you if the gods didn't believe you worthy. You must believe you're capable in order for the ritual to take.

I stared into the night. Could I do it? Could I become a goddess and wield the power accordingly? Could I keep it from rushing to my head? Could I become a goddess and remain Ember? Could I remain someone I respected? Could I be true to my values and still walk among the Immortals?

Herne does, the voice whispered. *And Morgana and Cernunnos and Brighid. Some of the gods don't set a good example, and some are corrupt, like Pandora. But do you really think you have the nature within you to be that destructive?*

I thought about it. Even though both sides of my heritage were predators, I could never do what Pandora had done to Raven. I would always stand for the under-dog, I would always choose to protect those weaker than myself. I would always choose ethics over inhumanity. And *that* meant that I could handle the responsibility. As long as I kept my true nature in sight, I could choose goddesshood with a clear conscience.

The next moment, I opened my eyes and I was lying in the field, staring up at the sky, and Morgana was there, waiting for me.

CHAPTER SEVENTEEN

"You have learned what you needed to learn?" Morgana asked.

I nodded. "Yes, I believe I did." I yawned. "How long was I out?"

"Less than an hour." She settled down on the log beside me. "I can feel the difference."

I rolled up, blinking. "Less than an hour? It feels like days."

"Some experiences leave a long-lasting mark. You're ready for tonight. For the ritual. Go, spend some time with Angel and Herne. Take a bath, take a nap. Eat a light dinner. I'll come for you when it's time."

I thought about what she had told me about the Gadawnoin. "So this wasn't facing my fears…"

"Let us say it was the beginning." She paused, then bent over and plucked a blade of grass from the ground, playing with it. "I was around your age when I met Cernunnos and went through the ritual."

YASMINE GALENORN

"Were you scared?" I asked, leaning back against the tree trunk.

"Oh, I was terrified. My father was angry that I wasn't following in his footsteps. He wanted me to eventually join the Force Majeure. Though now, I'm not so sure if he was angry or just…didn't like the gods. He blamed them for setting up Arthur, who had been a protégé of his until he was claimed for kingship."

"Then you've been a goddess for a thousand years or so?"

"Longer than that. Arthur was king during the fourth century CE. So…oh, not quite two thousand years." She dropped the blade of grass and leaned back, resting her hands on the log. "I remember so often he would leave home—my father—and not return for years at a time. My mother and I grew used to his absence. Then I met Cernunnos and my world changed. In my eyes, he was all there was. And I went through the ritual so that I could be with him."

"Do you ever regret it?" I asked. "Do you still love him?" I needed to know that love could last through time.

"Do I still love him?" she said, musing. "Cernunnos and I will always love each other. We live apart now so that our love continues. There are weeks and months where we don't see one another, but when we come together, it's always with passion and joy. But for a long time, we were inseparable. Then I realized…I couldn't die. There wasn't the need to be together all the time. So we live apart, and we rekindle romance whenever we feel the need for companionship. I believe we'll always be in love, but it's different now. Our love is the foundation for our connection, but we no longer need to wear it on our sleeves, so to speak."

I wondered if Herne and I would become that way, and would it be bittersweet? "Do you regret how it's changed?"

"No, our love's much deeper now than it was in the beginning. We belong together, as a couple, but we don't need to cling." She motioned for me to stand. "Let's return to the palace."

"Where are we?" I asked.

She grinned at me. "I thought you'd pick that up. We're in your mind, and I don't mind saying, it's rather interesting in here." She led me toward a door that magically appeared.

I wasn't sure what to say, so I kept quiet and followed her.

THAT AFTERNOON we were all hanging out in a common room except for Viktor and Sheila, who were still on their honeymoon. Raven and Kipa were curled up in an overstuffed armchair. Herne and I were eating cookies and petting Mr. Rumblebutt, who was on a leash so we could keep track of him. Angel was playing chess with Talia, and Yutani was looking glum.

"What's the matter?" I asked him, handing him the cookie platter.

"I miss my tech. I miss my computer. And I miss the city," he said. "I'm not cut out for life over here."

I wanted to tell him he'd adapt, but the truth was, I wasn't so sure. Yutani truly *wasn't* cut out for a non-tech-

nological world. I glanced at Herne, who cleared his
throat.

"I've been discussing matters with my father," Herne
said. "He received a note from Saílle and Névé. Like we
thought, they've started evacuations. They're moving
their cities to the realm of Wildemoone. They can't come
back to Annwn, unless they choose to yield their rule to
the ancient Fae Court queens. And they certainly have no
desire to move to the Forgotten Kingdom. Wildemoone
has plenty of space and they can establish a life there for
their subjects who choose to follow them. So we won't be
responsible for watching over them anymore."

"How does that apply to us?" Yutani asked.

"If you want to move back home, you are free to do so.
We won't force you to stay somewhere you're unhappy.
You'll always have the freedom to journey here to Annwn
if you like, but if you want to chance the dragons…that's
your decision."

My breath caught in my throat. The thought of the
team breaking up made me heartsore, but I knew that
there was nothing I could do about it. We couldn't drive
the Luminous Warriors back to their realm, and if Saílle
and Névé were gone, then the original reason the Wild
Hunt was formed was null and void.

"Can't you introduce something here for Yutani to
work on? Annwn has a connection with our world, so
why not bring technology over?" But even as I said it, I
realized that remaking the realm of the Celtic gods in the
image of Earth wasn't a good idea. For one thing, while
magic and technology could coexist, usually one was
dominant and the juggling of the two systems required a
lot of focus and work.

"No, if it spontaneously develops here, that's different. While we use some items—and very gratefully—from Earth, production usually introduces a vast amount of pollution and raping of the land. And we will not do that. We could not. Y'Bain would strike back at us, for it's the predominant life form in this realm."

The great forest of Y'Bain was, indeed, a sentient creature, a hive mind of all of its components. The gods weren't allowed through the borders of it, either. And the forest covered a great deal of Annwn from what I had seen.

"I understand, and it's all right. But I might return to my home after Ember has passed through the Gadawnoin," Yutani said. "Or perhaps, to my father's realm. I want to convince my aunt to leave Earth."

"Viktor said he and Sheila are considering moving here," Herne said. "They're mountain people rather than city folk, and Viktor knows how to live up in the shadows of the mountains. They're going to decide while they're on their honeymoon."

"Speaking of home," Raven said. "As soon as you make it through the ritual, we'll be going home until your wedding. Home as in Kalevala, of course. Raj will be waiting for us, and my father—we did send word that we're all right, so he won't worry."

I turned to Talia. "What about you? Where are you going?"

She sighed, leaning back against the sofa cushion. "I think… I think I would prefer life in Morgana's castle. My dogs are already here, and my most important possessions. I might see if I can cadge a job with her—maybe work in the treasury or with human resources in her castle. I'm not sure. She mentioned she might have a position opening soon."

And so we were ready to scatter to the winds. I turned to Angel, searching her face. "And you? Have you made a decision yet?"

She scanned my expression, letting out a slow smile. "DJ is here, now. I don't want to live a world away from him. And I've been thinking about Morgana's offer. I think…" she paused. After a moment, she said, "I think that I'll be taking her up on her idea, so I may be joining you if everything goes right."

I clapped my hands. "It will. It has to. You won't be sorry—"

"I already am. Listen, don't mention this to DJ yet. I don't want him to find out from anybody else but me, and I sent a note to Cooper so that we can meet and discuss it." Angel held my gaze. "I'm not making this decision lightly. It's been hard, in fact, for me to accept that I want this. You're going into this world with Herne. I'm going into it alone."

"No, you're not," I said. "You'll have me, and you'll have Herne. You won't be alone."

After that, we relaxed and made small talk until the dinner hour, when Herne and I retired to our chamber as I thought about what was coming my way, and whether I'd make it through.

I STOOD at the window and looked out over the frozen landscape. The snow had let up, and the moon was shining down on the brilliant white blanket that muffled the world. Everything seemed like a still life—a Yuletide postcard, even though Yule and Imbolc had come and gone.

"We're all splitting up," I said, my voice catching. "Raven and Kipa will be in Kalevala, Yutani's going home."

"But Talia and mostly likely Viktor and Sheila will be here," Herne said, wrapping his arms around me. "And Angel will walk with the gods. She'll be here."

"I guess…maybe it's the Wild Hunt splitting up that seems so abrupt and painful. Everything was moving along and then boom, one fell swoop of the dragons and we're no longer necessary."

"Oh, love, the Wild Hunt will continue, but not in the same form. Did you expect us to go on as usual after you became a goddess and we married?"

I nodded, dashing away a tear that had managed to squeeze out from my eye. "I think I did."

"Well, maybe it would have, if it weren't for the drag-ons. But everything is shifting and changing, and we have to adapt." He paused, rocking me gently, then whispered, "I love you more than you can ever know."

Turning to him, I threaded my arms through his, holding him around the waist as I rested my head on his shoulder. "I never expected to find love. I never expected much of anything out of life. I guess we have to remain open to change, because if I hadn't been, I never would have met you, or been part of this whole wild ride. I wouldn't be standing in Annwn, preparing to become a goddess. I wouldn't be…anywhere."

He leaned down and kissed me, wholly and fully. "Let me make love to you," he whispered. "I want to feel your body against mine, I want to run my fingers over your skin and touch you in those secret places that make you cry out."

We went to bed, then, and I rode my wild lord until near midnight.

Herne watched silently as I slipped out from the bed to dress in the tunic and trousers, wrapping the sash around my waist and fitting Brighid's Flame in the sheath. I slung a quiver over one shoulder, and rigged Serafina on her strap and slid her over my other shoulder. I braided my hair back, and finally, I slid on my boots and waited, petting Mr. Rumblebutt.

Not five minutes later, Morgana tapped on the door and I gently slid my cat from my lap and answered her.

"We're ready," she said. "Follow me."

I turned back to Herne, who was standing behind me. He caught my face between his hands and dipped down for another kiss.

"Come back to me," he said, his eyes glistening. "You come back to me, you hear?"

I nodded. "I'll try. I will do my best to survive." Feeling teary-eyed, I straightened and followed Morgana down the almost-empty hallway. "It's quiet here at midnight."

The palace was silent, and there was barely any foot traffic in the hallways.

"Yes, early bed and early morn—that's the timetable for most of the people here." She glanced back at me. "Afraid?"

I nodded. "Yes, but less so than earlier. The meditation helped." I paused. "Can you make sure that everyone's okay if I don't make it through?"

"Of course. But focus on facing the challenges and

working through them." She paused. "Remember, not all challenges are to be overcome or conquered."

I glanced at her. "What do you mean?"

She shook her head. "I can't explain. Just remember my words."

We continued along, winding through the labyrinthine hallways until we stood at a locked door. It was unassuming—there was nothing to mark it as anything special, but Morgana took out a long key and held it up to her lips, blowing on it after whispering an incantation to it. She fitted it into the lock and slowly began to turn it. Instead of turning smoothly, it clicked into position, and she turned the key six times, each a fraction of a turn, until she had gone half circle with the key. Each time it clicked into place, and I thought I could hear a chamber in the lock shifting with each movement. Finally, 180 degrees later, she turned the handle of the door and it opened.

"Once you enter, the only way out is to follow the path. Do not stray from it, or you'll end up lost forever. You have your sword and bow?"

I held up Serafina and patted the sheath containing Brighid's Flame. "Yes."

"Good. You may need them during the ritual." She paused, then added, "Do you have any more questions?"

I stared at the open door. Beyond it was a swirl of colors that snapped and crackled. I couldn't see what lay beyond them, but I knew a portal when I saw it. "Do I have a time limit?"

"The Gadawnoin will take as long as it takes, but no more than twenty-four hours. I can't tell you how long— there is no set pace. You'll know you've reached the end, however. That much will be apparent." She let out a breath. "Don't let doubt cloud your mind. Doubt and fear will fail you. Sometimes, even a wrong decision is better than making no decision." Then, kissing me on the forehead, she motioned for me to enter the chamber.

I didn't want to go—a sudden wash of insecurity rippled through me, but I didn't have a choice. I was set on this path, and I wanted to marry Herne, and to marry Herne I had to pass this ritual. Taking a deep breath, I gave Morgana a final look and plunged into the vortex.

CHAPTER EIGHTEEN

I WASN'T SURE WHAT I EXPECTED, BUT I ENDED UP ON THE slope of a mountain, with fog rolling past below me. It was dark of the night, and I should be cold given the mountain was covered with snow, but I felt neither cold nor heat nor breeze nor icy air. I glanced over my shoulder, but everything behind and below me was hidden by the swirling mists. The night sky was clear, filled with stars that reeled overhead in a dizzying array. Once again, I was reminded that I was a long ways from home.

Looking around, I tried to figure out which way I should go, but finally, when I examined the ground beneath my feet, I realized that I was already standing on a path. It, too, was blanketed with snow, but I assumed that I should continue in the direction I was facing, given that I could see clearly up the mountain but behind me was a haze of mist and faintly shifting colors.

"It would be much easier if I had a walking stick," I muttered. The next moment, one appeared in my hand. Startled, I looked around but there was nobody else near me, and I had no clue if there was anybody else but me on this mountain. But, to cover all bases, I muttered, "Thank you," and began the climb up the path.

One of my favorite books when I was young had been *Heidi*—I loved reading how she ran up and down the mountain with Peter the goatherd and the goats, and I had wanted to experience that, but this mountain wasn't exactly what I had in mind. It was snow covered, yes—like Heidi's mountains had been during winter—but it was steep and, I suspected, incredibly treacherous if you stepped off the path. Here and there, glacial patches shimmered beneath the moonlight.

The moon was a cold moon—she was huge and luminous and silver, but she seemed as icy as the mountain. Sometimes the moon was gentle, sometimes she was welcoming and ripe and it felt like she was watching over me, but tonight, the moon felt like an alien ice queen, brutal and cruel and unforgiving. Her light was harsh and cold, but I was grateful for it as I worked my way up the steep slope.

I had no clue where I was going, but I kept on. As I climbed, I wondered if the Gadawnoin had been different for Morgana. Did every person going through it climb this mountain, or did they have their own mountains to scale, their own landscape to traverse?

Then it truly hit me that this path was leading me to the biggest crossroads I would ever face. I wasn't trekking *to* the ritual, this was *part* of the ritual itself. That sobered me even more. I paused to look behind me. The mist had followed me up the slope. I couldn't see where I had started from—it was now covered with the roiling coils and swirls of the fog.

"Am I supposed to climb all night?" I whispered, but there was no reply on the wind that whistled past. I felt like I should be cold, and even though I could feel the currents of air, they felt warm, like body temperature. Confused, but curious, I started the ascent again, deciding to accept whatever came, even if all I did was walk all night.

AT ONE POINT, a shriek startled me, the first sound beyond my own breathing and voice that I had heard since I started. I had no idea how long I'd been hiking, but I froze, looking around for what made the noise. Overhead, against the dark night, a huge winged figure passed by, its wings gliding—not flapping. The bird must have had a seven-foot wingspan and I immediately thought of golden eagles, though I expected they would fly during the daylight. But it *looked* like an eagle, although a faint golden glow emanated from its body. I had to be seeing its aura.

"What are you looking for?" I asked, keeping my voice soft as I stood perfectly still. While I thought golden eagles could attack people, this looked like it might be a magical bird. Either way, I didn't want to be on the wrong end, in case it was more dangerous than a regular eagle.

The bird glided overhead, letting out another series of short shrieks. Then, it began to descend. It didn't seem to be coming directly at me, but I was still cautious, and I readied my bow, nocking an arrow in the crossbow. I was still carrying my allentar arrows, and I figured one would take down the bird if there was a problem.

But instead of attacking, the bird circled lower and lower until it landed on the ground in front of me. It was huge—over three feet tall—and it watched me closely.

I wasn't sure what to do. If I kept on walking, I'd run right into it. Finally, I decided to acknowledge it and see if that did anything. "Hello. I'm Ember."

The eagle hopped a step closer, then began to shimmer and a moment later, a gorgeous woman stood there, my height and sturdy. She was wearing a golden dress that glinted beneath the moonlight, and her hair—a rich brown color streaked with tawny strands—hung long, down to her hips.

"Welcome, Ember Kearney." She motioned to an outcropping that jutted from the mountain about twenty-five feet up the path. "Enter."

I squinted at the outcropping and saw an opening dark against the snowy front of the outcropping. "Thank you," I said, turning back to the eagle shifter. "May I know your name?"

"I'm the guardian of the mountain," she said, and then stepped back. "Go through the cave to the next stage of the journey. Do not continue up the mountain." Then, without waiting for me to say a word, she shimmered again back into her eagle shape and took wing, flying into the night sky.

Curious, but feeling like finally I was getting some direction, I bent and saw that the path did, indeed, turn toward the cave. Remembering that Morgana had warned me not to stray from the path, I did as the guardian bade me, turning to the left to the entrance of the cavern.

There, the inky blackness of the opening blazed to life as

I approached, shimmering with a sparkling array of lights. It reminded me of the portals, except this looked more like vertical blinds made up of light. I slid my arm between two of the long rays and they shifted, opening enough for me to see the path that led into the cave. Reluctant, yet encouraged, I stepped through the lights, into the mountain proper.

THE MOMENT I entered the cave, the walls lit up with a pale silver glow that seemed to come from within. It was bright enough to see the path led across the cavern floor, into a long passage. While there were other passageways along the face of the back wall, the path led to only one. To reach the others, I'd have to go off path, so I kept my focus on the trail in front of me, ignoring the lure of exploring the others.

"Stick to the path, Ember, stick to the path," I chanted to myself. "You need to stick to the path. Morgana told you, don't go off path."

And of course, the other entrances kept beckoning me. I found myself thinking about what might be at the end of each passage, but I dragged my attention away, figuring this was part of the test. I usually was good at following directions, but this time I had to avert my gaze from the other possibilities and finally, I ran as fast as I could, plunging into the passage at the end of the path to put a stop to my dithering.

The tunnel was a long one. From the pale light that shone from the walls, I could see it stretch into the distance. It felt like I was journeying to the center of the mountain. I kept telling myself that everything would be all right. Everything would be fine.

But leaving the others unexplored left me feeling anxious, as though I might miss something important by ignoring the other tunnels. The pull to run back out into the main cavern and peek down each hallway was strong, but I forced myself to continue along the path, even though every fiber of my being was shrieking that I was making a mistake.

"Good gods, get a grip," I muttered. "All you're feeling is FOMO."

Fear of missing out was very real for a lot of people and I hadn't realized that I suffered from it until now. How many times had I intended to do one thing while giving in and trying something else first? As I thought back, I realized it had been a regular occurrence in my life. But where had it come from?

"It's normal to want more," I said aloud, and the sound of my voice felt reassuring. "It's normal to think I'm missing out on something by making a definitive choice. But remember—Morgana said sometimes making a bad decision is better than making no decision. And you're following her instructions, so this isn't a bad decision."

The passage was dry and clear, and once again, I realized that I had lost track of time and had no clue of how long I'd been walking. But up ahead, I began to see what looked like another opening, where the passage widened out, and that buoyed up my heart.

"Is the Gadawnoin merely a series of paths to walk?" I said.

By now I was starting to get tired, so I paused to find a candy bar in my pack. The sugar gave me a buzz and I shook my head. It had to be well into two or three in the morning by now, and it felt like I had been walking for hours. I took another deep breath and started on again. A glance over my shoulder showed me that I'd been walking long enough that I could no longer see the entrance.

More time passed and then, I caught a glimpse of an opening up ahead. Anxious to get out of the tunnel, I jogged ahead. As I stepped through the opening, I paused.

I was in a wide chamber, but the walls were made of ice, and the floor too, and icicles hung from the ceiling—massive and long, with jagged points threatening anyone who walked beneath them. The walls glistened with a pale blue light, so smooth that I could have skated on them. The chamber went farther back, but the path—carved into the floor—led to the center, where a spiral staircase, also carved from ice, circled up through the ceiling. I glanced up at the hole through which it disappeared. The ceiling of the cave had to be fifty feet high, and it didn't look like the staircase ended there.

I made my way to the base of the staircase. I still wasn't noticing the temperature—everything felt mildly cool. The path ended at the bottom step and I was about to set foot on the stair when a sound from above startled me. I looked up to see a Star Hound guarding the top of the stairs near the ceiling.

Crap. What the hell was I going to do? It had taken both Raven and me to eliminate one. I wasn't sure I could manage one on my own.

The Star Hound stood at least seven feet tall, and for all the world looked like a statue of Anubis. Its eyes glowed with a gold light, and around its neck, it wore a silver knotwork collar. It was also wearing a kilt in a complex pattern in black and silver. In one hand—which was very much a cross between a paw and a hand—it held a silver scepter.

You can't do this. If you get close it's going to kill you.

Turn back. Find a different way. Surely Morgana didn't mean for you to stay on the path to certain destruction.

Right...get the hell out and goddesshood be damned.

The voices began to race through my mind, and I stood on the first stair, still locking eyes with the Star Hound, unable to move as panic flooded my brain. My muscles tensed, my body urging me to run, to put distance between me and this creature. It took every ounce of discipline that I had to stand my ground.

But then, a drop of reason filtered through. The Star Hound hadn't attacked me. Yes, it had what looked like a weapon, and yes, Star Hounds were dangerous, but this one was waiting, watching me. If it had been going to tear me to pieces, wouldn't it have made a move by now? Wouldn't it be at my throat already?

Morgana said to continue on the path. She's been through this ritual before. She must have faced either the same thing or something similar.

Finally, I managed to break my paralysis and force my foot to the next step. My heart pounding, I took another step, and then another, all the while keeping my gaze locked on the Star Hound. And I was twenty steps away, and then ten, and still it stood there, silent and waiting. I took a deep breath and continued and then we were face to face. I stood there, silent, waiting for it to act.

"Are you afraid of me?" the creature asked.

Surprised that I understood it, I nodded. "Yes, I am."

"Then why did you continue up the stairs?"

I thought about my answer, not wanting to blurt out something stupid. Finally, I answered honestly. "I trust Morgana not to lead me astray. She said to continue along the path—don't step off the path. And these stairs are on the path."

The Star Hound leaned forward and I could feel its breath on my face as it studied me for a moment, its long muzzle smelling vaguely of dog. After yet another interminable time, it straightened and turned to the side, allowing me access to the staircase.

"You may pass."

Gripped by fear, I forced myself to move, to continue up the stairs. As I passed the Star Hound, I kept my eyes directly in front of me. A moment later it was behind me. I glanced over my shoulder to see that it had turned around again, facing the bottom of the stairs once again. I leaned against the railing of the spiral staircase, breathing heavily.

The light faded as I entered the second story of the stairs, and only the steps were lit. I couldn't see anything else in the chamber I had just entered, except for what looked like glowing eyes from the darkness. Red and gold, silver and blue, the lights shifted constantly. I wasn't even sure if they were eyes—they reminded me of a cat's eyes caught in snapping a photograph, reflecting the light. A faint rustling picked up, like autumn leaves caught in the wind.

My stomach tightened and I glanced up. The circular lights of the staircase seemed to continue on and on with no end. My legs ached and I had to go to the bathroom. Luckily, I just needed to pee, and though I hated doing so, since there was nowhere else to go—no bushes or trees to dart behind—I pulled down my trousers and—holding onto the railing—scooted so my butt was over the edge of the stairs.

I hope nobody down below gets pissed on...or pissed, I thought, then let out a strained laugh at my unintentional pun. This wasn't a memory I wanted to share with anybody else. Somehow, I had expected the ritual to goddesshood to be more dignified and less awkward. But relieved and ready to move on, I cinched my trousers again and began to climb once more.

I had no idea how many steps I had climbed, but it had to be at least ten tall floors' worth. I looked up and was grateful to see yet another ceiling coming up. I prayed that when I climbed through it, that would be the end of the stairs.

"I'm never getting on a stair machine again," I muttered as I forced myself to continue. But a thought caught my attention. If the first guardian had been a Star Hound, what the hell would I be facing at the top of this part of the journey?

Nervous, I let out a long breath and pushed onward. I was nearly to the ceiling when a sound like a faint gong rang out.

Gongs meant alarms meant somebody was up here waiting for me.

And sure enough, as I approached the spot where the steps went through the ceiling, another figure appeared, coming down through the opening. Once again I froze as a great horned owl flew through, landing on the railing near the entrance. It gazed at me with round eyes, watching every move I made.

Cautiously I approached it. Owls were magical and

they could also be dangerous when provoked. I didn't want a face full of its talons.

But the owl tilted its head, watching me closely. A feather fell from its wing, drifting down to land at my feet. By now, I was running on autopilot, I was so tired. I bent over and picked up the feather, holding it up so the owl could see.

"Is this a gift?"

The owl let out a long *hoot* that echoed around me, reverberating until I couldn't hear anything else, getting louder with each echo. I was about to cover my ears but then I caught words among the echoes.

Are you willing to leave your past behind? Are you willing to let go of everything you've ever been and cross over the threshold into a new life? Are you willing to step off of the Wheel, out of the Eternal Return, and take your place among the Immortals? Are you ready to face your trial at the feet of She who rules the Silver Wheel?

The owl stared at me as I fingered the feather, gazing down at it. The owl signified magic and wisdom and sometimes—death. The bird watched me, waiting. And then I knew where I was headed. I hit the realization like a brick wall and every ounce of my courage evaporated.

She who rules the Silver Wheel.

Arianrhod.

I was on my way to face Arianrhod, the goddess of the Silver Wheel. The goddess of Caer Arianrhod. The goddess of Caer Sidi. She ruled over reincarnation…and becoming a goddess meant I'd never incarnate again. I would face life eternal in the body I had now, in the persona I wore in this life.

Could I do it? Could I live as myself, live as who I was

forever and ever? Could I face each day waking up as Ember Kearney?

Until that moment, I hadn't thought about it, but death offered the chance to start again. Death offered an out, if I couldn't stand myself. Death offered an end—and new beginnings. To become a goddess meant to transcend death, and it meant wearing the mask of who I was forever. Did I like who I was enough to make that leap?

My stomach knotted and I slowly settled down on the step next to the owl. It waited for me, gazing down at me placidly from its perch on the railing.

"Do I love who I am enough to make this work in the long run?" I knew I'd have help, but what if I went mad? What if I wasn't capable of facing an eternity, even to be with Herne? How could I know whether this was the right move?

Herne does it, Morgana does it—and she chose to cross this threshold. Cernunnos and Brighid have lived forever...and will live forever. Even if all of these realms vanish, they'll still live and grow and thrive. For them, the physical realm is simply one state of being.

Ah yes, another voice whispered. *But there's no going back. Are you sure, are you* so very sure *that you're ready to face eternity?*

I already face it, just in different bodies, with different names, and other parts of my own soul. When I become a goddess, I imagine I'll have access to all of my soul selves, all of my incarnations. That thought stopped me. I hadn't considered that, either.

I can be so much more than I am. I'll be Ember, but also every other life I've lived.

And that thought frightened me so much I began to shake.

What if I don't like the person I become? What if...I'm not Ember when I change?

But Morgana's been through the Gadawnoin. She didn't mention anything about any of these things. Then again, she seems happy with her choice.

I steeled myself and stood, facing the owl.

Sometimes, we had to make a choice. And like Morgana said, sometimes making a bad decision was better than no decision at all. I would either stay Fae, and mortal, or I would become a goddess. Those were my two choices. I had no idea if I'd come through this and be happy. But if I quit now, if I turned back, I'd regret it forever. I'd wonder until the day I died—and I would die —if I should have taken the chance.

I held out the feather to the owl and said, "I'll continue."

It let out a soft hoot and swiveled its head to look up the steps. And even though I didn't speak owl, I knew without a doubt, it was saying, *Go on. Continue. You're almost there.*

CHAPTER NINETEEN

As I passed through the opening, the staircase ended, and I was standing on what appeared to be a wide silver thread in the stars. Everywhere I looked, I saw similar threads running through space, intersecting in a massive web. I reached down to touch the thread, wondering if it was glass or rope or something else—but it sizzled under my hand, not burning, so definitely pure magical energy. A tingle ran up my spine.

The web spread out as far as I could see in every direction, and as I glanced over my shoulder, the staircase and cavern was gone, and everywhere I looked, I saw the webs streaming through the universe.

About a hundred yards away, balanced across the web I was standing on, a massive silver throne rose up, resting on what looked like a dais made of ice. The throne was embellished with blue and crystal gems, and the moon hovered nearby, casting its frozen light down on us.

Either I had entered an interstellar realm, or I was on some massive acid trip.

Atop the throne sat a woman who looked twenty feet tall, and just the sight of her took my breath away. Dressed in an indigo gown that shimmered with beads, her platinum hair flowed down her back, shrouding her like a cloak. Her eyes were silver with no pupils, and her face was as pale as winter's blush. As she turned her head to gaze at me, her power rushed through the chamber like a wave, knocking me to my knees. I was unable to avert my gaze.

Her headdress rose tall, a knotwork of silver and diamonds. The knotwork was so intricate that I couldn't follow the pattern, and sparkled so brightly that it almost blinded me. Beneath the flowing platinum locks, a white fur cloak cascaded down her shoulders, and she held a silver scepter. At her feet a small clearing appeared, a grove with a pond that bubbled and sprayed. Beside the pond hung a gown from a nearby bush and I knew—with absolute certainty—that it was my gown, the one I had been fitted for wearing the blindfold. Next to the bush was a marble bench.

I managed to gather my wits and crossed to the foot of the throne.

After a moment, Arianrhod spoke, and her voice echoed like the wind. "Ember Kearney, you are here by petition of Morgana, Cernunnos, and Herne, to hand over your mortality and join the gods. Are you here of your own free will?"

I took a deep breath and nodded. "I am."

"You passed through the long night. You faced my guardians. But now, you must answer to me." Arianrhod motioned for me to stand. "Once you take this step, you are forever removed from the Wheel. You will never return to it, never again experience the Eternal Return. You will exist outside of time and space, you will belong to the ages, rather than to the cycles. Are you prepared to give up your mortality and face eternity with the rest of us?"

I paused, then answered, letting my heart speak. "Yes, I'm ready to join the gods."

She scanned my face. "I believe you," she said after a moment. "Are you willing to learn what you need to learn, to apply yourself to the years of lessons you must take, and to take up the duties you must accept as Herne's wife?"

My voice started to shake. "Yes, I am."

"Are you willing to walk away from the world of mortals, even though you have friends there?" Arianrhod hit a nerve with this one.

I paused. "Herne still interacts with mortals, including me."

"Yes, but he is not of your realm. There will be a difference."

I thought of Angel. What if she wasn't able to make the change? What then?

"If you turn this down, you're a fool. I'd do it, for the right love," Angel's voice echoed in my thoughts. At one time, she had chided me for worrying about her. And even though I prayed and hoped she would follow me, that she would join the gods with me, I knew that I couldn't let even my twin soul dissuade me from what felt like the right path.

"I will walk away from the world of mortals," I said, my throat dry even as my eyes teared up. "But I will still keep hope that—" I stopped, realizing that it wasn't my place to beg Arianrhod to offer Angel the same chance, and Arianrhod wasn't part of the Triamvinate, so the chance wasn't hers to offer.

"Then, give me the feather my guardian presented to you."

I handed her the feather.

"Given Herne has petitioned the Triamvinate, and they have agreed, and you are willing, we will begin the Gadawnoin." She motioned to the pond. "Strip out of your clothing and enter the sacred pool."

I stripped off the trousers and the tunic, as well as my underwear and bra. I sat on the bench to pull off my shoes.

As I stood naked before her, Arianrhod pointed her scepter toward the pond. "Enter the water, dip fully beneath it, and come out the other side. Do everything you're told to do."

Taking another deep breath, I slowly began to enter the pond, which was filled with a teal-colored water and was about five feet at the deepest. As my feet hit the stones lining the pond, for the first time that night I felt something beyond my own skin. The water was warm— not overly so, but enough so that I noticed the difference. It lapped against my skin, moved by an ethereal wind. I slowly made my way to the center and—as I stood there— I closed my eyes, swaying in the water. I bent my knees, dipping my head below the surface so that I was fully covered, and the next moment, I sank into a deep trance.

THE FAINTEST BREEZE fluttered over my crib and I—new to the world—looked up into my mother's face. Even as I caught a glimpse of her, a long string of memories raced through my mind—bits and pieces of other lives all crowding in together, as so often happened with newborns.

A Light Fae woman on her knees, scrubbing a floor, begging her mistress to forgive her for being slow even while inside, she seethed at being a servant bound to the nobility. Her mistress, despising weakness, kicked her in the side and that kick ruptured the servant girl's spleen. Hours later, she died in pain and alone.

A young girl on a mountain, picking wild flowers. Her mother was nearby but was occupied with yet another new baby and didn't see the coyote that was sneaking up on the child. Within seconds, the flowers scattered to the ground, and the coyote dragged off the girl while the mother screamed and attempted to reach her.

An old woman rested in bed, ancient Dark Fae—and she held her eldest daughter's hand as her family gathered around her. Beloved, she was, and revered, and as she drew her last breath, she could hear the cries go up. She wanted to tell them she was young again, but her lips would not work, and she understood then that she was free, and that freedom tasted sweet.

On and on the memories went, life after life, back before time, and several times Angel was there with me, my twin soul saying good-bye, promising to meet again.

I kept my head below the water, and in that moment my breath vanished and I realized my life was passing. I was moving out of life as I knew it, and entering a new world, only this time it was in the same body. There would be no funeral, no mourning because I was still alive

—but it would be a very different form of life, with no going back.

Deep in my veins, my blood shifted and frothed, changing as it flowed through my body, and lungs and heart and every organ began to evolve. My DNA re-wove its sequence and all sense of aging fell away as my body took on more light and gave up its mortality.

Every strand wove itself anew, and I could feel myself expanding and changing as the memories of my other lives flowed through my mind and took up their place in a space easy to access, but that wouldn't interfere with the Ember part of me.

I spread my arms wide, feeling an inner glow beginning deep in my heart, and it spread through my body to fill every cell, every nook and cranny. I opened my eyes and saw that I was, indeed, glowing with a pale blue light. I also realized that I was hovering over the pond, no longer in it. Fearing I'd drop into the water, I steeled myself, but I remained in midair, and then, very slowly, as the light spread to every recess of my blood, body, and soul, I slowly descended back into the water.

A sense of strength flooded through me, and clarity, and even my magic leapt up, awake and aware. As the energy began to settle, Arianrhod stood, stepping down from her throne.

"Welcome, Lady Ember, into the realm of the Divine. Rise now, and take your place among the Immortals." With that, she bade me to exit the pool and dry myself. I donned the gown that waited for me, and Arianrhod herself placed a stunning aquamarine pendant on a silver chain around my neck. "You are now Goddess of the Grotto, Lady of Water Fae, and Mistress of the

Hunt. Let your actions never dishonor the path you now walk."

My entire body was humming so violently I could almost hear it. "Is this normal?"

"What are you talking about?"

"I feel like I'm vibrating so much I'll fall apart." I was trying to stand straight, but I felt like I was listing to the side. "I know I'm not drunk."

"You are feeling the aftereffects of the Gadawnoin. Your body will adapt over the next few days. But for now, you must rest and take time to adjust. You survived the transformation, but your body's been through a major disruption. You must heal. I will take you to Ferosyn now."

She paused, then added, "Welcome, Grotto Mother, into this new world. May you never regret your choice."

Everything began to spin and then, before I could cry out, I felt myself tumbling into the vast field of stars surrounding us, and everything else fell away.

I FELL THROUGH THE STARS, through the cold reaches of space. I fell through galaxies and passed comets speeding on their way and spun endlessly through the Milky Way, watching the universe careen around me, watching it spin on its axis. Stars rose and blossomed, while others vanished in an explosion of pure light, then sank inward on themselves, gobbling up time and space as they grew tighter and smaller.

I couldn't remember who I was. I knew that I existed, and that I was part of the universe, part of the dance that made up existence. I leapt along the Web, those glittering strands sparkling as they stretched out, touching other strands, weaving a pattern throughout space, where all worlds collided, where everything connected.

A single strand set up a song, vibrating as it hummed, and that vibration rolled along the Web, touching every other part of the massive universal construct, and even though I wasn't sure what or who I was, an image of a butterfly came to mind and then as it rose on its wings, I saw how its movement affected everything around it, spreading out, so that eventually the silent swish of its wings touched stars far, far away. Everything was connected and linked, every life, every planet, every star.

Eventually, I slowed down and my tumble through space began to decelerate, and then I saw a planet ahead, spinning on its axis, and that planet was overlaid with other realms, transparent and yet still there. My eyes began to close and I gave into the lure of slumber, and then all was quiet and I slept and dreamed of starlight and space, and as I dropped deeper into my sleep, everything went silent.

"EMBER, WAKE UP. EMBER?" A familiar voice echoed in my head and I slowly began to wake. As I forced myself to open my eyes, I saw Ferosyn standing over me. He was patting my cheeks. "Time to wake up, Ember."

I groaned, trying to move. Everything hurt and as I slowly sat up, every muscle gave its own little scream. "What...where am I?"

"You're in my healing center. Time to wake up, Lady Ember."

*Lady Ember...*and then it all came flooding back. The ritual, meeting Arianrhod, the transformation. It had all been real and not a dream. I eased myself up and scooted back against the headboard.

"Am I... Did it work?"

He nodded, reaching for my arm. "Let me check your blood pressure." He checked all my vitals and finally pronounced me fit. "You're strong, you're healthy, and yes, the Gadawnoin worked. You are a goddess."

The words echoed in my head. It was true. It had worked. I had gone through with it. "Am I...still me?"

"Yes, but it will take you awhile to adjust, so you'll need to go easy on yourself. For the next few weeks, you'll be in a precarious spot. Don't try to do too much, too fast, or you'll spin yourself into a crisis." He shook a finger at me. "No getting out of bed."

"But I thought—" How could I stay in bed for several months?

But Ferosyn motioned for me to look around. "You'll be in your own rooms, and you won't have to stay in the healing center as long as you obey the rules."

I started to smile at him and felt one of my teeth pierce my inner lip. "What the hell?" I asked, rubbing one of my teeth. It was sharp, pointed like a fang.

"Your Leannan Sidhe side took precedence when you went through the Gadawnoin. Your Autumn's Bane Heritage is a minor part, though still strong. Which means," he said, sitting in a chair beside me and taking one of my hands in his, "you are primarily a goddess of the Water Fae and Rivers, and secondarily—a goddess of the Hunt. Full Leannan Sidhe have retractable fangs. You'll get the hang of it. They're used to siphon off life energy—not blood—from your victims in the quickest, most expedient manner."

I asked for a mirror and he handed one to me. As I gazed at myself in the looking glass, I saw minor shifts that had happened during the ritual. My hair was curlier, the fangs were the most obvious, but there was something about my eyes that spoke most to the change I had been through. They were darker, more vibrant, and there was something behind them that almost scared me.

"When can I get up?"

"You can get out of bed to eat, use the bathroom, and walk around a few minutes each day. I'll have one of my healers come in to help you. For now, though, I want you to drink this healing draught and go back to sleep. You need to rest. Your body has to adapt." He handed me a small vial with some blood-red liquid in it. "Drink."

I reluctantly took the sleeping potion. "When can I see the others?"

"When I think you're past the crisis point. Now back under the covers, and rest." As Ferosyn turned to leave the room, he glanced back at me. "You do realize that 50 percent of those who undergo the Gadawnoin never make it, don't you? Though now that you're through the main ritual, you have a 90 percent chance of surviving the aftereffects."

I stared at him. Nobody had told me that, but even as I started to protest, the potion drew me back into sleep, and I let go of everything as I closed my eyes.

CHAPTER TWENTY

Two months later, I was finally allowed out of bed. Raven and Kipa had gone home to Kalevala, Viktor and Sheila were building a house in Eselwithe, Yutani had opted to stay over in Annwn for the time being and was hanging around with some of the mages who were doing their best to rig up a communications system with several of the other realms, Angel had moved into a cottage near DJ and his foster family—also in Eselwithe—and Talia was working as Herne's private secretary.

Herne and I were preparing to journey back through the portals to oversee that everything we needed had been packed up, ready to be delivered through the portals. I was adjusting fairly well to my new status, though it felt so odd to think of myself as a goddess. On one hand, it didn't feel like a lot had changed. On the other hand, everything had.

I no longer needed to eat often—though I still did, out of my sheer love of food. I didn't get winded or tired, my magic seemed stronger and yet more unstable than ever, and if I cut myself or hurt myself, I healed up faster than I could ever imagine healing. Oh, things still smarted, but I was able to roll with the punches.

"Are you ready for this?" Herne asked.

I nodded. I was carrying Serafina and my quiver of what was left of the allentar bolts. "Yeah, I think I need to see for myself what's going on—so that I don't keep thinking of my home the way it used to be."

Herne looked grim. "It's not pleasant, so be warned."

We rode our horses—mine was a black Friesian I had named Bolt—to the portal and then, leaving them with the guard, leapt through. Herne seemed much more relaxed since I had passed through the Gadawnoin, and I realized it was because he wasn't afraid I'd be killed. Now he could focus on things the way he needed to, without worrying about me all the time.

As we arrived in the park behind Herne's house, Orla, the portal keeper, gave us a tight smile. "Things are bad, be cautious."

"How bad?"

"Bad enough that Cernunnos is having me seal this portal for now and return home. I'll go after you return to Annwn." He shivered. "The Luminous Warriors have taken over the United Coalition, as you know. The rest of the representatives are there, but in name only."

I shivered. Even the air felt different, though it was probably my imagination. As we hurried down to Herne's house, we saw the members of Cernunnos's staff working to pack up the last of Herne's belongings. We toured the nearly empty house.

"Are you selling it?" I asked.

He shook his head. "No, we'll seal it up and keep it, should we be able to come back. Maybe the dragons will get tired of this game and go home. That's always a possibility."

"Unless they decide that they prefer human flesh to cows and other animals." I shook my head soberly. "It's amazing what a few months can do."

"Come on, let's drive over to your house and make certain they have everything set." He motioned for me to get in the Expedition.

I stared out the window as we drove along the rain-slicked streets. It was mid-April, and the spring rains were in full swing. Here and there we saw people hurrying past, and life almost seemed normal except for the look in their eyes that said, *Don't approach, get out of my way.*

I had put my phone on to charge the moment we arrived in the house, and now I scrolled through the news, my heart sinking. There was some sort of lottery that had been instituted by the Luminous Warriors, and people were entering for chances to win trips to the Forgotten Kingdom. I had a feeling that would be the last vacation they would ever take.

I thought about calling Ashera, but she had visited us in Annwn and brought the news that the Celestial Wanderers and the Mountain Dreamers were going undercover over here, those who hadn't returned to the Forgotten Kingdom. The ones returning had some plan to set up a trap for the Luminous Warriors but we weren't privy to it.

"Do you think the world is lost?" I asked.

"No, not lost. Eventually the dragons will move on. Or…they won't. Nothing will ever be the same again. But maybe that's not such a bad thing. Maybe this will bring people together and force them to form alliances rather than to fight each other."

Herne paused, then added, "I've watched this world evolve and grow for a long, long time. Now you will, too. Thirty-one years…Ember, it's a grain of sand on the beach of life. In a hundred years, we'll see how things are going. In a thousand years, we won't recognize the landscape from what it is today. Nothing stays the same forever. The gods have learned this, and you will too. Yes, there has been a drastic shift, but it will force the world to change with it. For good or ill. Let's hope for good."

I thought about the future. I was a goddess now, and I was beginning to notice that I sensed things deeper, that I found myself starting to think in terms of centuries rather than years. I was facing a future that extended beyond time, and I was learning to come to terms with it.

"Angel's accepted Morgana's offer to plead her case to the Triamvinate," I said.

"She'll make a wonderful goddess. Let me guess, a goddess of the hearth?" Herne asked.

I laughed. "What else? Oh, another thing that she hasn't mentioned. She and Sejun have been spending a lot of time together. I think something might be happening between them."

Sejun had been Raven's and Rafé's therapist, and Angel had started talking to him to come to terms with Rafé's death, but I had the feeling there was a growing connection there.

"That would be nice, for both of them," Herne said. "We're here," he added, parking in front of my house.

As we stepped out of the car, I stared at the home that Angel and I had shared. It felt so familiar, but now it also felt too small for my world. Everything was expanding. Everything was growing and evolving along with me. And now, this home, this lovely place, already felt like a memory.

"I think I'm done here," I said. "I have dreamed of coming home for weeks, but now that I'm here, I realize that my story here is done. I'm on a new path. We're planning our wedding. The Fae cities have moved on to Wildemoone. The Wild Hunt is—at least over here—dissolved. My mother and father are long gone, and Angel and her brother are living over in Annwn now. Raven and Raj and Kipa have moved on." I let out a deep sigh. The noise and the pollution had startled me when we had arrived through the portal. Three months without it had left me coughing when we returned, and I had begun to appreciate the slower pace of Annwn.

As we approached the door, I saw that it was ajar. My heart sank. "Please, don't let anybody have trashed the house," I whispered.

Herne and I opened the door, cautiously entering. Everything was boxed up, and ready to go, and Ender— one of Herne's huntsmen—was at the dining room table, waiting for us. He had a box with him that looked like an oversized hat box.

"What's that?" I asked.

Ender shrugged. "Névé sent one of her messengers here with it. She said this belonged to you and she found it when they were preparing to leave for Wildemoone."

I frowned, accepting the box. What could it be? As I began to slice open the strapping tape holding it closed, an energy reached out from the box to touch my own and I shivered. It felt like my mother. "What the hell...?"

"What is it?" Herne asked.

I opened the flaps of the box and gasped. Inside was a crown. I lifted it out, shaking my head. I knew exactly what it was. "This is the crown Morgana told me to find. The one that my maternal grandmother owned but disappeared when Raven and I went to visit her and found she had died. I know it in my bones."

As I held up the headdress, I shook my head in wonder. The crown was a sculpture in bone and gems. Dyed bones carved into the shape of roses formed a diadem, and two spiraling horns rose from the center. Ropes of sparking aquamarine cabochons looped from side to side, scalloping around the sides and back. In the front, a gem was set in the center—a black opal the size of a silver dollar, hanging down to fit over the third eye.

"Oh my gods," I whispered. "This is incredible."

"Destiny," Herne said. "This embodies your energy— the water mixed with the Hunt mixed with the Fae...this crown embodies your magic, and when we marry, you will wear it to mark the goddess you have become."

I nodded, knowing he was right. "When we marry..." And then it hit me—full force, like it hadn't before. I was a goddess, planning to marry the god of my dreams, the god who had won my heart and to whom I'd entrusted my life. And this crown was the final sign that every decision I had made had led me to this moment. "How on earth did my grandmother come by this? Who made it?"

"I don't know. Some seer from the past, catching a

glimpse that it would one day be needed? Some oracle who caught a glimpse of the future?" Herne turned to me as I gently replaced it in the box. "But it's made for you—and only for you. So, my love, are you ready to take your place in Annwn and become my bride?"

I glanced around, then nodded. "I'm ready to leave the past behind and take my place in my future. When shall we marry?"

"You wanted to marry in the autumn originally. We no longer have to adjust the date back, given you have passed through the Gadawnoin. What say that we marry on the eve of the new year? Samhain Eve? October thirty-first?"

And, with the scent of bonfires rising in my memory, I agreed. I would marry the Lord of the Hunt, and take my place in the world of Annwn. I still loved my home world, but change had come—for ill or good, it was too soon to know the final outcome. And so I was moving on. My friends would still be with me—even though some were scattered. We would have new adventures, and new lives, and new worlds to explore. And maybe one day, we'd return to Seattle to visit. But the future beckoned and I had to answer.

As we made sure everything was ready to go, and then —carefully carrying the crown—made our way back to the portal, I turned back to look at the world I was leaving. Wondering when I'd see it again, I extended my hand out in a silent farewell to everything I had known here.

"Ready?" Herne asked, his hand on my back.

"I'm ready," I said, reaching up to give him a kiss.

Then, thinking about Mr. Rumblebutt and how much I wanted to go cuddle him, I stepped through the portal. I was going home—to Annwn.

AND SO ENDS the second story arc of the **Wild Hunt Series**. If you enjoyed **Veil of Stars**, then you might want to read the rest of the series. Start with **The Silver Stag, Oak & Thorns**, and **Iron Bones**. Book 18: **Antlered Crown**—the wedding novella—is available for preorder now. The series will be finished with that novella, although I plan on writing a few more short adventures in the future.

If you enjoyed this series, preorder the first book in the new **Hedge Dragon Series—The Poisoned Forest**—which takes place in the Forgotten Kingdom and the world of Wildemoone realms that are mentioned in this book. Storm, a Hedge Dragon, leaves her home in the Forgotten Kingdom and journeys to the realm of Wildemoone where she goes in search of her sister, long ago sold off into slavery. *You just might catch a cameo of your fave Wild Hunt characters from time to time!*

If you like ooo-spooky fiction with an older female lead, check out my **Moonshadow Bay Series**. Begin with **Starlight Web**. January Jaxson returns to the quirky town of Moonshadow Bay after her husband dumps her and steals their business, and within days she's working for Conjure Ink, a paranormal investigations agency, and exploring the potential of her hot new neighbor. **Harvest Web** and **Shadow Web**, books 4 and 5 in the series, are now available for preorder, so grab them before you forget!

If you like paranormal mysteries/paranormal women's fiction, try my **Chintz 'n China Paranormal Mystery Series**. Begin with **Ghost of a Chance**. There are five books and two novellas available. This series is finished.

Return with me to **Whisper Hollow Series**, where spirits walk among the living, and the lake never gives up her dead. I re-released **Autumn Thorns** and **Shadow Silence**, along with a new book—**The Phantom Queen**! Come join the darkly seductive world of Kerris Fellwater, spirit shaman for the small lakeside community of Whisper Hollow.

If you prefer a lighter-hearted paranormal romance with some steamy vampire-witch action, meet the wild and magical residents of Bedlam in my **Bewitching Bedlam Series**. Fun-loving witch Maddy Gallowglass, her smoking-hot vampire lover Aegis, and their crazed cjinn Bubba (part djinn, all cat) rock it out in Bedlam, a magical town on a magical island. Start with book one of the series: **Bewitching Bedlam**. There are six books and several novellas in the series.

I invite you to visit Fury's world. Bound to Hecate, Fury is a minor goddess, taking care of the Abominations who come off the World Tree. Books one through five are available now in the **Fury Unbound Series**, so begin with **Fury Rising**. This series is finished.

For a dark, gritty, steamy series, try my world of **The Indigo Court**, where the long winter has come, and the Vampiric Fae are on the rise. Begin with the first book —**Night Myst**. There are five books and a novella available.

For all of my work, both published and upcoming releases, see the Bibliography at the end of this book, or check out my website at **Galenorn.com** and be sure and sign up for my **newsletter** to receive news about all my new releases.

QUALITY CONTROL: This work has been professionally edited and proofread. If you encounter any typos or formatting issues ONLY, please contact me through my **website** so they may be corrected. Otherwise, know that this book is in my style and voice and editorial suggestions will not be entertained. Thank you.

CAST OF CHARACTERS

The Wild Hunt & Family:

- **Angel Jackson:** Ember's best friend, a human empath, Angel is a member of the Wild Hunt. A whiz in both the office and the kitchen, and loyal to the core, Angel is an integral part of Ember's life, and a vital member of the team.
- **Charlie Darren:** A vampire who was turned at 19. Math major, baker, and all-around gofer for the Wild Hunt.
- **Ember Kearney:** Caught between the world of Light and Dark Fae, and pledged to Morgana, goddess of the Fae and the Sea, Ember Kearney was born with the mark of the Silver Stag. Rejected by both her bloodlines, she now works for the Wild Hunt as an investigator.
- **Herne the Hunter:** Herne is the son of the Lord of the Hunt, Cernunnos, and Morgana, goddess of the Fae and the Sea. A demigod—given his

mother's mortal beginnings—he's a lusty,
protective god and one hell of a good boss.
Owner of the Wild Hunt Agency, he helps keep
the squabbles between the world of Light and
Dark Fae from spilling over into the mortal
realms.

- **Rafé Forrester:** Brother to Ulstair, Raven's late
fiancé; Angel's boyfriend. Was an actor/fast-
food worker, now works as a clerk for the Wild
Hunt. Dark Fae. Deceased.
- **Talia:** A harpy who long ago lost her powers,
Talia is a top-notch researcher for the agency,
and a longtime friend of Herne's.
- **Viktor:** Viktor is half-ogre, half-human.
Rejected by his father's people (the ogres), he
came to work for Herne some decades back.
- **Yutani:** A coyote shifter who is dogged by the
Great Coyote, Yutani was driven out of his
village over two hundred years before. He walks
in the shadow of the trickster, and is the IT
specialist for the company.

Ember's Friends, Family, & Enemies:

- **Aoife:** A priestess of Morgana who guards the
Seattle portal to the goddess's realm.
- **Celia:** Yutani's aunt.
- **Danielle:** Herne's daughter, born to an Amazon
named Myrna.
- **DJ Jackson:** Angel's younger half-brother, DJ is
half Wulfine—wolf shifter. He now lives with a
foster family for his own protection.

- **Erica:** A Dark Fae police officer, friend of Viktor's.
- **Elatha:** Fomorian King; enemy of the Fae race.
- **George Shipman:** Puma shifter. Member of the White Peak Puma Pride.
- **Ginty McClintlock:** A dwarf. Owner of Ginty's Waystation Bar & Grill
- **Louhia:** Witch of Pohjola.
- **Marilee:** A priestess of Morgana, Ember's mentor. Possibly human—unknown.
- **Meadow O'Ceallaigh:** Member of the magic-born; member of LOCK. Twin sister of Trefoil.
- **Myrna:** An Amazon who had a fling with Herne many years back, which resulted in their daughter Danielle.
- **Sheila:** Viktor's girlfriend. A kitchen witch; one of the magic-born. Geology teacher who volunteers at the Chapel Hill Homeless Shelter.
- **Trefoil O'Ceallaigh:** Member of the magic-born; member of LOCK. Twin brother of Meadow.
- **Unkai:** Leader of the Orhanakai clan in the forest of Y'Bain. Dark Fae—Autumn's Bane.

Raven & the Ante-Fae:

The Ante-Fae are creatures predating the Fae. They are the wellspring from which all Fae descended, unique beings who rule their own realms. All Ante-Fae are dangerous, but some are more deadly than others.

- **Apollo:** The Golden Boy. Vixen's boytoy. Weaver of Wings. Dancer.

- **Arachana:** The Spider Queen. She has almost transformed into one of the Luo'henkah.
- **Blackthorn, the King of Thorns:** Ruler of the blackthorn trees and all thorn-bearing plants. Cunning and wily, he feeds on pain and desire.
- **Curikan, the Black Dog of Hanging Hills:** Raven's father, one of the infamous Black Dogs. The first time someone meets him, they find good fortune. If they should ever see him again, they meet tragedy.
- **Phasmoria:** Queen of the Bean Sidhe. Raven's mother.
- **Raven, the Daughter of Bones:** (also: Raven BoneTalker) A bone witch, Raven is young, as far as the Ante-Fae go, and she works with the dead. She's also a fortune-teller, and a necromancer.
- **Straff:** Blackthorn's son, who suffers from a wasting disease requiring him to feed off others' life energies and blood.
- **Trinity:** The Keeper of Keys. The Lord of Persuasion. One of the Ante-Fae, and part incubus. Mysterious and unknown agent of chaos. His mother was Deeantha, the Rainbow Runner, and his soul father was Maximus, a minor lord of the incubi.
- **Vixen:** The Mistress/Master of Mayhem. Gender-fluid Ante-Fae who owns the Burlesque A Go-Go nightclub.
- **The Vulture Sisters:** Triplet sisters, predatory.

Raven's Friends:

- **Elise, Gordon, and Templeton:** Raven's ferret-bound spirit friends she rescued years ago and now protects until she can find the secret to breaking the curse on them.
- **Gunnar:** One of Kipa's SuVahta Elitvartijat—elite guards.
- **Jordan Roberts:** Tiger shifter. Llewellyn's husband. Owns *A Taste of Latte* coffee shop.
- **Llewellyn Roberts:** One of the magic-born, owns the *Sun & Moon Apothecary*.
- **Moira Ness:** Human. One of Raven's regular clients for readings.
- **Neil Johansson:** One of the magic-born. A priest of Thor.
- **Raj:** Gargoyle companion of Raven. Wing-clipped, he's been with Raven for a number of years.
- **Wager Chance:** Half-Dark Fae, half-human PI. Owns a PI firm found in the Catacombs. Has connections with the vampires.
- **Wendy Fierce-Womyn:** An Amazon who works at Ginty's Waystation Bar & Grill.

The Gods, the Luo'henkah, the Elemental Spirits, & Their Courts:

- **Arawn:** Lord of the Dead. Lord of the Underworld.
- **Arianrhod:** The Goddess of the Silver Wheel; Lady of Reincarnation and the Stars
- **Brighid:** Goddess of Healing, Inspiration, and

Smithery. The Lady of the Fiery Arrows, "Exalted One."

- **The Cailleach:** One of the Luo'henkah, the heart and spirit of winter.
- **Cerridwen:** Goddess of the Cauldron of Rebirth. Dark harvest mother goddess.
- **Cernunnos:** Lord of the Hunt, god of the Forest and King Stag of the Woods. Together with Morgana, Cernunnos originated the Wild Hunt and negotiated the covenant treaty with both the Light and the Dark Fae. Herne's father.
- **Corra:** Ancient Scottish serpent goddess. Oracle to the gods.
- **Coyote, also: Great Coyote:** Native American trickster spirit/god.
- **Danu:** Mother of the Pantheon. Leader of the Tuatha de Dannan.
- **Ferosyn:** Chief healer in Cernunnos's Court.
- **Herne:** (see The Wild Hunt)
- **Isella:** One of the Luo'henkah. The Daughter of Ice (daughter of the Cailleach).
- **Kuippana (also: Kipa):** Lord of the Wolves. Elemental forest spirit; Herne's distant cousin. Trickster. Leader of the SuVahta, a group of divine elemental wolf shifters.
- **Lugh the Long Handed:** Celtic Lord of the Sun.
- **Mielikki:** Lady of Tapiola. Finnish goddess of the Hunt and the Fae. Mother of the Bear, Mother of Bees, Queen of the Forest.
- **Morgana:** Goddess of the Fae and the Sea, she was originally human but Cernunnos lifted her to deityhood. She agreed to watch over the Fae

who did not return across the Great Sea. Torn
by her loyalty to her people and her loyalty to
Cernunnos, she at times finds herself conflicted
about the Wild Hunt. Herne's mother.

- **The Morrígan:** Goddess of Death and
  Phantoms. Goddess of the battlefield.
- **Pandora:** Daughter of Zeus, Emissary of
  Typhon, the Father of Dragons.
- **Sejun:** A counselor in Cernunnos's employ.
  Raven's therapist. Elven.
- **Tapio:** Lord of Tapiola. Mielikki's Consort.
  Lord of the Woodlands. Master of Game.

The Fae Courts:

- **Navane:** The court of the Light Fae, both across
  the Great Sea and on the east side of Seattle, the
  latter ruled by **Névé**.
- **TirNaNog:** The court of the Dark Fae, both
  across the Great Sea and on the east side of
  Seattle, the latter ruled by **Saílle**.

The Force Majeure:
A group of legendary magicians, sorcerers, and
witches. They are not human, but magic-born. There are
twenty-one at any given time and the only way into the
group is to be hand chosen, and the only exit from the
group is death.

- **Merlin, The:** Morgana's father. Magician of
  ancient Celtic fame.
- **Taliesin:** The first Celtic bard. Son of

Cerridwen, originally a servant who underwent magical transformation and finally was reborn through Cerridwen as the first bard.

- **Ranna:** Powerful sorceress. Elatha's mistress.
- **Rasputin:** The Russian sorcerer and mystic.
- **Väinämöinen:** The most famous Finnish bard.

The Dragonni—the Dragon Shifters:

- The Celestial Wanders (Blue, Silver, and Gold Dragons)
- The Mountain Dreamers (Green and Black Dragons)
- The Luminous Warriors (White, Red, and Shadow Dragons)
- **Ashera:** A blue dragon.
- **Aso:** White dragon, bound to Pandora, twin of Variance
- **Echidna:** The Mother of All Dragons (born of the Titans Gaia and Tartarus)
- **Gyell:** Shadow dragon, working with Aso and Variance to bring chaos to Seattle
- **Typhon:** The Father of All Dragons (born of the Titans Gaia and Tartarus)
- **Variance:** White dragon, bound to Pandora, twin of Aso

TIMELINE OF SERIES

Year 1:

- May/Beltane: **The Silver Stag** (Ember)
- June/Litha: **Oak & Thorns** (Ember)
- August/Lughnasadh: **Iron Bones** (Ember)
- September/Mabon: **A Shadow of Crows** (Ember)
- Mid-October: **Witching Hour** (Raven)
- Late October/Samhain: **The Hallowed Hunt** (Ember)
- December/Yule: **The Silver Mist** (Ember)

Year 2:

- January: **Witching Bones** (Raven)
- Late January–February/Imbolc: **A Sacred Magic** (Ember)
- March/Ostara: **The Eternal Return** (Ember)
- May/Beltane: **Sun Broken** (Ember)

- June/Litha: **Witching Moon** (Raven)
- August/Lughnasadh: **Autumn's Bane** (Ember)
- September/Mabon: **Witching Time** (Raven)
- November/Samhain: **Hunter's Moon** (Ember)
- December/Yule: **Witching Fire** (Raven)
- February/Imbolc: **Veil of Stars** (Ember)
- September/Samhain: Antlered Crown (Ember)

PLAYLIST

I often write to music, and VEIL OF STARS was no exception. Here's the playlist I used for this book.

- **Air:** Moon Fever; Playground Love; Napalm Love
- **Airstream:** Electra (Religion Cut)
- **Alexandros:** Milk (Bleach Version); Mosquito Bite
- **Android Lust:** Here & Now; Saint Over
- **The Black Angels:** Currency; Hunt Me Down; Death March; Indigo Meadow; Don't Play With Guns; Always Maybe; Black Isn't Black
- **Black Mountain:** Queens Will Play
- **The Bravery:** Believe
- **Broken Bells:** The Ghost Inside
- **Crazy Town:** Butterfly
- **Danny Cudd:** Double D; Remind; Once Again; Timelessly Free; To the Mirage
- **DJ Shah:** Mellomaniac

- **Eastern Sun:** Beautiful Being
- **Eels:** Love of the Loveless; Souljacker Part 1
- **FC Kahuna:** Hayling
- **The Feeling:** Sewn
- **Fluke:** Absurd
- **Foster The People:** Pumped Up Kicks
- **Garbage:** Queer; Only Happy When It Rains; #1Crush; Push It; I Think I'm Paranoid
- **Gary Numan:** Hybrid; Cars; Petals; Ghost Nation; My Name Is Ruin; Pray For The Pain You Serve; I Am Dust; Betrayed; The Gift; I Am Screaming; Intruder; Is This World Not Enough; A Black Sun; The Chosen; And It Breaks Me Again; Saints And Liars; Now And Forever; The End of Dragons; When You Fall
- **Godsmack:** Voodoo
- **The Gospel Whisky Runners:** Muddy Waters
- **Hang Massive:** Omat Odat; Released Upon Inception; Thingless Things; Boat Ride; Transition To Dreams; End Of Sky; Warmth Of The Sun's Rays; Luminous Emptiness
- **The Hu:** The Gereg; Wolf Totem
- **Imagine Dragons:** Natural
- **In Strict Confidence:** Snow White; Tiefer; Silver Bullets; Forbidden Fruit
- **J Rokka:** Marine Migration
- **Lorde:** Yellow Flicker Beat; Royals
- **Low:** Witches; Nightingale; Plastic Cup; Monkey; Half-Light
- **M.I.A.:** Bad Girls
- **Many Rivers Ensemble:** Blood Moon; Oasis; Upwelling; Emergence

- **Marconi Union:** First Light; Alone Together; Flying (In Crimson Skies); Always Numb; Time Lapse; On Reflection; Broken Colours; We Travel; Weightless
- **Matt Corby:** Breathe
- **Pati Yang:** All That Is Thirst
- **Rue du Soleil:** We Can Fly; Le Française; Wake Up Brother; Blues Du Soleil
- **Screaming Trees:** Where the Twain Shall Meet; All I Know
- **Shriekback:** Underwater Boys; Over the Wire; This Big Hush; Agony Box; Bollo Rex; Putting All The Lights Out; The Fire Has Brought Us Together; Shovelheads; And the Rain; Wiggle & Drone; Now These Days Are Gone; The King In The Tree
- **Tamaryn:** While You're Sleeping, I'm Dreaming; Violet's In A Pool
- **Thomas Newman:** Dead Already
- **Tom Petty:** Mary Jane's Last Dance
- **Trills:** Speak Loud
- **The Verve:** Bitter Sweet Symphony
- **Wendy Rule:** Let the Wind Blow

BIOGRAPHY

New York Times, *Publishers Weekly*, and *USA Today* best-selling author Yasmine Galenorn writes urban fantasy and paranormal romance, and is the author of more than seventy-five books, including the Wild Hunt Series, the Moonshadow Bay Series, the Fury Unbound Series, the Bewitching Bedlam Series, the Indigo Court Series, and the Otherworld Series, among others. She's also written nonfiction metaphysical books. She is the 2011 Career Achievement Award Winner in Urban Fantasy, given by RT Magazine. Yasmine has been in the Craft since 1980, is a shamanic witch and High Priestess. She describes her life as a blend of teacups and tattoos. She lives in Kirkland, WA, with her husband Samwise and their cats. Yasmine can be reached via her Website at Galenorn.com. You can find all her links at her LinkTree.

Indie Releases Currently Available:

Moonshadow Bay Series:

Starlight Web
Midnight Web
Conjure Web
Harvest Web
Shadow Web

Hedge Dragon Series:
The Poisoned Forest

The Wild Hunt Series:
The Silver Stag
Oak & Thorns
Iron Bones
A Shadow of Crows
The Hallowed Hunt
The Silver Mist
Witching Hour
Witching Bones
A Sacred Magic
The Eternal Return
Sun Broken
Witching Moon
Autumn's Bane
Witching Time
Hunter's Moon
Witching Fire
Veil of Stars
Antlered Crown

Lily Bound Series
Souljacker

Chintz 'n China Series:
  Ghost of a Chance
  Legend of the Jade Dragon
  Murder Under a Mystic Moon
  A Harvest of Bones
  One Hex of a Wedding
  Holiday Spirits
  Well of Secrets
  Chintz 'n China Books, 1 – 3: Ghost of a Chance,
Legend of the Jade Dragon, Murder Under A
Mystic Moon
  Chintz 'n China Books, 4-6: A Harvest of Bones, One
Hex of a Wedding, Holiday Spirits

Whisper Hollow Series:
  Autumn Thorns
  Shadow Silence
  The Phantom Queen

Bewitching Bedlam Series:
  Bewitching Bedlam
  Maudlin's Mayhem
  Siren's Song
  Witches Wild
  Casting Curses
  Demon's Delight
  Bedlam Calling: A Bewitching Bedlam Anthology
  The Wish Factor (a prequel short story)
  Blood Music (a prequel novella)
  Blood Vengeance (a Bewitching Bedlam novella)
  Tiger Tails (a Bewitching Bedlam novella)

Fury Unbound Series:
    Fury Rising
    Fury's Magic
    Fury Awakened
    Fury Calling
    Fury's Mantle

Indigo Court Series:
    Night Myst
    Night Veil
    Night Seeker
    Night Vision
    Night's End
    Night Shivers
    Indigo Court Books, 1-3: Night Myst, Night Veil, Night Seeker (Boxed Set)
    Indigo Court Books, 4-6: Night Vision, Night's End, Night Shivers (Boxed Set)

Otherworld Series:
    Moon Shimmers
    Harvest Song
    Blood Bonds
    Otherworld Tales: Volume 1
    Otherworld Tales: Volume 2
For the rest of the Otherworld Series, see website at **Galenorn.com.**

Bath and Body Series (originally under the name India Ink):
    Scent to Her Grave
    A Blush With Death

Glossed and Found

Misc. Short Stories/Anthologies:
    Once Upon a Kiss (short story: Princess Charming)
    Once Upon a Curse (short story: Bones)
    Once Upon a Ghost (short story: Rapunzel
Dreaming)

Magickal Nonfiction:
    Embracing the Moon
    Tarot Journeys

CPSIA information can be obtained
at www.ICGtesting.com
Printed in the USA
LVHW101146130423
744169LV00006B/307

9 798460 354818